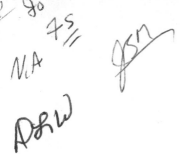

# A CATERED VALENTINE'S DAY

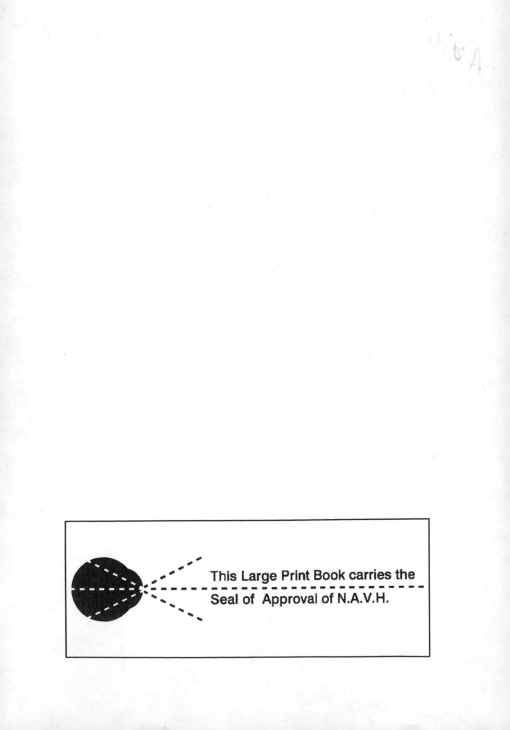

This Large Print Book carries the
Seal of Approval of N.A.V.H.

A MYSTERY WITH RECIPES

# A CATERED
# VALENTINE'S DAY

## ISIS CRAWFORD

**WHEELER PUBLISHING**
An imprint of Thomson Gale, a part of The Thomson Corporation

**THOMSON**
———✦———™
**GALE**

Detroit • New York • San Francisco • New Haven, Conn. • Waterville, Maine • London

**LIBRARY OF CONGRESS CATALOGING-IN-PUBLICATION DATA**

Crawford, Isis.
    A catered Valentine's Day : a mystery with recipes / by Isis Crawford.
        p. cm. — (Wheeler Publishing large print cozy mystery)
    ISBN-13: 978-1-59722-472-7 (pbk. : alk. paper)
    ISBN-10: 1-59722-472-3 (pbk. : alk. paper) 1. Simmons, Bernie (Fictitious character : Crawford) — Fiction. 2. Simmons, Libby (Fictitious character) — Fiction. 3. Caterers and catering — Fiction. 4. Women in the food industry — Fiction. 5. Cookery — Fiction. 6. Large type books. I. Title.
    PS3603.R396C3725 2007
    813'.6—dc22                                                    2006039592

Published in 2007 by arrangement with Kensington Books, an imprint of Kensington Publishing Corp.

Printed in the United States of America on permanent paper
10 9 8 7 6 5 4 3 2 1

For Marna

# ACKNOWLEDGMENTS

I'd like to thank the usual suspects.
Dan, for his suggestions and corrections.
Mike, for listening.
Sarah, for her cooking sense.

# CHAPTER 1

Bernie entered the room ahead of her sister. *Drats,* she thought as she looked around. There were no empty seats, at least none that she and Libby could get to easily. Plus, the minister was already giving his eulogy, which meant they'd missed most of the ceremony. This was not good. Not good at all. Being late to a movie was one thing; being late to a funeral was quite another.

"I told you we should have left earlier," Libby hissed in her ear.

Bernie grunted. She wasn't taking the blame for this one. She wasn't the one who had decided they had to go to the funeral at the last minute. And she wasn't the one who'd decided that wearing her Dolce & Gabbana slacks and a mauve blouse wasn't "respectful enough," an archaic concept if she'd ever heard one.

The lady in the last row was wearing red and the woman right next to her had on a

9

pink jacket, for heaven's sake. It wasn't Bernie's fault her navy suit was hiding underneath her ski stuff or that her navy suede pumps had gotten stuck behind her travel bag. How often did she wear this kind of stuff? Never. That's how often. At least not since she'd quit her straight job five years ago. More like ten actually.

Bernie automatically rebuttoned her top suit button so the lace on her cami wouldn't show. So maybe she had taken a little more time than was strictly necessary putting on her eyeliner and mascara. So maybe she did hate funerals.

Okay, loathed them. Had ever since Uncle Tom's coffin slid out of the hearse on the way to the funeral and got hit by a milk truck. She hadn't had a milk shake since that day, and they had been her favorite food. Bernie repressed a shudder. Uncle Tom all over the highway had not been a pretty sight. Fortunately Aunt Ethel had been too drunk to make much sense of what was going on.

Bernie sighed. When she died she wanted to be cremated and have her ashes shot into space. Or sent down in the deepest chasm in the ocean or scattered in the Himalayas. The walk would do Libby good. After all, she kept saying she had to get more exercise.

Bernie luxuriated in the thought of Libby trudging up the side of the mountain, bearing her ashes through a blizzard.

One thing was for sure. Bernie didn't want to be laid out in some funeral parlor — a term that harkened back to the days when the dead were laid out in their houses, not carted off to funeral homes. And why did this funeral home have to feature beige as its dominant color? Talk about drab. Bernie shook her head. No, siree, Bob, as her dad liked to say. Now, if she were doing this place she'd do it in shades of light green, green being the color of renewal.

Bernie moved her silver and onyx ring up and down her finger while she surveyed the room. Okay, so Libby was correct — not that she'd ever tell her that. They should have gotten here earlier. In a situation like this, being conspicuous was not necessarily a plus. After thirty seconds or so Bernie spotted two seats. Unfortunately they were smack dab in the middle of the third row. Better to stand in the back, she reasoned, never mind that the shoes she had on weren't made for standing, but then four-inch heels rarely were. She was just going to make that suggestion to Libby when an usher appeared and started herding them toward the third row. By now the minister was in full oration mode.

Bernie caught the words "kindly" and "charitable" and "loved the outdoors" and "dog lover." This was not the mother of Mrs. Vongel that she'd heard about, she reflected as she began making her way down the row. The mother she'd heard about had allergies to every living thing and spent most of her time behind her triple-sealed windows watching the Shopping Channel and buying exercise equipment she never used. But that was the thing with eulogies.

Most of what was said wasn't true anyway. At least not in her experience. Look at what the priest had said about Ann Higgenbottom and her scones. The pride of the parish, he'd called them, when actually they'd been responsible for more cases of dyspepsia than anything else served at the potlucks.

"Excuse me. Excuse me," Bernie whispered as a chorus of "ouchs" and "reallys" followed her down the row.

Finally she arrived at her seat.

"I told you this would happen," Libby hissed as she plopped herself down next to Bernie.

Bernie noted she was red in the face. Bernie wondered if it was from anger or embarrassment. Probably both.

"Yes, you did. Several times in fact,"

Bernie retorted.

She was about to add something to the effect that Libby's habit of repeating things didn't help anything when she caught a glimpse of the puckered lips of the lady sitting next to her and decided that in this case silence really was golden.

Instead Bernie settled into her chair, which kept shifting from side to side whenever she crossed and uncrossed her legs, and attempted to focus on what the minister was saying, but despite her best intentions she found her attention drifting.

She started thinking about the new oven they'd installed at A Little Taste of Heaven. Had she known what a big deal it was going to be she never would have purchased it. According to the sales rep, the oven was supposed to do everything from bake bread to darn socks in half the time. And as a bonus it was supposed to save on energy costs. Maybe it would too — if they could ever get it up and running.

First they'd had problems securing it; then they'd had problems with the gas line, and now they were having problems with the baking times, but that was the least of it because there was one thing the sales rep hadn't mentioned — even though she should have known it. The oven put out more BTUs, considerably more BTUs, than their old oven. Which meant they needed a new exhaust system, including a recirculating fan. Just the thought made her wince.

This was going to involve major construction. Wait until she told Libby. Libby didn't know yet. She'd been at the market when the housing inspector had stopped by. Bernie flicked her hair back. She was going to tell Libby — once she found the right time — which seemed to be never.

All this aggravation for only six thousand dollars too. What a deal. And the exhaust system was probably going to cost another four thousand, one thousand to have it installed, and three thousand for the duct-work by the time the construction company was done, never mind the mess and disruption the workmen were going to cause.

Libby was ready to kill her, and she didn't blame her sister one bit.

Fortunately, they still had one of the old ovens left, one of the old reliable ovens as Libby was fond of saying, but that wasn't enough with Valentine's Day coming up and all the cakes and cookies they were contracted to make, not to mention the fundraiser they were doing at Just Chocolate.

They'd have to subcontract some of their baking. That was all there was to that. Libby would object, but what else could they do? Unless of course they could get the new oven up and running. Libby was right. They should have stuck with what they had. Sometimes new is not a good thing. Bernie sighed as she thought of the havoc she'd unintentionally wrought.

She'd just have to speak to the serviceman's supervisor and see if she could get him to speed things up. She hated to do it, but they were running out of options. She was composing her conversation when she felt a poke in her ribs.

Libby cupped her hand and whispered into her ear, "I don't recognize anyone here."

It occurred to Bernie that she didn't either, which was strange with Longely being a fairly small place. "I don't either," she allowed.

Libby tugged at her sleeve. "Do you suppose we're in the wrong place?"

"Don't be ridiculous," Bernie shot back.

How could they be in the wrong place? That wasn't possible.

Libby tugged at her sleeve again. "I hate to tell you this, but Mrs. Vongel's mother's name was Janet."

"So?" Bernie answered. She was still wondering how to tell Libby what the code enforcement officer had told her.

"Will you two be quiet?" the lady next to her snapped. "Bad enough that you had to be late. At least have the decency to be quiet. Have some respect for the dead, for heaven's sake."

"Sorry," Bernie murmured.

The woman snorted and turned her attention back to the minister. Well, they certainly weren't making friends and influencing people today, Bernie thought as she felt another tug on her arm.

She turned and put a finger on her lips. "Not now," she told Libby as the man in front of them turned around and sniffed.

"But, Bernie," Libby persisted.

"What?"

"The minister is talking about Janet Voiton. Voiton. Not Vongel. We're in the wrong funeral."

# CHAPTER 2

Libby closed her eyes for a moment. She was so sorry she was right. She wanted so badly to be wrong. But she wasn't. How had this happened? She couldn't believe she and Bernie had done this. No, actually she could. It seemed as if these days anything that could go wrong did. She felt like Lot. Okay, maybe that was a slight exaggeration, but not by much. Witness the batch of dough she'd made this morning. She'd forgotten to put in the yeast. She never did that. Ever. At least she hadn't since high school when the rolls she was making for Thanksgiving hadn't risen. They'd been like little rocks.

And then there were her new black pants, the ones Bernie called her old lady pants, just because they had an elastic waist. Was it so wrong to want to be comfortable? Was that such a crime? But the elastic in the waistband had ripped as she and Bernie were driving here, and on top of that the heels on her good black shoes were so run-down they looked as if they'd been chewed on by her neighbor's Jack Russell terrier. Her mother would not have approved. And Libby didn't even want to think about what her grandmother would have said.

And then Amber and Googie had both been late arriving at the shop — both claimed they'd been sick, which Libby didn't quite believe — but that didn't matter. What mattered was that the special lunch salad A Little Taste of Heaven was featuring — roasted sweet potatoes and fennel on a bed of arugula with a sprinkling of roasted walnuts — still needed to be prepped.

But possibly the worst thing that had happened this morning was that her oven — her one remaining oven — was turning unreliable so that the first batch of scones she'd baked had been raw in the center, a fact she hadn't noticed until Mrs. Schneider had called it to her attention by spitting out a piece of scone in front of the ten other customers. This was not what you called good business.

Libby glanced at her watch. The repairman was supposed to be at the shop in an hour and a half to recalibrate the oven, and she and Bernie had to be back by then. She'd told Amber what to tell the repairman, but the truth was she didn't quite trust Amber to relay the information correctly. She tended to get things mixed up, or as Bernie would say, "ditz out," especially now that she was in love. All she ever talked about these days was what her boyfriend Dickie said. It was "Dickie said this" and "Dickie did that." Libby hoped she wasn't that bad with Marvin.

And then on top of everything else they were late to the funeral. If it had been up to Libby they never would have come, but then Bree had called her up and suggested she and Bernie put in an appearance.

"Dear Catherine will appreciate it," were Bree's exact words. Libby didn't feel as if she could say no. Of course, she never said no to Bree, as Bernie was the first one to point out. But how could you say no to the social arbiter of Longely? Half of Libby's business would be gone. She pushed a lock of hair behind her ears. The names Voiton and Vongel were so similar. What were the odds?

And she'd wondered why no one looked familiar here when she'd come in. Why hadn't she acted on that feeling? Why had she told herself she was crazy? Why hadn't she taken a moment to read the sign more closely instead of rushing in like some crazy woman?

If she hadn't been so preoccupied with the ovens at A Little Taste of Heaven she would have. She wanted to kick herself. Instead she reached into her bag to get a square of 70 percent pure Venezuelan chocolate before she remembered she'd eaten the last piece when they'd walked into the funeral home. And just when she'd needed it the most too.

*Okay, Libby,* she told herself. *Relax. This isn't the end of the world.* The question was what to do about it. Of course, they could just sit through the funeral. But then they'd miss Mrs. Vongel's mother's funeral. And that would be bad.

Libby thought about what her mom would have done in this situation, but it wasn't much help because her mom would never have gotten herself into this situation in the first place. She wouldn't have been late and she would have stopped to read the card on the easel by the door. Libby bit at her cuticle with her front teeth. No. They'd just have to leave. Leave now. Libby turned toward Bernie and jerked her head in the direction of the door.

"Let's go," she mouthed.

Bernie raised an eyebrow.

Libby shook her head.

"Are you sure?" Bernie whispered.

"Absolutely," Libby whispered back.

The man in front of her turned his head and said, "Have the decency to behave yourself."

Libby could feel herself turning red. She wanted to shrink into the floor. She hated calling attention to herself. She was the person who waited to pee in the movies until it was over because she didn't want to disturb other people, and now she was going to do something that would make everyone look at her. She could feel her heart start to race. *Don't be such a chicken,* she told herself. *Just do it. Now.* She took a deep breath and stood up.

"Excuse me," she murmured as she stepped on people's feet. "So sorry."

In the background she heard Bernie say, "She gets these really bad migraines. Can't stop throwing up. That's why we have to go. Now."

*Leave it to Bernie to make me into a public spectacle,* Libby thought bitterly as she reached the end of the aisle.

"Migraine?" she said when they got outside. "I throw up? That's attractive."

Bernie shrugged. "It was effective. People

let us through really quickly."

"That isn't the point."

"I thought it was. Anyway, what else was I supposed to say? That we wandered into the wrong funeral by mistake?"

"You could have made up something else."

"I did."

"Something else."

"This was the first thing that occurred to me."

"Fine."

"And by the way, your blouse is open."

Libby looked down. The third button on her blouse had come undone. "Why didn't you tell me before?" she wailed.

"If I had seen it I would have. It must have opened when you stood up. Remember, I followed you out."

*Wonderful,* Libby thought. Now she was an exhibitionist as well as a funeral disturber.

"I'm coming apart at the seams," she moaned.

"If you bought better quality clothes you wouldn't have that problem."

"There's nothing wrong with Marshall's," Libby heard herself snap. "Not everyone can shop at The Most." *Let alone fit into their clothes.*

Bernie made a rude noise.

Libby wanted to say that she didn't see the sense in spending hundreds of dollars on a skirt, especially these days, what with the condition the oven was in, but she decided now was not the time to start a fight with her sister.

"Can we leave my clothes alone and concentrate on getting to the correct funeral?" Libby said instead.

"By all means. So where do you think the Vongel funeral is anyway?" Bernie replied. "This place is huge."

Libby looked around. On this they could both agree. It was true. The Hanson Funeral Home was now extremely large. Libby remembered when the place could only accommodate two funerals, but in the past year Marvin's father had gone on a building spree. He'd kept on adding room after room. Now the place could fit ten to twelve "bereavements," as Clayton liked to call them.

"This is like one of those bridal palaces out on the Island," Bernie remarked. "It just goes on and on forever. I'm surprised they don't have the gold funeral room for the rich, the purple one for those with royal persuasions, and the green one for the ecologically minded among us. You know, themed burials like they do out in Hollywood. You could have the Viking funeral, the Roman funeral, the French Revolution funeral — that of course would come with optional knitting."

Libby massaged her temples. "You're giving me a headache."

"No. The air freshener in here is giving you a headache."

"Bernie," Libby pleaded. "For once be quiet."

"Fine."

Libby watched her sister's eyes rest on the huge bird-of-paradise flower arrangement in front of them. "And don't say anything about that either," she instructed.

"I wasn't," Bernie said, sniffing, even though Libby knew that she had been thinking it. "Except to point out that they're bad feng shu. They're blocking the energy flow." And Bernie pointed in the direction of the entrance hallway. "I bet there's some sort of directory in there."

"Good thinking," Libby said. She started trotting off in that direction.

She'd taken two steps when she could feel her pants begin to slide. As she yanked them up, she saw Marvin come down the hall. *Oh no,* she thought. *Why do I always see him when I look like such a mess?* She knew that he didn't care, but she did.

"Thank heavens I found you," Marvin said as he came toward them.

He was panting slightly and his tie was askew. That made Libby feel better. Bernie always called her and Marvin the two schleps, and she hated to say it but her sister was right.

"Why? What's the matter?" Libby asked him. *He looks tired,* she thought. *He's been working too hard.* Which, if you're a funeral director, Bernie would point out, isn't such a good thing for the rest of the community.

Marvin looked around. When he was sure no one was watching he hugged her. "I thought you'd be at the Vongel funeral."

"We made a mistake," Bernie said. "We ended up at the Voiton affair."

Marvin shook his head as if to say that was something he would have done, and as he stepped back Libby remembered yet again why she loved him.

"We'd better go. My dad is waiting to speak to you and Bernie," Marvin told her.

"Why?" Libby asked again.

"He'll tell you," Marvin replied as he motioned for her and Bernie to follow him down the hall.

"Why can't you?"

"I'd rather he did," Marvin said, and he looked so unhappy Libby decided not to insist.

Three steps later he tripped over the leg of a chair that had been placed out in the hallway and stumbled into a table with one of the bird-of-paradise flower arrangements on it. Bernie caught the vase just as it was about to tumble over. That was the other thing she liked about Marvin, Libby thought. He was clumsier than she was.

As Marvin thanked Bernie for saving the flowers Libby wondered what on earth his father wanted to talk to them about. Clayton wasn't particularly fond of her, her sister, or her father. He thought they were a bad influence on his son, distracting him from the family business and giving him, in Marvin's father's own words, "fantasies about being a detective when he should be concentrating on other more important things." Notably the family business.

It was a business, it must be said, that Marvin wasn't particularly fond of. Libby didn't blame him. She still hadn't reconciled herself to what he did. It gave her the creeps if she thought about it, so she tried not to. How could anyone want to be a funeral director? No matter how much she tried she just couldn't see it.

But then, Marvin didn't really have a choice. At least not when you had a dad like Clayton. She and Bernie were lucky they had their father. Very lucky. Libby bit her lower lip as she tried to remember what Bernie called Clayton. A martini? A martin? No. A martinet. She was trying to remember what the word meant when she realized that Marvin had said something to her.

"Excuse me?"

"What's the matter with your pants?" he asked.

Libby looked down. They were beginning to slide down her waist again.

"Nothing," she said. As she hoisted them up she could hear Bernie snickering in the background. "Nothing at all."

It was at that moment that Marvin's dad materialized from a door in one of the rooms. When she'd first seen him, Bernie had said he looked as if he'd been dipped in shellac. And it was true. Everything about him gleamed, from his hair down to his shoes.

He nodded curtly at Marvin. "That took long enough," he told him.

Marvin looked down at the floor.

"You know how important this is."

"Hey," Libby said. "It wasn't . . ."

But before she could finish, Clayton dismissed her comment with a wave of his hand. "Don't bother with excuses. We have to go," he said, turning to the door where Libby knew the hearses were parked. "We have to go now."

"We can't," Libby heard her sister say.

Libby watched Clayton stiffen. He was about to reply when a woman started walking down the hall. He plastered a simpering smile on his face, nodded at her, and asked her if everything was all right. "Mrs. Frost, if there's anything, anything at all I can do in your time of need . . ."

"No. You've been wonderful," she told him.

Libby watched Marvin's dad produce another of his smiles.

"Thank you. Thank you so much." And he patted her hand. When she was gone he rounded on them. "You have to come with me," he growled at them.

"Please," Marvin added.

Libby looked at her sister and gave a little nod.

"Are you sure?" Bernie asked.

Libby nodded her head more vigorously. What else could she say? She didn't want to have anything to do with whatever this was, but given the circumstances — mainly the fact that her boyfriend's father was doing the asking — she felt she didn't have a choice.

# CHAPTER 3

Bernie looked out the rear window of Clayton's limo. The view was not inspiring. It was gray and dreary. The sky was slate. The ground was frozen solid. Little patches of dirty snow remained from the storm they'd had two weeks ago. The trees were all bare. It reminded her of a Thomas Hardy poem. Depressing. No doubt about it, February sucked. It was the time of year when she wished she were back in L.A. No, make that Costa Rica or Cancún. Somewhere with sun and palm trees. Scratch the palm trees. She'd just take the sun and a couple of Cuba Libres.

February was her least favorite time of the year. Always had been. Spring was too far away to think about. Except if you were a gardener. Then you got to think about what you were going to plant. The holidays were all done, except of course for Valentine's Day. Which was usually fun.

In grade school she'd made lace valentines and given out those little candy hearts to what her mom had called her "special friends." Now, however, she gave her "special friend" different gifts. She'd gotten a great red thong and matching lace bra to wear for Rob. Except now she was mad at him.

Why had he signed up for the bachelor auction at the Just Chocolate benefit for Sudanese orphans? That had been totally unnecessary. She'd like to give him a kiss all right. A kiss with her fist. Pow. Right in the kisser. Rob had called her jealous. Which was ridiculous.

She didn't have a jealous bone in her body. None. Okay, maybe her pinky. It was the principle of the thing. She just had to figure out which principle it was. She just wanted to spend time with Rob. Was that so bad? She'd tried to explain, but he hadn't gotten it. Of course, he hadn't gotten a lot of things lately.

All she knew was that Rob had better get her something really, really nice to make up for this. Like the pink cowboy boots she'd seen in Saks. Or dinner out at the new Moroccan restaurant down in Dumbo. Yes. That's what she'd ask for.

The thought made her feel slightly better

— having a plan always did — and she turned her attention back to the view. They were out of Longely now and heading down Townsend Road. Which meant they were heading either to Longely's minimall or the cemetery. Considering the circumstances, Bernie was betting on the cemetery.

She leaned forward and tapped Marvin's father on the shoulder. "Are we going to the Oaks?"

Clayton turned his head around and glanced at her. "You'll see," he said.

Then to Bernie's relief he looked at the road, always a good thing for a driver to do, in her opinion.

"Because I'd prefer the mall," Bernie said to the back of his head. "They have a sale on there at E.J.'s."

E.J.'s was a funky little shop that sold T-shirts and the odd sweater or two.

Marvin's father grunted.

Bernie tried again. "I have a friend that teaches the chemistry of embalming."

Nothing.

"Do you use pomade on your hair?"

"I don't think you're funny," Clayton replied.

"Most people don't," Libby commented.

"Nice answer," Bernie told her.

"But true," Libby said.

Bernie sighed, sat back, and watched the trees going by. *At least I'm not in the front seat with him,* she thought. *Things could always be worse.* That was what her mother had always said. But then, they could always be better too. She glanced at her watch.

They had another hour to go before the repairman arrived at the shop. She hoped they'd make it back to A Little Taste of Heaven by then, but she had a feeling they wouldn't. Whatever this was about had to be pretty serious, and in her experience pretty serious always meant time-consuming — extremely time-consuming. Of that she was sure.

Otherwise Marvin's father wouldn't be doing this. Normally, he didn't even talk to her or Libby. She'd heard through the grapevine that he still wanted Marvin to marry Emily Funkenwagel. Her dad owned a chain of funeral homes. She was the heiress of the Funkenwagel Mortuary Places. Everything with Marvin's father was all about the business. She felt bad for Marvin. There hadn't been any goofing off time for him when he was growing up.

Bernie twisted her silver and onyx ring around her finger while she tried to figure out what this was about, but for the life of her she couldn't. Oh well. She guessed she'd just have to wait and see. She bent down and readjusted the strap on her blue suede stiletto. The dratted thing kept slipping. But one thing she did know. Walking in the Oaks in these things was not going to be fun. If she had known where the day was going to take her she would have chosen a different pair of shoes.

The Oaks was the oldest cemetery in the surrounding area. It had been built almost a hundred years ago by a famous landscape architect and conceived of as a place where the dead could be buried and the living could come and visit them on weekends.

People did things like that a hundred years ago — linked the dead and the living. Unlike now, when people moved all the time and families, let alone communities, were fragmented. As a consequence, the old part of the cemetery had loads of winding paths that were way too narrow for cars. You had to hike up and down hills.

Bernie leaned forward and tapped Clayton on the shoulder again.

"What?" he snapped.

"Are we going to the new part?" she asked.

"The new part of what?" he demanded, turning back to look at her again.

"Car," Bernie yelled as a Toyota came toward them. She could hear Libby shrieking up front.

"I see it," Clayton told her as he turned his eyes back to the road.

Another person who couldn't drive and talk at the same time, Libby reflected. At least she now knew where Marvin got his driving ability from, but that was the only thing he had in common with his dad. Bernie leaned her head back against the seat and decided that the only talking she'd be doing in the limo from now on was with her sister.

"So," she said to Libby, "how are the chicken breasts coming?"

The chicken breasts were supposed to be made into a salad by now, but when she and Libby had left they were still marinating in their bath of yogurt, lime juice, cumin, and coriander. Some shops would just use precooked, prepackaged chicken breasts, but that wasn't Libby's style. Bernie smiled as she remembered the look of outrage on her sister's face when the food salesman from Sysco had suggested it. You'd have thought he was asking her to use vanillin instead of vanilla or margarine instead of butter.

"I could call Amber and ask her to get the salad started," Bernie suggested.

Libby didn't answer. She probably hadn't

heard her, Bernie reflected. That's because she had her nose pressed against the limo's window. Bernie was just about to repeat her offer but decided against it. For some reason she had no desire to talk to Libby or anyone else in Clayton's presence. He was, she reflected, like some negative force that just sucked the fun out of things. She'd noticed that Marvin was even more nervous than he usually was when he was around him.

The silence was beginning to get oppressive. Bernie decided it would be better to concentrate her energies on other things, so she sat back and closed her eyes and thought about how she and Libby were going to set up for the benefit at Just Chocolate.

Just Chocolate was obviously supplying the chocolate and they were doing the wine, but she and Libby were responsible for the food part of the operation. At latest count Bree Nottingham had sold over three hundred tickets out of a possible five hundred, but Bernie was sure that by the day arrived the event would be sold out. It was the perfect Valentine's Day event.

She and Libby had the menu loosely worked out, but they had to refine it. And then they needed to figure out the numbers so they could phone their orders in. The benefit was only two weeks away and they needed time to prepare.

Of course they were doing the tried and true. Platters of strawberries and tangerine sections as well as baskets full of grape clusters and melon and mango slices. They were serving three different types of chocolate cake, not including cheesecake, all of them baked in heart-shaped pans, as well as eight varieties of chocolate cookies, among them chocolate cookies with black pepper and chocolate cookies with ginger, a combination she was particularly fond of, as well as a takeoff on a Linzer tart cookie.

Then they were making six different kinds of brownies, among them rocky road, cashew, mint, and double fudge. Just thinking about all the baking they had to do made her tired. But at least they weren't doing pies or tarts. Those took forever.

Less obviously, she and Libby were doing figs stuffed with almonds and chocolate, a Portuguese delicacy. They were also doing chicken mole, a Mexican chicken stew made with about twenty ingredients, including chocolate, as well as a South American beef stew that used dark chocolate as a thickening and flavoring agent. With the stews, Bernie was thinking they should serve some sort of stretch bread to sop up the sauce.

Bernie thought again about what a tremendous amount of work they'd undertaken. They really did have to order and start baking now in order to be ready in time. At least they should. Fortunately, a lot of the stuff could be baked in advance and frozen, not that Libby would agree. Unfortunately, what with the oven and the building inspector and the construction, Bernie didn't know how they were going to do that on top of their usual stuff, at least not if they didn't want to work until three in the morning.

Bernie felt a stab of panic. What if the building inspector said they had to stop working until the exhaust system was installed? He had the ability to shut them down. Maybe she could bribe him. Ha. She wouldn't know how to even start. Or maybe Bree could talk to him and plead their case. That would work better.

Bernie was beginning to think her mother was correct when she said, "In life it's not what you know but who you know that counts."

Bernie moved her ring up and down her finger.

Libby was right, though. It was important to go to Mrs. Vongel's mother's funeral, and now they'd missed it. This was all her fault.

As usual. If she hadn't taken so long put-ting her mascara on, they wouldn't have been in such a hurry, and they would have noticed what the sign on the door said. She hadn't even actually read it. She'd just seen the V and sailed right in.

Maybe if she baked Mrs. Vongel a cake. Scratch that. Like Bree Nottingham she was a size 2. She didn't eat, she grazed. Maybe an expensive bottle of wine? Yes. That might work. Or better yet, a good brandy. Bernie was tapping her fingers against the seat, try-ing to decide what kind, when she realized Libby was speaking to her.

Bernie's head went up.

"What?" she asked.

"I was just saying that we're here."

"Indeed we are," Bernie replied as they entered the front gate of the Oaks.

"Remember good old Charlie?" Libby asked her.

"How could I forget him?"

"What you did was really mean."

"Mean?" Bernie retorted. "I was mean? What about him?"

When she was in high school she'd come up here with Charlie Quincy and they'd made out on the bench next to Elizabeth Engel's grave. They'd done that three times when she'd heard a moaning noise behind

38

them. Then something that looked like a ghoul had come at her. At which point she'd done what any normal person would have. She'd spun around and clocked the thing over the head with her backpack. He'd screamed and grabbed his nose. Who knew you could break a ghoul's nose?

The ghoul turned out to be Chris Parker, Charlie's pal. Charlie had hired him to scare her, figuring that he'd play the big hero and she'd be so grateful that he'd get into her pants later that evening. Ha, ha. Not happening. She'd felt a little bad about Chris's nose, but she was really pissed at Charlie. And she'd gotten him back.

When she'd walked out of his closet at three in the morning he'd let out the loudest shriek she'd ever heard. Maybe it was because she'd painted herself with phosphorescent paint. She glowed in the dark — except for her face, which she'd blacked out. It had been hell to get off — she'd had to scrub herself with a brush — but it was all worth it.

Bernie smiled as she watched the limo drive up and down the meandering paths. In the spring, the place was lovely, but now it was spooky. Her counter girl, Amber, would love it. Whenever she saw a horror movie — and she saw them all — she insisted on telling everyone else in the kitchen the plot. Nothing like prepping chicken for chicken salad to a detailed description of *The Texas Chainsaw Massacre.*

"Where are we going?" Bernie heard Libby ask as they drove by the angel holding the lantern.

"You'll see," Clayton said.

As Bernie watched they drove by the mausoleum of the founder of Longely. It was built along the lines of a Roman temple. They passed the monument to the people who died from the flu in 1918. They passed Bernie's favorite monument, the statue of a cocker spaniel with a young man. The placard read LOVE IS ETERNAL. Then they were through the old part of the cemetery and into the new part. Here the land was much straighter and the graves were arranged in orderly rows. There were fewer statues — no angels, no dogs, no large symbols, and no mausoleums.

"I like the old part better," Bernie commented to Libby.

"Pain in the ass to dig in, though," Clayton answered. "Too many tree roots."

"I thought people used backhoes for that," Bernie observed.

"I'm talking about in the old days," Clayton replied.

This time Bernie was relieved to see that he didn't turn around while he spoke. They kept driving. Now they were at the new part of the cemetery. Bernie wondered where they were going because they were coming to the end. When they got to the grounds-keeper's house, a small yellow cottage, Clayton's father took a hard right.

"I didn't even know there was a road here," Libby said to him.

"Me neither," Bernie agreed.

Marvin's father laughed. Snickered really. "I thought you famous detectives knew everything."

"Almost everything," Bernie told him.

"She has a photographic memory," Libby added.

"Semiphotographic," Bernie corrected.

Clayton grunted and kept driving. Now they were on a narrow unpaved road. As they traveled along, Bernie noticed rows of small crosses on either side. They had a homemade look about them. Despite her vow she tapped Marvin's father on the shoulder again.

"Who is buried up here?" she asked him.

"People who can't afford a funeral."

"So this is a potter's field."

Marvin's father didn't answer.

41

Bernie looked around. She'd read about them, but she hadn't known they actually existed in this day and age.

"Well, is it?" Bernie repeated.

"We don't use that name," Clayton said.

"I wonder where the word *potter* comes from," Bernie mused. "Of course in old Scottish dialect a pot used to mean a deep hole, and then there's going to pot, which means going to ruin, in the sense of deteriorating which is what bodies do."

"Fascinating," Clayton commented.

Bernie ignored the sarcasm and continued. "Now, the concept itself comes from a verse in the Bible, Matthew, I believe, which states that there's supposed to be a place of burial for the stranger and the friendless poor."

"You're just a mine of useless information, aren't you?" Marvin's father noted as he pulled the limo to a stop.

For once Libby was in agreement with him.

"I guess it depends on your point of view," Bernie told him.

"We're getting out here," Clayton said.

"Why?" Bernie asked. "I don't see anything."

"There." He pointed. Bernie followed his finger. "We're going up there." And with that he got out of the car and hurried toward what looked like a mound of dirt.

Libby got out of the car as well. Bernie joined her.

"I think that's a grave site he's heading to," she said to her sister.

Libby pulled her jacket around her. "I think it is too. Yuck."

"What do you think this is about?" Bernie asked her.

Libby shook her head, "Nothing good." The gesture said that she really didn't know.

By now they were behind Clayton because Bernie's heels kept getting stuck in the dirt.

"I told you not to wear those," Libby said.

"Like you knew we'd be doing this," Bernie told her.

Libby opened her mouth and closed it again. What was the point?

Marvin's father had stopped by the edge of the pile of dirt and was waving at them impatiently to hurry up.

"Definitely a grave site," Bernie said.

Libby shuddered. "On second thought," she said, "I'm glad you're wearing those shoes."

Bernie grinned at her. "Me too. Let's get a grip. How bad could this be?"

"About two bars of chocolate bad. No. Make that three."

"I'd make it three shots of scotch myself."

Bernie agreed. After all, what could be so bad? Being in a cemetery? An open grave? A distressed funeral director? You put them all together and you got something icky. Unless you were like Amber and liked this sort of thing. Now, she would be running up the hill.

Bernie stopped for a moment to pull her stiletto out of the dirt. And she was the one that had fixed Libby up with Marvin. She actually pushed the two of them together. If she hadn't done that, then Marvin's father wouldn't be showing them whatever it was he was about to. Bernie shook her head. Sometimes even she admitted she went a little too far. Not too often, but sometimes. Okay, more than sometimes.

"Hurry up," Marvin's father called to them.

"I'm moving as fast as I can," Bernie lied. Which wasn't exactly true, but she wasn't planning on breaking the heels on her Jimmy Choos.

Finally she and Libby reached the edge of the dirt pile. Yup. Just as she suspected. An open grave. Libby hung back while Bernie peered over the edge. She could see a casket lying there. The hole wasn't very deep. In fact, it was pretty shallow — as if someone had dug it in a hurry. Libby came up and looked over her shoulder.

"The coffin looks flimsy," she observed.

"Like a cardboard box," Bernie said.

"Well, not that bad," Libby objected.

Maybe, Bernie thought, but it sure didn't look like the ones in Marvin's father's funeral home. Those were made out of mahogany and teak. They had brass fittings. The woods were polished to a high gloss. Some were lined with steel or lead and they all cost a lot of money. Bernie decided that if she was going to be buried at all, she'd like to be buried in a coffin shaped like a giant high heel, maybe a strappy wedge. Libby's coffin, on the other hand, would probably be a chocolate bar or a blueberry muffin. She was just going to ask Clayton if that were possible when he coughed and started to speak.

"This is the problem," he said as he pointed to the casket.

"Someone vandalized the grave?" Libby asked. "If that's the case I think you should go to the police. I'm sure they'll do a much better job than Bernie and I can."

"That's not the problem," Clayton said.

"Then what is?" Bernie asked. "Grave robbing? That's so nineteenth century."

"I wish it were that simple," Clayton answered.

Libby felt herself at a loss. What else could it be?

Bernie watched while Clayton rubbed his hands together. Did she detect a crack in his veneer?

"What I'm about to show you is strictly between ourselves. You are not to tell anyone about it," he said.

Bernie looked at Libby and Libby looked at her.

"Well?" Clayton demanded when neither of the sisters answered.

"Maybe you shouldn't show us," Bernie said.

"We won't tell anyone," Libby said.

Clayton looked at Bernie.

"How can I promise when I don't know what I'm promising?" she asked. It didn't seem like an unreasonable question to her.

Libby took Bernie's hand in hers. "Please," she begged.

Bernie snorted. "If it means that much to you, fine." She lifted her hand up. "I promise. Girl Scout word of honor."

So what if she'd never been a Girl Scout? Big deal.

Clayton looked from one of them to the other and nodded.

"Fine," he said.

Then before Bernie could say anything, he got into the grave.

"What are you doing?" she cried.

"You'll see," Clayton said.

"I'd prefer I didn't," Bernie told him.

But Clayton didn't listen. Instead he leaned over and began to lift up the coffin lid.

"Don't," Libby cried.

But it was too late. The coffin lid hit the ground with a thud.

For a second Bernie thought Libby was going to pass out. Instead she closed her eyes.

"Are you okay?" Bernie asked.

Libby nodded.

Bernie took a deep breath and let it out. Then she made herself focus on the man lying inside the coffin. She blinked. Then she blinked again. It wasn't possible. She leaned forward to get a better look.

"It's Ted Gorman," Bernie cried. He looked a little worse for the wear, but given the circumstances who wouldn't?

"I know who it is," Clayton snapped. "What I don't know is what the hell he's doing here."

# CHAPTER 4

Sean looked at his two daughters while he took a sip of the tea Libby had brought him. She still looked a little shaken. So did Bernie for that matter, and it took a lot to shake up Bernie. Like him, she had nerves of steel. Then he nodded toward Clyde. Clyde nodded back and took another bite of his lemon square.

Sean knew what Bernie had told him over the phone about this being privileged information, but he wanted Clyde to hear this as well. When he had headed the Longely police force he'd considered Clyde his best man. He still was, even though Sean was no longer on the force. But Clyde was, and given the circumstances, Sean figured it couldn't hurt to have Clyde's opinion on the matter at hand. He hoped he wasn't wrong.

Sean indicated the cup in his hand with his chin. "Nice tea," he said, nodding toward the cup.

"Organic Russian," Libby replied.

Sean adjusted his wheelchair. The damned thing kept on tilting. He'd have to get it fixed.

"Libby, I'll take another cookie if that's all right with you," Clyde said.

Libby smiled as she passed him the plate.

Sean tried to keep the smile off his face as he watched Clyde buttering up Libby. He knew that the shortest way to Libby's heart was through eating her cooking.

"I still don't think you should be here," Libby protested to Clyde.

"That's your dad's decision," Clyde said.

*Thanks, Clyde,* Sean thought as he watched Libby turn toward him. "I just think that we might need a little extra help, and Clyde happened to be here when you called." Which was a big, fat lie. He'd called him and told him to get down to his place ASAP. "Another pair of ears is always a good thing."

"But Clayton made us promise —" Libby began when Bernie cut her off.

"I didn't promise," she said.

Sean added some more sugar to his tea. It didn't help. "Well, one thing is for sure," he said. "That wasn't a nice thing for him to do."

"No, it wasn't," Libby agreed.

Sean didn't answer. If truth be told he was still digesting what the girls — they were still girls to him, at least — had told him when they'd come into his bedroom twenty minutes ago.

Sean watched while Libby broke off a piece of a heart-shaped sugar cookie, a trial run for Valentine's Day, and popped it in her mouth. His wife, Rose, had never cared about the holiday much, he reflected. Said it was silly. Inez on the other hand . . . He shook his head to dislodge the pang of guilt in his chest. It was just a card, for heaven's sake. Why shouldn't he send a Valentine's card to a friend? A friend who was down in the dumps? It would give her a lift. Just yesterday she'd been telling him how isolated she felt. He knew what that was like. That was one of the problems with getting older — no one paid attention to you anymore.

"Dad, are you listening?" Libby asked.

"Of course I was," Sean lied. Now, he thought, he could feel guilty about not giving his eldest daughter his full attention, especially considering the circumstances.

Libby took another bite of her cookie "The least Marvin's dad could have done was warn us. It wouldn't have been such a shock."

Bernie took a sip of her scotch and re-arranged her legs across the arm of the flowered armchair. Why she insisted on sitting that way Sean didn't know. But she did. Had ever since she was a small child. Nothing his wife tried had ever broken her of the habit, and Rose had tried plenty of things. A plethora, as Bernie would say.

"That was the whole point," Bernie said.

"What was?" asked Libby.

Bernie waved her hand in the air. "Shocking us, silly. If he had told us what he was going to do we would have been prepared."

"If he had told us what he was going to do I wouldn't have come." Libby brushed cookie crumbs off her blouse.

"I don't know if I would have either," Bernie admitted.

"Count me in on that as well," Sean said. Viewing dead bodies wasn't one of his favorite things, and he should know. He'd seen enough of them in his time on the force in Longely. People thought that nothing like that ever happened in a small town, but boy, were they wrong!

"But why would Clayton want to do that to us?" Libby asked.

Clyde shrugged. "Who knows? Maybe it gives him a sense of power? Maybe it gives him a sense of control? Maybe he's so used to dealing with dead bodies that he doesn't realize the effect they have on other people."

Bernie scratched her shin. "We should ask him the next time we see him."

Libby started on her second cookie. "I don't want to see him."

"Neither do I, sister dearest, but you're going to have to. Remember, Clayton is our client."

"So now this is my fault?"

"I didn't say that," Bernie retorted.

"You implied it."

Bernie rolled her eyes. "Given the circumstances, what else could I do? You'd say yes if Rob asked you to do something."

"Not these days."

Sean coughed. The girls turned toward him.

"Ladies, can we get back to the matter at hand?"

"Sure," Bernie said. She gave him a closer look. "You're really mad at Clayton, aren't you?"

"What makes you say that?" Sean asked.

"Because your jaw is clenched," Bernie replied.

Actually, he wasn't mad at Clayton. He was furious with him. He didn't look kindly at someone scaring his girls. Matter of fact, he didn't look kindly at someone raising his voice to his girls. Back in the day he would have given Marvin's father a good talking-to. Or something a little stronger. Unfortunately those days were gone. Or maybe not.

"Don't," Libby said.

"Don't what?" Sean asked.

"Do whatever you're planning."

"I'm not planning anything," Sean protested. *At the moment,* he silently added.

"Marvin is my boyfriend," Libby said.

"I know that," Sean replied. How could he forget it, although there were times when he'd like to.

"Well, it's considered bad form to hurt the father of your daughter's enamorata," Bernie pointed out.

"I wasn't going to hurt Clayton. Anyway" — Sean pointed to his wheelchair — "what could I do?"

"I'm not sure," Libby said, "but I know you'll figure something out."

"You give me too much credit," Sean told her.

Libby ate another piece of her cookie. "Somehow I don't think so. And anyway, he's our client."

"So you've said. Don't I get a say in taking the case?"

"No," both his daughters said simultaneously. "You're outvoted."

"I'm not sure I approve."

Bernie threw him a reproving stare.

"We're stuck with this case, so you might just as well accept it," she told him.

"Because Marvin is Libby's boyfriend, does that mean we have to accept his entire family as clients?" Sean asked.

"In a word, yes," Bernie said. She turned to Libby. "Isn't that right?"

Libby flashed her a grateful look.

"And mom would have agreed with me if she were here," Bernie continued.

"That is a low blow."

"But a true one," Bernie said. "Anyway, don't you want to find out some answers? Aren't you just a little bit curious to figure this out?"

"Not really," Sean told her.

Bernie snorted.

Clyde looked up from finishing off his third lemon bar. "They have you, Chief. Admit it."

"Fine," Sean said grudgingly.

Libby laughed. So did Sean. He didn't know what he'd do without his daughters. He really didn't. He drummed his fingers on the arms of his wheelchair while he thought over what Bernie and Libby had told him. He knew they were right. He just hated to give in. Rose had always said that pride was his besetting sin, and she was correct.

The trouble was, he'd never liked Clayton when he was chief of police in Longely, and he liked him even less now. The man was — what was Bernie's word? Smarmy. Yes. That was it. The man was smarmy. He made his flesh crawl, and it wasn't because of what he did, either. It was because of what he was. But when a man needs your help, he needs your help and you got to give it to him — even when you'd rather not.

"Okay," he said. "Start from the beginning and don't leave anything out."

Libby got up and hugged him. So did Bernie.

"That's enough," he said, pushing them both away. He didn't want them to think he was getting soft in his old age, even though he always had been when it came to them. And didn't they just know it?

Sean watched Clyde lean forward as his daughters began to speak. He knew that if he missed anything, Clyde would pick it up.

"There isn't much to tell," Bernie said. "Like I said, a Ms. McDougal was supposed to be buried in that grave and she's not. Ted Gorman is."

Sean took another sip of his tea and set

the cup down on the saucer. He liked plain old Lipton's better, but he'd never tell Libby that, not when she was so proud that she was serving him the best. He noticed that his hand was shaking slightly, the way it always did these days. But, he reminded himself, it wasn't as bad as it had been when he first got sick.

"Ted Gorman's funeral was three weeks ago, wasn't it?" he asked Bernie and Libby.

"Almost four," Libby corrected.

"That's right." Sean shook his head. Three years ago he wouldn't have made that mistake. "If I recall correctly, they couldn't identify the body."

"That's correct," Clyde said. "According to the reports, Ted Gorman was burned beyond recognition. He wrapped his BMW around a tree and it went up in flames. Not much left of him or the car."

Bernie cut in. "So you can see why I was a little surprised to see him lying there in his jeans and Harley Davidson T-shirt."

"I certainly would have been," Clyde said.

Sean brushed a crumb off his lap. "The story got a big play in the local paper."

"And on TV," Clyde added. "The media were all over it."

"I can imagine," Sean said. And he could.

"His wife had to ID him through his class

ring," Clyde continued. He turned to Bernie and Libby. "You're positive that was Ted Gorman you saw lying there in the coffin?"

"Positive," Bernie said.

"I think it was," Libby said. "Honestly I was so upset I can't be sure."

Sean stroked his chin. "Because if Bernie's right, we definitely have a problem."

*"Several,"* Clyde corrected. "We have *several* problems."

# CHAPTER 5

Everyone in the room was silent for a moment. Finally Bernie said, "I don't know how Clayton expects to keep this quiet."

Clyde took a sip of his tea and put the cup on the table. "You'd be surprised," he observed. "He and Miss Lucy are the best of friends. There'll be an investigation, but it'll be very discreet."

Sean smiled. Miss Lucy was Clyde's nickname for the Longely chief of police.

"Then why does Clayton want us to look into this?" Libby demanded.

Sean shrugged. "That's easy. Because we can go places and say things that the police can't."

Clyde tapped his fingers on the arm of his chair. "How old . . ." He stopped and started again. "From what you observed . . ."

Bernie rescued him. "Do I think Ted Gorman has been dead for a while?"

Clyde nodded in gratitude. "Exactly."

Bernie thought for a moment. "I've never seen someone who's been dead for a while, but Gorman looked okay to me." She turned to her dad. "I mean I'd notice, right?"

"You certainly would," Sean told her. He didn't feel it was necessary to go into all the details of decomposing bodies.

Clyde snagged the last lemon square. "So the question is, where has Ted Gorman been all this time?"

"And who died in the car crash?" Sean added.

Libby leaned forward. "How about Ms. McDougal?"

Sean shook his head. "I looked up the obit on line. She died several weeks before."

"Then where is she?" Libby demanded.

"I wish I knew," Sean said.

Libby began fidgeting with the hem of her blouse. "This is going to be a shock for Marnie, Ted's wife," she said.

"For sure," Bernie said.

"Do you know how she's doing?" Sean asked.

"She's still running the store," Libby replied. "They closed Just Chocolate for two days."

"That's what you did when Mom died," Bernie pointed out.

"I was afraid to lose the business. You're

not around and people go elsewhere. Marnie must have felt that too."

"Retail is tough," Sean heard himself say.

Libby nodded. "The store opens no matter what."

This was true, Sean thought. In that way it was harder than being a police officer. "So how much are we being paid for taking on the case?" he asked.

Sean watched Libby's expression. Her lips were turned down. He felt bad he'd asked.

"I didn't ask for any money," she stammered.

"I didn't either," Bernie chimed in. "It didn't seem right."

"But Clayton has money," Sean pointed out. "Lots of money."

Libby reached up and fixed the doodad that was holding her hair in place.

"Not really," she said. "Marvin says he's way overextended."

Bernie chewed on her cheek. "Rapid growth will do that to you. Did you know that funeral homes are one of the most rapidly growing businesses in America right now? They —"

Sean interrupted. "Not now."

"Don't bark," Bernie told him.

Sean took two deep breaths.

"I'm not barking," he replied when he was

done. "I just thought we'd established a policy. I thought we'd agreed that if we took any more cases we would ask for payment."

"No. We discussed it. We didn't agree to it."

"I could swear we did."

"Well, we didn't."

Sean turned to Clyde. "Don't smirk," he told him.

Clyde put both his hands up in the air. "I'm not."

"Yes, you were."

Clyde didn't answer. Sean sighed again. In the old days, back when he was working with his men, this wouldn't have happened. Discussing something meant that it happened the way he wanted it to, but somehow he'd never been able to make that happen with his wife and daughters. He gave up. Like he always did.

"Marnie is not going to be happy when she finds out about this," Sean observed. "Not happy at all."

"That's putting it mildly," Clyde replied.

"Yeah," Sean said. In his experience people took it badly when they found out that someone who was supposed to be buried wasn't.

Clyde nodded. "Remember Ned Hawkins?"

Sean laughed. "How could I forget." He turned and explained to his daughters. "About twenty years ago, a funeral director ended up burying bodies in a dump site instead of in the cemetery and, to make a long story short, this guy Ned Hawkins shot him. Just went into the funeral home and popped him one. Said he deserved it for all the pain and grief he'd given to everyone's families. The judge let him go. Allowed him to plead not guilty by reason of insanity."

"I don't think Clayton is worried about getting shot. I think he's worried about getting sued," Bernie said.

"Different times, different worries," Sean observed.

"He could get sued for millions," Bernie said. "Although I honestly don't see how this is his fault. I mean he's supposed to bury bodies. I would think the cemetery would be the place that got sued."

"He owns part of the cemetery," Sean informed her.

"You're kidding," Libby cried.

"Not at all. Anyway, it doesn't matter whether this is his fault or not," Sean told his daughter. "After all, these days people get a million for spilling hot coffee on their laps."

"Where do you think Ms. McDougal is?"

Libby blurted out.

"Heaven only knows," Sean said. "Maybe whoever did this reburied her somewhere else in the cemetery."

He doubted it, though. It was more likely that they chopped Ms. McDougal up and threw her in the Hudson River, or used her body in some satanic rite, but he kept quiet in deference to Libby's sensibilities. He rubbed his forehead. Something told him things were going to get very complicated by the time this was over, very complicated indeed.

"Now, who discovered this?" Sean asked instead. "How did this come to Clayton's attention?"

"We already told you," Libby protested.

"Yes, but you were both talking at once when you burst in here. I missed half of what you were saying."

Bernie stood up and began pacing around the room. "The groundskeeper. He noticed the dirt around the grave site had been disturbed, and when he came over to take a better look he realized that someone had been digging something up . . ."

"It's hard digging when the ground is frozen like it is now," Clyde observed. "Although the winter has been pretty mild."

"Hmm." Bernie moved her ring up and

down her finger. "I hadn't thought of that."

"That's because you've never had to dig holes," Sean told her. "Anyway, go on with your story."

"The groundskeeper called Marvin's father, who came out immediately."

"Did the groundskeeper see anyone?"

Bernie shook her head. "If he did, Clayton didn't say anything about it to me."

"What's the groundskeeper's name?"

Bernie and Libby looked at each other. Sean waved his hand in the air. "Not a big deal. We can get it later. Someone will have to talk to him. Go on."

Libby continued. "Clayton said that when he got there he could see that the ground had been dug up and replaced, so he got the groundskeeper to clear the hole. He went in to take a closer look, and that's when he realized the coffin lid had been unscrewed."

Sean studied a lady getting out of her car down the street. She was dressed in a fur cap, fur coat, and suede boots, clothing that might be appropriate for the arctic, but this was Westchester and it was thirty degrees out. Oh well. There was no accounting for people's taste. Or their personal thermostats. He, for example, was like a furnace. Or anyway, that's what Rose used to tell

64

him. Funny, but Inez had said the same thing to him the other day.

He directed his gaze back to his daughters. "To recapitulate what Clyde said, it seems to me like we have three, maybe four problems here. One being, what happened to Ms. McDougal? Two, who did Marnie identify as her husband. Three, how and when did Ted Gorman die. Finally, what the hell is going on here?"

He could see Bernie looking at him. "You have an idea, don't you?"

Sean reached for his teacup but decided against it. The tea made his mouth pucker. What he really wanted was some of Bernie's Scotch, but Libby would just yell at him if he asked.

"Let's just say I have a theory," he replied.

He was just about to lay it out for them when Amber burst into the room.

"The building inspector and some construction guy are both in the kitchen and they want to speak to someone," she cried.

"Building inspector?" Libby repeated.

"That's what he said. Said he was from the town."

"Who are you talking about?"

"I just told you." Amber smoothed back her ponytail. "They're in the kitchen and they want to speak to someone. Now."

Bernie groaned. She closed her eyes for a second, and opened them again.

"I probably should have told you this before —" she began, but Libby cut her off.

"No kidding. This is about that friggin' oven, isn't it? Well, isn't it?"

"Yes. But I've been hoping . . ."

"Hoping what?" Libby asked.

Bernie took hold of Libby's arm and started steering her toward the stairs. "I'll tell you on the way down."

Sean caught a glance from Clyde.

"Why don't your dad and I continue talking?" Clyde said.

Bernie threw him an absentminded kiss. "That'll be great."

Sean watched as Amber, Libby, and Bernie headed out his bedroom door.

"Not good," Clyde commented.

"Not good at all," Sean agreed.

He didn't know what Bernie was going to tell Libby, but he did know *that* it wasn't going to be good. Anything having to do with building inspectors and kitchens never was. They rarely came around to tell you what a good job you were doing. They only came around to tell you how bad you were screwing up.

# CHAPTER 6

Libby stepped into her kitchen ahead of Amber and Bernie.

"They're over there," said Amber, pointing to the two men chatting in front of the cooler. One was dressed in a parka and knit slacks, while the other was wearing jeans and a windbreaker.

"I can see that," Libby replied.

She loved this room, she thought, as the guy in the knit slacks broke off his conversation and headed toward her. She remembered when her mom had set this kitchen up, and she hadn't changed anything in it since she'd taken over the business, at least not in any meaningful way, and she'd been right not to, given what had happened when she'd let Bernie talk her into making changes.

It was perfect the way it was. She loved the tile floors, the large window overlooking the back, and the pots hanging down from the ceiling, the stacks of flour on their shelves, the bags of sugar next to them. The rack of her mom's knives lined up next to the prep table and the scales she used to weigh the ingredients. They all felt good in her hands.

Her mom had always told her that this was backstage, whereas the place where they waited on people was the performance area. Everything started from here.

Libby's eyes reflexively swept the kitchen for possible health code violations, but everything was okay. The sinks were clean, as were the scrubbies. No food was lying out. Everything that should be in the cooler was.

The cleaning products were on their own shelf. All food products were off the floor. Amber and Googie were wearing hats, something Googie had a tendency to forget about. Libby watched the guy in the knit slacks walk toward her. Definitely the building inspector. She'd bet money on it.

She wondered what had happened to George. She'd liked George. He was a nice guy. Probably gone down to Florida to live with his children. He'd been talking about it for years. This one was young. That wasn't good. His bearing was stiff. That wasn't good either. And, even worse, he had a grim expression on his face. Executioner grim.

Given what Bernie had just told her as they went down the stairs, she could understand why. Although she had to remind herself it could be worse. She took a deep breath. She'd like to strangle her sister, but this wasn't the time or the place. Maybe later. No. Absolutely later. One thing was sure: Bernie created chaos wherever she went. Maybe someone could study her. She could be like a science project. Libby was thinking about what kind of science project when she realized that the building inspector guy was talking to her.

"So your sister told you, right?" he asked.

Libby tried not to glare at Bernie. "I'm afraid she hasn't had the chance," Libby said.

Their dad always said never admit, never deny, and that was what Libby intended to do.

"We've had several emergencies," Bernie added.

The building inspector shrugged. "They have nothing to do with this."

"What happened to George?" Libby asked.

"Went down to Florida a couple of months ago."

"That's nice for him."

"If you like bugs. And heat. Which I don't."

Libby followed his eyes as he glanced around the kitchen. She felt a burst of pride at its orderliness and cleanliness. Bernie coughed. Libby's gaze shifted to her.

"I was going to tell her," Bernie explained to him. "I was just looking for the right time."

Libby decided to ignore her, mostly because she didn't trust herself to speak to her sister yet, at least not in what her mother would have called a civil manner.

"You have a name?" Libby asked the building inspector. "A card?"

"The name is Peter Hager." He slapped his pockets. "Sorry. No cards. Must have left them in the office."

"I haven't seen you around before," Libby observed. She felt an overwhelming desire for a piece of chocolate.

"That's because I'm new."

Libby shuddered inwardly. The new ones were always the worst. They had something to prove, whereas the old guys were more inclined to honor the spirit rather than the letter of the law. Not that she wasn't punctilious, because she was. No one had ever gotten sick from food from A Little Taste of Heaven, and as far as she was concerned they never would.

Libby watched as Peter Hager folded his arms over his chest. His expression got even grimmer. "You need a bigger venting system with this new oven."

"You're kidding," Libby heard herself say. They were tight on money these days. The roof had to be fixed and they were going to need a new vehicle soon. The van was in the shop more than not.

"Nope. Your new oven is putting out a lot more BTUs. Sorry, but I don't see any way around it."

Peter uncoiled himself, extended his arm, and pointed to the new oven. "And you need to have your oven tethered to the wall because it's on rollers."

"We're just waiting for the clamp to come in. The one they gave us didn't work. Anything else?" Libby asked.

Peter smiled. Libby reflected that his smile wasn't pleasant.

"Well, I'm not a hundred percent sure," he continued. "I'll have to go back and consult the codebook, but I think you might need a sprinkler system."

"A sprinkler system?" Libby squeaked. "Why? We have an Ansul system. We've always been fine with that."

"Yes, but when you bought your new oven

you went from a light-hazard to a medium-hazard operation. Now, if public space is over four hundred feet away . . ."

Libby groaned. A sprinkler system would cost two thou, easy. All this because they'd installed a new oven that was supposed to be more energy- and time-efficient. Talk about *no good deed goes unpunished. From now on,* Libby vowed, *I'm sticking with the tried-and-true. If it works, it stays. Screw Bernie and her technology.*

"We are over four hundred feet away," Bernie said. She gestured to the other man. "You have a tape measure?"

He laughed. "In my profession I never leave home without it."

"You want to measure?" she asked him.

Libby watched while he whipped his tape measure out of his pocket. "I guess you're in luck," he said to her when he finished. "It's four hundred and thirty feet, so you can just squeak by. "By the way, my name is Tim Conner. I own Conner Construction. Your sister asked me to drop by." He extended his hand and Libby shook it. He looked up at the exhaust fan. "Doesn't look too bad to me. We'll just rip everything out."

Libby gasped.

"Hey. I'm kidding. Just a little contractor humor."

72

"You know what you have to do?" Peter asked him.

Tim nodded.

Libby felt as if she was losing control of the situation.

"What if we got our old oven back?" she asked.

She could see the two men exchanging glances. Peter Hager shrugged. "Then I guess you wouldn't have to make any changes."

"Good," she said. "Because that's what we're going to do."

Bernie rolled her eyes.

Libby turned to her.

"What's that supposed to mean?" she demanded.

"It means exactly what you think it does."

"That's not an answer."

"Ladies, ladies."

Both Libby and Bernie turned. It was Peter Hager.

"You have to make up your mind here," he said.

"We have made up our minds," Bernie said.

"I suppose," Libby said grudgingly.

Peter Hager crossed his arms over his chest. "Good. I'm glad that's settled because now you can concentrate on the meal you're cooking for the Just Chocolate benefit."

"You're going?" Libby asked. She was surprised. He didn't look like a food person.

"Wouldn't miss it for anything. You two always come up with interesting takes on things." He gestured to the door. "You coming?" he asked Tim Conner.

"Might as well," Conner replied. "If I need to I can come back and take measurements later."

"So," Libby heard Hager say to Conner as they both headed out of the kitchen, "I hear you had some trouble down at the shop."

"Naw. Not really. Just the usual stuff. Someone borrowed one of our backhoes. We found it off Lakeland. Happens all the time."

"You're kidding."

"Nope. Probably someone who worked for us. Did you hear what happened at the Smollet Restaurant? I about died . . ."

Then they were through the door and Libby couldn't hear anything else.

"Who says men don't gossip?" Bernie said. "I wonder what did happen at the Smollet Restaurant. When I go to R.J.'s I'll have to ask Brandon."

"You do that," Libby told her sister. Personally she didn't care. "You should have told me. I feel like a moron."

Bernie hung her head. "I know. I kept meaning to, but the time never seemed right. Were you really thinking of getting a deck oven back in here?"

"Definitely."

"But we'll be able to bake so much more with the new one."

"We would if it worked."

"It does work. We just have to iron out a few kinks."

"We've been ironing out the kinks for way too long in my humble opinion." Libby was set to continue in that vein when she felt someone pull her sleeve.

She turned around. It was Googie.

"What's up?" she asked him.

"I'm baking the lemon squares now."

"That's great." On the way downstairs Amber had told her that they were nearly out of their best seller.

Googie tugged at his hair. Recently he'd grown it back again after shaving it off. "I thought you said you were going to give me more hours."

"I did," Libby said.

"I need more."

"I'll see what I can do."

Libby thought for a moment. There was always something to do around the shop. The question was, could they afford to pay to get it done, especially now that they were going to be spending money on enlarging the venting system? On the other hand, Googie was usually a good worker and she didn't want to lose him.

"Well," Libby told him, "you can clean the mixer out tonight and inventory our supplies after we close." That was one of those jobs that always needed to be done and no one ever had the time to do.

"I have to leave tonight," Googie protested.

"Well, when do you want to put the hours in?" It was not, Libby thought, an unreasonable question, but judging from the expression on Googie's face he thought it was.

Googie tugged at his hair again. "How about tomorrow?" he mumbled. "I could come in early tomorrow."

"That'll be fine."

His phone began to play some tune Libby didn't recognize. Hip-hop? Or was it rap? Libby couldn't tell them apart, although Googie had explained the difference numerous times. Bernie probably knew, Libby reflected. But then, Bernie was hip. Really, she defined the term. Libby watched Googie take the phone out of his pocket and move away from her.

Bernie turned toward her. "What was that

all about?"

Instead of replying immediately Libby opened the cooler door, reached in, and took a bite of their classic chicken salad. The chicken was slightly dry. It had cooked too long in the oven. Mayo would help. Like butter, mayo helped practically everything.

"He has a new girlfriend," Libby explained as she threw a few finely chopped walnuts into the salad. A little texture wouldn't hurt either. Neither would some black pepper. She reached for the grinder and turned. Nothing.

"Googie," she yelled.

"Yeah?" He moved the phone away from his ear.

"I thought you were going to fill up the pepper mills."

He flushed. "Right. Yeah. I'll get on it right away."

Libby shook her head. He'd been with her for two years now. Usually he was pretty good, but every once in a while he just lost focus.

Bernie nodded for Libby to move away from Googie.

"He seems totally spaced out," she said once they were standing near the sink.

"I told you. He's got a new girlfriend."

"He always has a girlfriend."

"This one is different."

"How so?"

"He's in love." Libby bracketed the word *love* with her fingers.

"I would think he'd want fewer hours, not more."

"She's got expensive taste."

"How expensive?"

"She wants something from Prada."

Bernie whistled. "That's expensive. Even for me."

"Do tell," Libby answered. "And she wants it for Valentine's Day."

"That's not very far away," Bernie protested. "Maybe he should give her some nice chocolates."

"Nope. Not good enough. I've already suggested that. And while we're on the subject, Amber wants that day off."

"Valentine's Day? But we need her."

"I know." Libby took another nibble of the chicken salad. Much better. "Yeah. It's going to be a real problem. Especially since we'll be prepping for the benefit." She shook her head. She wished she could do everything by herself. That way she wouldn't need to deal with staff. "All I can say is that I'll be glad when Valentine's Day is over this year."

"Hmm," Bernie said. "Do you know the

origin of Valentine's Day?"

"No. And I don't want to."

"Rather grumpy, aren't we?"

"I can't imagine why," Libby said. "First Ted Gorman and now Peter Hager. It has not been a good day."

"No, it hasn't," Bernie agreed, "although I have to say there's a big difference between dealing with a wayward corpse and a building inspector."

"True." Libby watched while her sister spun her silver and onyx ring around her finger.

"And let's not forget that we missed the funeral on top of everything else."

"I'm sure we'll hear from Bree Nottingham."

"I'm sure we will," Bernie said. She smiled.

"What are you thinking?" Libby asked her.

"I'm thinking that we should go shopping."

"We could go to Central Restaurant Supply and see about getting a meat slicer. They have a good one on sale there."

"I was thinking more along the lines of buying shoes. Sexy shoes. How about a pair of red, sexy sling-backs? You could wear them on Valentine's Day."

"You just want to get my mind off the

oven because you think I'll forget about it."

"I wasn't thinking about that at all."

"Yes, you were. Anyway, Marvin doesn't care about stuff like that."

"Of course he does. All men do. He's just not admitting it."

"He thinks shoes like that are stupid."

Bernie snorted. "Right. He thinks that down-at-the-heel black flats are more attractive."

"That is so not true," Libby protested.

"That's what I was saying."

"I didn't mean that and you know it."

Libby was about to say something more when she heard the phone ring out front. Amber picked it up.

"Hello," Libby heard Amber say. "A Little Taste of Heaven. How may I help you?"

"Libby," she cried. "It's for you. A Marnie Gorman. She sounds really upset."

"Why am I not surprised?" Bernie said. "I guess Clayton told her."

"I guess he did," Libby agreed. "I think we can forget about shopping."

"Unfortunately, so do I."

# CHAPTER 7

Just Chocolate was located in a little shopping mall about four miles outside Longely. As Bernie drove she thought about the store. Unlike A Little Taste of Heaven, Just Chocolate had grown and grown and grown. The Gormans had started their shop a little over ten years ago in a small storefront. Bernie remembered going there before she'd gone off to L.A. They'd been the first store in the area to do hand-dipped chocolates.

Business was good so they started selling chocolate novelty items. Then they'd bought the store next door and knocked down the walls, so they'd had a fairly large production area and a cute little counter area.

Next they'd gotten into corporate gifts and the mail order business, and before they knew it they were netting over a million a year — at least that's what she'd heard from a couple of their suppliers. They were hosting the benefit in the rear of the shop because Bree Nottingham insisted that people always liked to see the behind-the-scenes stuff of successful places, and maybe Bree was right, Bernie reflected. Maybe they did. Unfortunately, Bree was usually right about everything.

"I feel so bad for her," Libby said to Bernie as they rounded a turn on Palm Street.

Bernie didn't answer. She was busy wondering about the name since there were no palm trees anywhere in the vicinity, let alone the state. Maybe it was the name of a person? But Palm was an odd name. When she had the time, she'd go down to the Historical Society and see what she could find out.

"Don't you?" Libby asked.

"Of course I feel bad for her," Bernie said.

Libby didn't say anything, but out of the corner of her eye Bernie could see her nodding. After a few seconds Libby turned toward her.

"Having her husband die like that, and now this. They were like two lovebirds, always kissing and holding hands."

"Remember Mom's lovebirds?" Bernie said.

Libby's mouth tightened. "Don't remind me."

The family dog had eaten one of them when the male lovebird — Bernie had forgotten what her mom called him — had flown through the dog's mouth. The bird got away with the stunt the first time; the second time, however, it was sayonara. Needless to say, there'd been nothing to bury. They'd held a memorial service instead.

"I should never have let them out of their cage," Libby continued.

Bernie took a left. With Libby, guilt was forever. "They were pretty stupid."

"But pretty," Libby protested.

"That's what I just said. They were pretty and stupid."

Libby didn't reply. Instead she rooted around in her bag until she found a piece of chocolate and popped it in her mouth.

"You should cut back on that," Bernie observed. "Especially since you said you wanted to lose another ten pounds."

"I need it," Libby protested.

"Nobody needs chocolate. You need a drink or a tranq. You *want* chocolate, you don't have to have it."

"I do."

Bernie laughed. "You're not going to rob a bank if you don't get it."

Her sister gave in. "All right. I don't need it, I want it."

"There is a difference," Bernie pointed out.

"Maybe, but nothing else works as well in the calming department."

Bernie leaned forward a little, the better to look at the window of BeSpoke. They had a neat blouse she'd had her eye on, but by the time she got in, it would probably be sold.

"Maybe you're right," she conceded.

Libby put her hand over her heart. "You're agreeing with me?" she said. "I'm in shock."

Bernie took her eyes off the road for a second and glanced at her sister. She was smiling at her.

"Miraculous, isn't it?" Bernie said. "But chocolate is one of the most chemically complicated foods that we have. Do you know it entered Europe a little while after coffee did? I find that fascinating."

"I don't," her sister said.

Bernie ignored her and continued on.

"Chocolate has over 423 separate components in it, several of which act on the brain and promote feelings of well-being. It acts on the same neuroreceptors that being in love does."

"That's news?" Libby asked.

"No, but they just proved it scientifically."

"Like there's a woman alive who doesn't know that? They should have paid me to do the study."

"And they've never been able to reproduce chocolate in the lab."

"They can't produce vanilla either. Vanillin is terrible. So are most of the imitation flavors for that matter. Look at orange extract. It usually tastes like perfume."

"True." Bernie looked at the piece of chocolate Libby was about to eat. "Do you have another square of that? Because if you do I'll take it."

Libby started rummaging through her bag. How she managed to carry that thing around Bernie never knew. It contained half her belongings. No wonder Libby always slouched. Given the weight of what she carried every day, it was amazing she hadn't hurt her shoulder. A moment later Libby put a square of chocolate in her hand.

Bernie broke off a piece and popped it in her mouth. "What kind is it?" she asked as the chocolate dissolved on her tongue.

"It's pure Colombian. First growth," Libby explained. And she started fishing around in her bag for the box.

"Interesting how food evolves," Bernie mused. "Look at chocolate."

"Here we go with the history lesson," Libby grumbled.

"Well, I think it's interesting. Think about this. A hundred years ago there wasn't any mass candy market."

"Like Reese's Peanut Butter Cups or Three Musketeers?"

"Exactly."

Libby turned her head and stilled her hand. Bernie could tell that she'd captured her attention.

"It's true," Bernie continued. "There were just small candy makers back then — kind of like Just Chocolate. Each town had its own candy maker, just like each town had its own brewery and bakery."

"Why?" Libby asked.

"Think about it. Transportation was different back then. It took time to get from one place to the other. Our interstates are a relatively recent development. I believe they were built in the 1950s for the purpose of getting the army from one side of the country to the other in case the Russians invaded our shores. And there were no large food conglomerates, no one that distributed things on a national level. And chocolate is fragile. It doesn't travel well when it's hot out.

"In fact," Bernie said, warming to her

subject, "until the Mars company figured out how to mass-produce and market chocolate, most of the candy in this country was sugar-based. Taffy and licorice were popular back then. Chocolate was strictly a luxury item, something the upper crust ate."

"It still is a luxury item," Libby said. "This bar we're eating cost almost six dollars. And it's not very large."

"Yes, but back in the day it probably would have cost the equivalent of twenty-five dollars, and you wouldn't have been able to afford it at all. In fact, you wouldn't have wanted it because you wouldn't know what it tasted like. People like you and me and Dad didn't eat chocolate. The closest we got was fudge, because that can be made with cocoa powder, which is way cheaper.

"The guy who founded the Mars company made chocolate affordable. He was the one who figured out that if you diluted it with milk solids you could cut down on the cost. Good dark chocolate contains at least seventy percent chocolate, bittersweet usually has fifty-five percent, but milk chocolate only thirty-five percent chocolate . . ."

"And since chocolate is so expensive, he saved a ton of money," Libby chimed in.

Bernie nodded her approval. "Exactly," she said. "For a while, all Americans ate was milk chocolate. It was extremely common and cheap. But look what's happened in the last ten years. Dark chocolate has become extremely popular again. Now we've been told it's good for us. Supposedly it has more antioxidants than red wine."

"See?" Libby said. "I knew there was a reason I liked it."

Bernie pulled into the parking lot. "Can we say the word moderation?"

"Like you're one to talk?"

"Moi?" Bernie replied as she scanned the lot. It was almost full.

"Yes, you," Libby retorted.

Bernie spied a space in the middle of the last row of cars and made for it.

Libby sighed.

"What's up?" Bernie asked as she carefully maneuvered the car in. Since she was driving Rob's car while their van was in the shop she wanted to be extra careful in the scratch department. Not that he would care, but she sure would.

"I'm just not looking forward to this, is all," Libby commented.

"Like I am?"

"Things don't affect you the way they affect me."

Bernie snorted. "What a load of crap."

"But they don't," Libby insisted. "You and

Dad don't get upset the same way I do."

"Of course we do," Bernie said. "We just don't show it, that's all."

Libby tore at one of her cuticles with her front teeth. "I still wish we didn't have to go in."

"Me too. But we do. And the faster we do this the faster we can leave."

Bernie put the car in park. For a moment neither she nor her sister got out of the car. Bernie sat there studying the facade of the shop. The Gormans had chosen to go in the opposite direction from A Little Taste of Heaven. Their facade was all clean lines and metal, while A Little Taste of Heaven had a cozy feel to it. The window display was minimalist with boxes of chocolate suspended in midair with wires. Just Chocolates' specialty, the Love Knot, a combination of bittersweet, white chocolate and crushed praline, was featured in the center.

Bernie pointed to the large, brown seed-like things on the floor. "I think those are cacao beans."

"They're bigger than I expected," Libby said.

Bernie nodded. They were.

"And uglier," she added.

"Agreed," Libby said.

"I'm not a big fan of the display," Bernie

mused. "Too cold."

It was odd, Bernie thought as she got out of the car. She should like this aesthetic better, it was more her style, but she preferred A Little Taste of Heaven. Somehow, she decided as she walked toward the shop, Just Chocolate projected cool, but whenever Bernie thought about food, she thought warm. Food was about family and friends, not about clean lines and space. She was still thinking about that when she pushed open the door and walked into the shop.

The smell of chocolate, sweet and spicy at the same time, greeted her. The shop was full. Marnie had two counter girls, plus herself, on duty waiting on people. She looked up.

"Thank God you're here," she said when she saw them. And she ran around the counter and headed straight toward them.

# Chapter 8

Libby watched Marnie approaching. "She looks as if she's been crying," she said sotto voce to Bernie.

Bernie grimaced. "Who wouldn't be?"

"But she still looks really good. When I cry my eyes swell up so much they look like slits. You could have disagreed," Libby said when Bernie didn't say anything.

"Okay. I disagree. Satisfied?"

"No." And Libby went back to looking at Marnie.

On closer inspection Marnie's eyes were slightly puffy and red from crying, and the skin on her cheeks was a little blotchy from where she'd wiped at her makeup. But Libby couldn't help thinking she still looked pretty darn good. No. She looked great.

In fact, Marnie looked the way Libby had always wished she could look — effortlessly pretty. She had fine, regular features, perfect teeth, blue eyes, and long blond hair. And she was thin, not skinny but thin. Probably a size 6.

Libby reflected that she'd never be that size and she'd never look like that — never had, never would. But it would be nice if she did. It would be so great to go into a store and have everything you put on look good. It would be so great to put on a pair of jeans and not worry about how big her ass looked — not that Marvin cared.

At least that's what he said, but she suspected that in his heart of hearts he felt differently. How could he not? Libby felt what her mother used to call the green eyes of jealousy peeping out. Then Libby remembered why she and Bernie were there and felt guilty about being jealous. Jeez. Maybe Bernie was right. Maybe her conscience was overdeveloped after all.

Marnie came at them with open arms. "I'm so glad you're here," she cried as she neared them. "So glad. I don't know what I'm going to do." She put her hand over her heart. "When Clayton called me, I just about died. I don't know that I can deal with this. Burying my husband the first time was bad enough." She took a gulp of air. "But this. I don't understand. I don't understand at all. I can't begin to fathom . . ." Her voice trailed off for a moment.

"He said —"

"Who?" Bernie interrupted.

Marnie turned toward her. "Clayton, of course. He said you'd take care of this . . . this problem."

"Did he?" Bernie said.

Libby could tell from the tone in her voice she was not pleased.

"I was so relieved when I heard it was you two who were going to be involved. The famous Simmons sisters."

"Hardly," Libby demurred.

Marnie grabbed Libby's hand. "But you have to find the answer," she told her. "Promise me you'll find out what happened to my Ted. When I saw him . . . I mean there was nothing . . . and now. I can't believe it. I simply can't. You have to find out what happened. You simply must."

"We can try," Libby replied.

"But the police might be able to do a better job," Bernie observed.

A tear trickled down Marnie's cheek. "They were so insensitive . . . when . . . you know. I'm not sure . . . I can deal."

"Don't worry," Libby reassured her. "We'll do what we can."

"Clayton said you would."

"The police will probably be here anyway," Bernie warned. She was surprised they weren't here already. Then she remembered what Clyde had said about Lucy and Clayton being friends. Obviously, he was right. "We have no control over them."

"But I'll feel so much better if you two are working on this," Marnie wailed. "I need answers and I don't think the police can supply them. I need the best, and that's what you are."

Marnie's eyes misted over.

*I can't say no,* Libby thought. *I just can't.* "Don't worry," she told Marnie. "We'll see what we can do. Won't we, Bernie?"

Bernie moved her ring up and down her finger.

"Won't we?" Libby repeated.

"Oh yes," Bernie said.

Libby watched as a small smile appeared on Marnie's face. "You know, Ted and I have been, excuse me, were together since high school. High school." She paused for a moment. "We got married on Valentine's Day. Ted insisted. He was always such a romantic."

Libby could hear Bernie making what she called sympathetic murmuring noises.

"That's one of the reasons we agreed to host the benefit," Marnie continued. "We wanted everyone to share in our good fortune. I feel like Saint Valentine."

Bernie peered at her. "Really?" she asked.

*Uh-oh,* Libby thought as Bernie's eyes glinted. *History lesson, here we come.*

"Yes. I'm a martyr to love," Marnie declared.

"In truth," Bernie began before Libby could stop her, "there were three Saint Valentines who were beheaded by the Romans, but no one knows which one of the three, if any, Valentine's Day is based on. Right now the favorite money is on the Saint Valentine who secretly married couples when the Roman Empire had forbidden clerics to do so, but it could be the one who was beheaded during the reign of Claudius the second, or the Catholic bishop of Terni who was also beheaded during Claudius the second's reign. Actually, a lot of Christians lost their lives then."

"Fascinating," Marnie said.

"Well, maybe not," Bernie conceded. "But here's something that might interest you. Even though chocolate was considered an aphrodisiac in the Aztec court, in Europe it was considered positively vile. In fact, I read somewhere that in 1569 Pope Pius the Fifth considered the substance so noxious that he said that drinking it would not break the communion fast. Actually, it was considered a medicine."

Marnie smiled for the first time. "I guess whatever comes around goes around. I've been reading that the doctors are saying chocolate is actually good for you." She glanced at the clock on the wall. "I have a rep coming in to talk to me in another hour. So if we could talk now . . ." Her voice trailed off.

"Definitely," Libby replied, thinking of everything they had to do back at their place.

The three of them started toward the door. As they did, Libby could suddenly hear her mother saying, "You have to smile at the customers no matter what. No one coming in here wants to know about your problems. They want to come in here to buy something and be treated in a friendly fashion. No one wants to come in and buy something in a place where bad feelings exist."

Libby was thinking about the wisdom of her mother's words when Marnie pushed the door to the back open and they went inside.

# CHAPTER 9

The smell of chocolate assailed Bernie's nostrils. It was so thick she could almost taste it in the back of her throat. Maybe you could have too much of a good thing. She knew that after a while she would have found the smell of chocolate cloying.

"Do you ever get tired of the smell?" she asked Marnie.

Marnie gave a little laugh. "Why do you ask?"

"Just curious."

"When people asked Ted that, he used to say, can you ever get tired of the smell of money? I think I have to go with his answer."

"I know I never get tired of the smell of cookies baking," Libby said. "It means home to me."

Personally, Bernie liked the smell of Chanel. She didn't think she'd ever get tired of the aroma, but she didn't say that as she looked around. The room they were standing in was twice the size of A Little Taste of Heaven's kitchen, maybe even larger. Her mom had done wonders fitting as much as possible together in a small space, but the kitchen of Just Chocolate was open and spacious. Everything was within easy reach. And if they wanted to expand they could.

The walls were lined with drying racks on two sides, while the third side was lined with paper goods, and the fourth contained boxes full of the finished product. Ceiling fans gently circulated the air. The place was completely tiled in white ceramic for easy cleanup. There were five different candy-making stations, large vats where the chocolate was tempered. Three of the vats were in operation now.

Employees were busy dipping a variety of centers into the vats with their gloved hands and carefully placing them on trays lined with white paper. When the chocolate hardened they'd be boxed up and placed in a cooler.

"People don't realize that hand-dipped actually means hand-dipped," Bernie heard herself comment. Was that a stupid comment or what? she wondered.

"It's true," Marnie said. "They don't realize that our products aren't made on an assembly line, that our centers are each individually enrobed . . ."

"Enrobed is such a nice word," Bernie couldn't resist saying. "It sounds as if you're dressing a king. You know, getting him in his robes. Of course, an even better word would be the French embonpoint, which means plump. I think it fits your product, don't you?"

Marnie gave her a nervous look. *Guess she doesn't agree,* Bernie thought. *Oh well.* But she liked it. Embonpoint. She turned the word over in her mind.

"Embonpoint is really quite onomatopoetic, don't you think?" Bernie asked.

Now Marnie looked quite alarmed.

"It sounds like a disease," Libby observed.

"Hardly," Bernie retorted. "It —"

Marnie interrupted. "I know what the word means. I guess I agree, I just never thought of it in relation to our product, but you may be right." She cleared her throat. "Anyhow. As I was saying, hand-dipping is one of the reasons our products cost what they do. Both our ingredients and our labor costs are extremely high." Marnie rebuttoned the top button of her black blouse. "We've been having good luck with our chocolate flavored with chili powder," she said, changing the subject altogether. "People seem to really like it."

"From the Aztecs," Bernie commented. "Interesting. They flavored their chocolate with chilies. Of course they drank their chocolate."

This time Bernie noted that Marnie seemed genuinely interested in her comment.

She nodded her head. "Exactly."

"I don't know," Libby said. "Chocolate with chili, chocolate with lavender, chocolate with lime. I think I'd rather stick with the tried-and-true."

"I agree, but a lot of people like novelty."

"Can I ask where you got the cacao beans from?" Bernie inquired.

"From one of our suppliers," Marnie replied.

"You don't see them very often," Libby observed.

"No, you don't," Marnie agreed. Her eyes swept the production room.

Bernie recognized the look. It was something she did at her place all the time to make sure everything was working well, that nothing was out of order.

"You've done a great job setting this operation up," Bernie commented.

"That was Ted," Marnie answered as the three employees who were working there looked up. "He had a wonderful sense of spatial perception. Much better than mine."

As Marnie gestured for them to go back to what they were doing, Bernie laughed.

Marnie gave her a puzzled look. "What's so funny?" she asked.

"Oh," Bernie replied. "I was just thinking how different this is from *Charlie and the Chocolate Factory.* I don't think many people expect to see such a streamlined, sterile facility."

Marnie bobbed her head up and down. "I know. Odd, isn't it? Originally we were going to have an open kitchen, but we decided against it. Maybe we should have, but that would have meant more regs to deal with."

"Tell me about it," Libby said and she explained what was happening at their store.

Marnie shook her head. "Amazing, isn't it? It's like they don't want you to go into business. Anyway, that's why Bree Nottingham thought it would be a good idea to hold the benefit in here. She told me that people would love to get a look at how our chocolate is actually made, and judging from the ticket sales I think she's right."

"Are you going to be making candy, then?" Libby asked.

"Not really. We can't. The last thing we would need is for something to fall into one of our chocolate vats. Which would be extremely expensive, given the amount of chocolate that's in one of them. What we'll do is a couple of small-scale demos with a couple of our little kettles. You know, we'll dip nuts, caramel centers, fresh fruit, maybe some potato chips. I don't know exactly. I haven't worked it out yet."

"We should talk about our menu at some point," Libby said nervously. She hoped Marnie didn't take the suggestion amiss.

"By all means," Marnie replied.

Libby breathed a sigh of relief while Bernie walked over to one of the vats and peered in.

"Do you think the cost of chocolate is going to go higher?" she asked Marnie.

"Considering the situation on the Ivory Coast, undoubtedly." Marnie strolled over and stood next to the man who was working there. "This is our premier bittersweet, right, Bolt?"

"Bolt?" Bernie said. What kind of a name was that? she wondered. Had he been born in a hardware store?

"It's short for Bolton," he explained even though she hadn't asked. "It's my family name. And no. I wasn't conceived in Home Depot. And no. I don't have a sister called Nut. You know, as in nuts and bolts." And he grinned.

"Guess you've been getting this all your life?" Bernie replied.

"Guess so."

"You go to R.J.'s, right?"

"On occasion. I'm on the softball team."

"Bolt is involved in all sorts of activities," Marnie said. "We're lucky to have him."

"Too true," Bolt said to Marnie as he shot Bernie one last smile.

He turned and went back to dipping slices of ginger into the swirling dark mass.

"Here, have one," Marnie said.

As Bernie watched she reached onto the white paper where the ginger slices were drying, plucked off two, and handed one to Libby and the other to Bernie.

Bernie took a bite. The spicy snap of the ginger combined with the smooth taste of the chocolate. She took another bite.

"This is wonderful," she said. And it was.

Marnie nodded her head. "It's one of our best sellers. Recently our hand-dipped fruits have taken off, and for Valentine's Day we can't do enough of our chocolate-dipped strawberries to keep up with the demand. I can't find long-stemmed strawberries at a semireasonable price anywhere this year. Can you?"

Bernie shook her head. "Our shipments are coming from Mexico. I'd prefer California, but with the weather being what it was out there, the supply is very limited. And when you factor in the transportation costs it's really expensive. We're getting a surcharge on each bill from our suppliers."

Marnie shook her head. "Me too. I'm going to have to pass the cost on to my customers eventually, even though I'd rather not." She sighed. "Ted used to take care of dealing with the vendors. Ted and I used to do everything together. Absolutely everything. Do you know that I met him in the third grade? He was in my class." And she sighed again and her eyes began to mist over.

Bernie decided now might be as good a time as any to bring up the subject they were here to talk about — namely how Marnie's husband had gotten into Ms. McDougal's coffin — but before she could Marnie straightened her back, wiped her eyes, and favored both her and her sister with a brilliant smile.

"But life goes on, right? I know Ted would have wanted me to continue." Marnie flung her arms out. "This store is like our child, a very well loved child, and I think the best thing I can do for Ted is honor his memory by tending to it with love and care." She turned to Libby. "Don't you?"

"Oh yes," Libby stammered. "Of course."

Bernie had opened her mouth again, but before she could get any words out Marnie was leading them across the floor to another candy dipper. When she looked up, Marnie said, "This is Cyna, Cyna Mullet. Another one of our valuable employees."

The girl nodded and looked up at them. She radiated sullenness, Bernie decided. She was as pretty as Marnie, but in an entirely different way. She had black hair, almost blue black, white skin, and green eyes. Bernie found her eyes fastening on Cyna's jeweled nose ring and pierced lip.

"I almost didn't hire Cyna because of that," Marnie said, gesturing toward Cyna's piercings.

"Everyone has them now," Bernie said. It was hard to hire staff that didn't have a tattoo or a piercing these days.

"Cyna has been with us since she quit going to high school, haven't you, Cyna?" Marnie said.

The girl nodded.

"I wasn't going to hire her. I didn't think she would be responsible enough, but Ted saw the potential in her and insisted that we try her out for a month. We had a tremendous fight over it. But he was right, wasn't he?"

"Yes," Cyna said softly.

"Cyna turned out to be one of our best workers. She sees what has to be done and does it no matter what it is."

"I wouldn't go that far," Cyna said.

"I would." Marnie turned her head away. "Ted always saw the potential in everyone, absolutely everyone. That was one of his greatest gifts. It's something I'm trying to do, but it's hard, very hard."

Then before Bernie could say anything, Marnie turned and ran out the door.

# CHAPTER 10

"That went well, don't you think?" Libby asked when she and Bernie were back in the car.

She was amused when Bernie grunted and turned the key in the ignition. The car made a whining sound as it turned over.

"I think I've finally met someone who can outtalk you," Libby continued. She knew she should stop, but she wasn't able to.

"Untrue," Bernie retorted.

Then her sister threw the car into reverse and backed out of her parking space, way too quickly in Libby's opinion.

"True," Libby countered. "Aside from that little rant about chocolate you couldn't get a word in edgewise."

"It wasn't a rant," Bernie protested. "It was a history lesson."

"Is that what you're calling it?"

"What are you calling it?"

Libby hunted around in her backpack and

came up with a chocolate chip cookie. She broke it in half and plopped the larger half in her mouth before replying.

"I'd call it a waste of time," Libby said after she swallowed. She could see two spots of color appearing on her sister's cheeks.

"Marnie thought it was interesting," Bernie said. She looked right and left before heading out onto Ash Road.

The traffic seemed to be heavy for this time of day. Libby wondered where everyone was going. She glanced at her watch. She still had to stop at Sam's Club. They were out of paper towels and scrubbies and portion cups.

"I take it from your silence that you didn't?" Bernie asked her.

*She's like an interrogator,* Libby thought. "No. I did," she admitted. "Sort of . . ."

"Then what's the problem?" Bernie demanded.

"Who said there's a problem?"

"You did."

"When?"

"Just now."

"No, I didn't."

"Your tone did."

"What's my tone?"

"Angry."

"Really?"

"Yes, really."

Libby ate the rest of her cookie while she thought over what Bernie had just said. "I'm not angry," she said even though she knew she was.

Bernie kept her eyes on the road.

"Okay, I am angry."

"I'm waiting," Bernie said when Libby didn't say anything else.

Libby took a deep breath. Why did she have such trouble talking about her feelings? It was ridiculous. "I guess, maybe, I'm still angry with you about the oven."

Bernie shot her a glance out of the corner of her eye. "But we agreed."

Libby didn't say anything.

"You could have said no."

"I got tired of your talking about it all the time. That's why I agreed. I knew it was a bad idea from the start."

"Then you should have told me to forget about it."

"But you wouldn't have. You never forget about anything. You just go on and on and on."

"So what? Is it wrong to want to try out something new?"

"Well —" Libby began, but Bernie cut her off before she could finish.

"Even the ovens we're using were new

once," she pointed out. "Think about it. I can just see it now. Honey, why are we using gas for the ovens? We should stick with wood. More reliable that way. Less likely to poison us. Someone had to invent an oven. In the beginning people just cooked on an open fire. In fact someone had to invent a range . . ."

"Range?" Libby asked.

"Yes. A range. Something that combines both a cooktop and an oven. The word *range* comes from the French word that means things in a row, like a range of mountains. I think the first use of the word *range* in the cooking instead of the mountain sense was somewhere in the fifteenth . . . or was it the sixteenth century . . . ? I forget.

"There's also a German word like it that means ring. I mean, in the beginning people didn't want toilets in their houses. They thought outdoor privies were a much better idea. More sanitary. Indoor plumbing is relatively recent. Of course, in some castles in the fourteenth century they had . . ."

Libby couldn't help herself. She started to laugh. Bernie was so over the top that no matter how she tried she could never stay mad at her for long.

Bernie laughed too. "Okay. Sometimes I get carried away. I admit it. And the oven does have problems. The next time we do something like this —"

"There won't be a next time."

"You mean we're never going to remodel, ever again?"

"I didn't say that," Libby said.

"Anyway," Bernie continued as if she hadn't heard her sister, "we should do more research into the implications of the changes we're going to make."

Libby didn't reply. How could she? It was hard to argue with what her sister was saying. So why did she still feel slightly upset? Another moment went by while Libby mulled that question over. And then she realized the answer. She was mad at herself, not Bernie. Bernie was right. She should have just said no instead of letting her sister ride roughshod over her. In the future, she vowed to herself, she would trust her own judgment.

"We need to go to Sam's Club," she reminded Bernie as they came up to Clarkson Avenue.

"I haven't forgotten," Bernie said as she took a sharp right. "Okay," she admitted. "I did forget. Happy?"

Libby smiled. "Yes. You know," she said after another moment had gone by, "that girl Cyna didn't seem very happy."

Bernie took another right. "No. She didn't, did she? She seemed . . ." She paused for a moment while she searched for the correct word. "Disgruntled."

Libby nodded. "Maybe she and Marnie are having an argument about something."

"Possible." Bernie swerved to avoid a car that had decided to stop in the middle of the road. "Or maybe she was just having a bad day."

"Could be," Libby said. What was it her mother used to say? Something about how a disgruntled employee was a destructive employee?

"But Bolt was pretty cute. Did you see his forearms? Nice muscles."

Libby shot her sister a look. "Interested?"

"No. It was just an observation."

"Rob wouldn't be happy to hear you say that."

Bernie snorted. "Just because I'm going with someone doesn't mean I can't look."

Libby shrugged. Another way she and her sister were different. "Maybe. One thing is certain, though. We still don't know any more about how Ted Gorman's body got where it was now than we did before we walked into the shop."

Bernie flashed a grin at her. "I was thinking the very same thing. But what could

Marnie really say? And anyway, given the subject I can understand why she didn't want to discuss it."

"But she called us to come over."

"She wanted us to reassure her that we would do something."

"Good point," Libby conceded. "I hadn't thought about it like that." She began to bite her cuticles.

"Stop it," Bernie told her.

Libby glared at her.

"You told me to tell you to stop biting your nails, so I am."

"You're right. I did." Libby took her hand out of her mouth. It was a bad habit. Half the time she wasn't even aware that she was doing it. "So who should we talk to?" she asked, changing the subject.

"One of us should talk to Marnie again," Bernie suggested.

"Agreed."

Bernie thought for another moment. "And someone should talk to Ms. McDougal's family."

"Maybe Dad knows them." After all, Libby thought, their dad knew practically everyone.

Bernie stifled a yawn. "Good idea. Marvin could drive him."

"He hates having Marvin drive him,"

Libby protested.

"He hates having anyone drive him."

"This is true." He screamed at Libby every time he was in the car with her as well. "Okay," Libby said. "Marvin didn't seem to mind that much."

"It will give them more time to bond," Bernie said to her.

Libby giggled.

"Meanwhile," Bernie continued, "we can talk to the groundskeeper and then go to Sam's Club."

Libby nodded. That would work.

"There's one thing I want to say, though," she continued.

Libby turned to look at her. "About who we should talk to?"

"No. About chocolate and blood."

Libby groaned. "No more."

"Seriously."

"I am serious."

Bernie ignored her and went on. "The Aztecs maintained there was a ritual relationship between blood and chocolate because they both have the same color."

"I don't see that at all," Libby said firmly.

"Maybe," Bernie said. "But don't you think there's a relationship between love and death?"

"No."

"Think about it."

"I am thinking about it and I still say that the answer is no. Sometimes you really are crazy."

"But in a good way," Bernie said.

"A very good way," Libby agreed. She was about to say something else when Bernie's cell phone began playing "Stayin' Alive."

"Could you get that for me?" Bernie asked.

Libby nodded and fished it out of Bernie's purse.

"Hello?" she said into it.

"Hello," came back the reply.

"Is this Marnie?" Sometimes it was hard to identify people when you talked on a cell.

"Yes, it is." Then Marnie stopped talking.

Libby looked at the cell to make sure it hadn't gone dead. Nope, they were still connected.

"Is there anything I can do for you?" Libby asked after a few more seconds had gone by. When there was no answer she said, "Do you want to wait and call Bernie back? She's driving right now."

"No," Marnie said. "That's all right."

Marnie's voice was so low Libby had to strain to hear it.

"There's something I need to tell you," Marnie said.

"Do you want us to come back?"

"No. No, don't do that." Marnie's voice rose. She sounded panicky. "I'm not sure I can say this to you face-to-face."

"Go on," Libby said.

Bernie raised an eyebrow. Libby shook her head and pointed to Bernie's phone. "This is important," she mouthed. She could hear people talking in the background. Then Marnie started speaking again.

"All that stuff I told you about Ted . . ."

"Yes," Libby prompted.

"It's true. But there was talk that Ted was going out with someone. Jealous rumors."

"Do you know who started them?" Libby asked.

There was no answer. She cursed herself for interrupting. She should have just let Marnie talk. The time for questions would come after Marnie had finished. Libby thought she had completely blown it when Marnie started speaking again.

She said, "People said he was out with her the night of the accident. Now they're saying he killed her and burned her body so everyone would think it was him who died in that crash."

"Why would they say that?"

"It's all lies." Now Marnie was sobbing so hard Libby had trouble understanding her.

"People are so mean. I loved him and he loved me."

"Do you know who killed your husband?" Libby blurted out.

More sobs on the other end of the line. "I don't know. You're the geniuses. You figure it out." And she hung up.

"Here," Libby said as she handed the phone back to Bernie. "She's hysterical," she commented after she'd told Bernie what Marnie had said.

Bernie took a right. "We should call Dad and tell him. He's good at figuring this kind of stuff out."

# CHAPTER 11

Sean took a sip of his tea while he thought about what Libby had told him yesterday. He'd been pondering Marnie's comments on and off since then and had come up with several questions.

He took a bite of his chicken salad sandwich. Why did Marnie assume it was a female in the car? It could have been a male. Maybe Ted Gorman was a gambler and owed a lot of money. Maybe he was gay? One thing was for sure. They had to find out more about Ted Gorman.

Sean had called Clyde and he was gathering information about Gorman while Sean dealt with the other end of the puzzle — Ms. McDougal. Over the years he'd found that when you don't know which direction to go, you work as many sides of the puzzle as possible. Eventually, one side stands out and you follow that one to the end. At least that was the theory.

Sean sighed, put down his sandwich, and tried to focus on what he was supposed to be doing, which was dealing with his computer. He knew they were wonderful things. At least they were now that he knew how to use one. He'd just finished searching through the obits of the local paper online. In the old days he would have had to go through the old papers down in the morgue.

He shook his head to clear it. These days they used microfiche. Saving the trees and all that. He felt sorry for anyone who'd been away from civilization for a while. When they came back they wouldn't even be able to make a phone call. Hell, it had taken him two hours to figure out how to answer his new cell, not that he'd ever admit that to his daughters.

Just look at the new oven in the shop if you wanted an example of technology run amok. The old one had worked perfectly fine. So it had to be recalibrated once in a while. So what? Then the girls had gone and gotten something that looked like a conveyor belt. Hell, it *was* a conveyor belt. He didn't know what Rose would have made of it. But this he did know: the thing had been nothing but trouble from the time it had been installed.

Ridiculous if you asked him. Of course no

one did. Why ask the old man? What did he know? He sighed and shifted his weight around. Why hadn't someone invented a more comfortable wheelchair? Something that molded to his body. Maybe with an automatic back massager. Heated. Oh well, at least he wasn't stuck in this thing. He could get up and walk when he had to.

No sense in bitching. He supposed he had it better than most. Some men in his position would be in a nursing home. Ha. He'd shoot himself before he let that happen. Not that it would. Not with Libby and Bernie around. They were super. Unfortunately, they always wanted to know stuff. His stuff. It wasn't that they'd care that he was sending Inez a Valentine's Day card. In fact, they'd be delighted. It was just that it was a private matter.

"Okay, Sean, admit it," he said out loud. "You just don't want to have to listen to your daughters gloat."

They'd been trying to set the two of them up for months. Bernie would never let him forget it. Ever. She was just like him in that way. He sighed and turned his attention back to his computer. Libby had assumed that given his job he would know something about Ms. McDougal. But he didn't. Couldn't even put a face to the name.

So far he'd only come up with a small death notice. Just a statement about how Ms. Clara McDougal had passed away on November 19. That was it. No more details given except her DOB. No cause of death was listed. She'd been seventy-nine at the time of her passing. *Time of her passing.* How was that for a euphemism? She evidently didn't have any kin, or if she did none were mentioned in the notice. Hmm. Interesting. Another thing he or the girls would have to check out.

Sean pushed his chair away from the computer, rolled it toward the window, and looked out. February was a barren time of year. He almost preferred the snow on the ground — at least it hid the gray. As he watched Murray's black and white cat run across the street, it occured to him that Ms. McDougal was probably buried where she was because she had no family and no money. Hence the death notice. The paper had to publish death notices gratis as a matter of public record, but obits were paid for by somebody.

And that area of the cemetery was reserved for the indigent. It wasn't a potter's field exactly — he had to remember to ask Bernie where that expression came from — but it was pretty much as close to one as the township of Longely got. The logical thing in this case, not to mention the quickest, would be to call Clayton and ask for the information he needed, but he hated talking to Clayton. Sean drummed his fingers on his chair. The man was a self-righteous prig. He'd had to be nice to him when he was chief of police; now he had to be nice to him — or at least civil — because he might be Libby's father-in-law someday. Sometimes life just wasn't fair.

Maybe it was time to get out and see what he could find out about Ms. McDougal on his own. He'd told Bernie he would. She'd been surprised to hear that he didn't know anything about this lady. She must have led a very quiet life.

And it would be interesting to see the crime scene as well. When he'd been the police chief he'd always done better cruising around, instead of relying on the reports his men brought in. Unfortunately he needed a driver for that. Even he had to admit that he could no longer drive himself.

And that meant Marvin, who he knew from experience would be more than happy to drive him. And Marvin would be able to tell him about Ms. McDougal as well, or if he couldn't he could find out anything Sean needed to know.

Sean took a deep breath. The only problem with riding with Marvin was Marvin's driving. Even Libby had done better her first day out than Marvin did after years on the road. Sean didn't want to think about how many accidents he'd inadvertently caused.

And of course there was the fact that Marvin was one of the clumsiest human beings he'd ever met. Okay, that was a slight exaggeration. Tipton Gray the Third had been clumsier. Sean closed his eyes for a moment as he pictured extricating Tipton from the toilet bowl at the Lucky Seven Bar and Grill, an establishment he had no business patronizing, a fact he'd pointed out at length as he'd tried to extricate Tipton's foot from the toilet bowl.

Tipton had gotten his foot wedged so far down that they'd finally had to smash the bowl with a mallet. Sean shook his head at the memory. Water and ceramic shards all over the floor. What a mess that had been. The bar owner had wanted the town to pay him damages; he kept insisting until Sean had a little chat with the guy and told him he was thinking about stationing a cop at the door weekend nights for the next year or so. For everyone's own good, of course. Funny how that had worked.

But as he always told his men, you had to work with what you had and mold it into what you wanted it to be. And what he had was Marvin. He had to make the best of him. Plus, Marvin could always drive him over to the Big W over in Hadley. If he remembered rightly, they had a card section in the back after the canned fruits and salad dressings. Sean squared his shoulders, took a deep breath, and reached for the phone. Sometimes a man had to do what a man had to do. Whatever that meant. He'd never understood the phrase himself.

"New van?" Sean asked Marvin as he fiddled with the seat belt. The things seemed to get harder to work every year.

Marvin grunted as he unzipped his jacket. It was one of those big puffy down things. Sean reflected that he looked like the Michelin Man going on an Arctic expedition.

"We can fold the seats down and slide two coffins in if we have to," Marvin told him when he was finished.

"Wonderful," Sean said. He didn't know why, but he hated the idea of riding in a vehicle used for transporting dead bodies. When he was young, he wouldn't have given it a thought. Now he thought about things like lingering germs and virsuses waiting to

attack him. "Kind of a multipurpose vehicle," Sean observed. He wasn't going to
ask if Marvin or his dad had already tried
out its coffin-carrying capabilities, because
he didn't want to know.

Marvin smiled at him. "Exactly. Hearses
are so . . . so." He paused while he searched
for the word he wanted.

"Obvious," Sean supplied.

"Exactly," Marvin repeated as he slipped
off his jacket and got his left arm stuck in
the sleeve.

Sean watched in fascination as he tried to
pull himself loose. Libby would probably
have helped, but Sean figured that would
only make the whole incident more embarrassing. A moment later Marvin succeeded
in extricating himself. He punched the
jacket into place.

"People would rather not be reminded
that we're carrying someone who's deceased," Marvin continued. "Weird, isn't
it?"

"Absolutely," Sean agreed as Marvin
pulled into the street without looking.

Sean closed his eyes. It didn't help. When
he opened them again, Marvin was looking
at him while he was driving down Main
Street. Sean gritted his teeth. *I won't say
anything,* he told himself. His resolve lasted

for all of three seconds.

"Eyes front."

"They are front," Marvin said as he continued looking at him.

"No, they're not," Sean said in a somewhat — okay, a very — loud voice.

Marvin redirected his gaze to the street. "I was just concerned because you had your eyes closed. I thought maybe something was the matter."

"Well, I'm fine," Sean snapped. "Next time focus on the road." Then he felt guilty and added, "But thank you for caring."

Marvin didn't say anything. Sean didn't either. Finally Sean couldn't stand it any longer. "So what did Libby tell you?" he asked.

Marvin remained silent.

*This is ridiculous,* Sean thought. "Look, if you want to take me back to the house . . ."

"I just don't think I'm that bad a driver," Marvin said.

This time Sean noted he was careful to keep his eyes on the road. *Oh, the things I do for my children,* Sean thought as he told Marvin he wasn't a bad driver, he was an inattentive one. Actually they were one and the same thing, but Marvin must have thought they weren't, because Sean noticed his jaw muscles loosening slightly.

Sean guessed all was forgiven because when they got to Western Avenue Marvin said, "Libby told me to take you up to the newspaper, but I don't think you're going to find much. Ms. McDougal didn't have any living family except for a third cousin who lives a little out of town. When we contacted her she said, 'Clara lived alone and she can bury herself.' Or words to that effect. And we were going to give her the cheapest rate too."

"Not nice," Sean said.

"Not nice at all," Marvin agreed.

"How hard did you look for a living relative?"

Marvin stopped at the stop sign. "You know my father. Do you think he'd bury anyone for free?"

"You looked very hard," Sean said.

Marvin nodded. "Very hard indeed."

"And you didn't find anyone."

"No one. She was an only child. Her mother and father both died years ago. She never married. And that, as they say, is all she wrote."

"What about her neighbors?"

Marvin clicked his tongue against the roof of his mouth as he continued driving. "What about them? She lived up around Brighton Ridge."

127

Sean groaned. That area was mostly state parkland. Few people lived up there because the roads were hard to navigate. Those that went up there were mostly backpackers and campers.

"So who found her? How did it happen?"

"A couple of campers knocked at her door. Their car had broken down and they wanted to use the phone. When she didn't answer, they knocked one last time and the door swung open. She was lying on the floor."

"Cause of death?"

"The death certificate reads heart attack," Marvin said, and then made a left turn.

"No, Marvin," Sean instructed. "Go right."

"But the newspaper is to the left."

"I know, but you've already told me everything I could find out from there. So now I want to go up and talk to the cousin, but before we do that I want to see the crime scene."

Marvin took his eyes off the road for a second.

"Road," Sean said. "Watch the road."

"There's nobody on it," Marvin protested.

"Watch the road anyway," Sean instructed, trying to keep his voice on a low frequency. *I will not yell,* he told himself.

"Anyway," Marvin told him as he swerved to miss a cardboard box lying in the road, "it's not a crime scene."

"Then what is it?" Sean demanded.

"My dad is calling it a case of misplacement."

Sean laughed. "Misplacement?" That was a good one. He wondered what the police would call it. Or were calling it. But he hadn't heard from them yet, so they weren't investigating. After all, if no one reported the incident, then they didn't know. Of course not reporting what had occurred was a crime in itself. Sean let out his breath. *I'm not going to think about that,* he told himself. He'd worry about it if it came up.

"Misplacement," Marvin repeated.

"Call it what you will, I still want to see it."

"But Libby is going to kill me if I do that."

Sean leaned forward a little. "I'll make you a deal," he told Marvin. "I won't tell her and you won't either. That way she'll never know. How's that?"

Marvin shook his head. "She'll find out. She always does."

Sean snorted. "So what? You're not afraid of her, are you?"

"Of course not. I just don't like when we fight."

129

"Fair enough. I don't like it when Libby and I fight either. But since she's not going to find out, it's not going to matter."

"I suppose," Marvin said in a hesitant voice.

From the look on Marvin's face Sean knew he had him.

"Then take the next left," he instructed.

"I know," Marvin groused.

They drove for a minute in silence. When they got to Ashdon Road, Marvin slowed down.

"Signal," Sean said. "Use your signal light."

"I was going to," Marvin informed him.

*He does this just to annoy me,* Sean thought as Marvin made a sharp left. They drove for another minute while Sean told himself, *I will be calm, I will be calm, I will be calm.* The trick, he decided, was to concentrate on something else — like the problem at hand.

Sean took a deep breath. "Out of curiosity, what did you do with Ted Gorman?"

Marvin gave him a stricken look. "I didn't do anything with him."

"I didn't mean you literally. I meant you as in your business."

"I don't want to talk about it. I don't want to talk about it at all."

And Marvin didn't say anything else for

the rest of the trip. Which was fine with
Sean.

## CHAPTER 12

Libby didn't look happy. But then, these days she never did, Bernie thought. Pressure and Libby did not go well together. Some people rose to meet the challenge. Unfortunately, Libby wasn't usually one of them.

"I want to go home," her sister said.

"You wanted to come along," Bernie pointed out. Which Libby had.

Libby gestured toward the cemetery. "Well, I've changed my mind. I keep seeing Clayton lifting the lid off the coffin."

"Do you know that horses have a coffin bone in their foot?" Bernie asked. Maybe that would distract Libby. At least she hoped it would.

"No. I don't know and I don't care."

"Well, I think it's interesting." Bernie looked around. She thought again about how bleak the cemetery looked this time of year.

Libby pulled her scarf around her neck. It was old and ratty and Bernie had tried to throw it out last week. She would have made it too if the garbagemen had come earlier.

"Anyway," her sister said, "it looks as if it's going to start raining soon. Or snowing."

"It'll be fine," Bernie told her, zipping up her jacket. It was getting colder. Snow seemed like a definite possibility even though she wouldn't admit that to Libby. "We used to come out here and make out all the time when I was in high school," Bernie said to her sister as she knocked on the door of the groundskeeper's house. According to her dad the man's name was Simon Brown.

"So you said. I never had the nerve," Libby admitted. "Orion always wanted to, but I always thought it was too scary."

Bernie laughed. "That's what made it fun. Especially when the caretaker decided this place was off-limits. Running from him was the best part."

"Good thing he never caught you," Libby observed.

Bernie grinned. "Isn't it, though? Mom wouldn't have been pleased if she'd had to bail me out."

"Not to mention Dad."

"Dad would have had a cow," Bernie agreed as she knocked on the door again.

No answer. She pressed her ear to the wood. She could hear the sound of the television playing through the panels. She knocked a third time. Still nothing. She studied the front window. The blinds were down. But maybe they weren't in the other parts of the house. She turned to Libby. "I think I'm going to go around and see if I can find a window to look through."

Libby put on her schoolmarm expression. "And the point of that is?"

"To see if he's home, obviously."

"Something tells me that catching you peering in his window will definitely not put this man . . ."

"Simon. Simon Brown. . . ."

Libby made an impatient gesture with her hand. ". . . Simon Brown in a mood to talk. I think we should come back later."

"But we're here now."

"And he's not."

Bernie found herself stamping her foot. Why did her sister have to be so stubborn? "We don't know that. Maybe he's in the bathroom or maybe he's stepped out for a moment and forgotten to turn off the TV. Lots of people do that."

"But that doesn't help us, does it?"

Libby said.

Bernie admitted it didn't. She rang the bell one last time. Nada.

"What can Simon Brown tell us anyway?" Libby demanded.

"He can tell us if he saw anything, anything at all."

"If he had he would have told Clayton."

"Not necessarily," Bernie pointed out.

"Why not necessarily?"

"Let me put it this way. Would you tell Clayton anything? Especially about something that you're supposed to be responsible for and have screwed up?"

Libby thought it over for a moment. "Good point," she finally said. "No, I don't suppose I would."

"Me neither."

"No one would."

"Exactly." Bernie held up a finger. "Just give me one sec to look around. You won't even know I'm gone." And before Libby had a chance to object Bernie took a couple of steps and turned the corner of the house.

Like she'd told Libby, all she was going to do was take a quick look around. If she didn't find Simon Brown, they'd drive around the cemetery for a bit, and then if they couldn't find him they'd go do their errands and try again another day. After they looked at the grave site where Ms. Mc-Dougal had been buried, that is.

Libby would probably freak when she told her, but she could stay in the car. Bernie wanted to have a second look. She'd been upset enough the first time around that she hadn't noticed much.

She walked around to the back of the house. The going was easier because someone had paved over the back half. Which was good. Bernie decided she definitely wasn't a nature lover. Mud and high heels didn't go together. Actually, life without her blow-dryer was not a pleasant thought either.

She stopped for a moment when she saw the woodpile. There was an axe embedded in a tree stump next to it. If she were Amber she'd be thinking about Freddie — or was it Jason? — now. But she wasn't Amber, so she was just going to concentrate on the business at hand. Like checking out the garage.

There wasn't a light on in there. But there was a car parked outside. That was a good sign. Or not, Bernie thought. For all she knew, Simon could have two cars. She was just wondering if she should call her dad and ask him when she felt something round and hard nudge her in the small of her back.

She spun around.

A man she assumed was Simon Brown was pointing a shotgun at her. Or maybe it was a rifle. She tried to remember the difference and failed. But one thing was for sure. Whatever type of weapon it was, it was very large.

"Are you Simon Brown?" she asked.

"So what if I am? What do you want?" he demanded.

"I want you to put that thing down."

"Not till you tell me what you're doing here."

"You point your gun somewhere else and I will." Now, why had she said that? Bernie wondered. Libby was right. She did have a big mouth.

"You're in no position to bargain, missy."

"Missy? Missy? You've got to be kidding me. What century are you in?"

Simon Brown pulled back the bolt on his rifle. "Do I look as if I'm kidding?"

"That would be a negative."

She was just about to explain who she was when she spied Libby sneaking up behind Simon Brown. She'd obviously come from the opposite direction. And she was holding a skillet, Libby's nine-inch all-clad skillet to be exact, the one she was taking to the store to have the handle resoldered, in her hands.

"Don't," Bernie cried. But it was too late. Libby had already brought the skillet down on the back of Simon Brown's head by the time the words had left Bernie's mouth.

Bernie watched as he crumpled to the ground. She strode over and yanked the skillet out of Libby's hands.

"What were you thinking?" she said to Libby.

"I thought you'd be pleased. He was going to shoot you."

"No, he wasn't."

"He had his rifle pointed at you."

"That doesn't mean he was going to shoot me."

"Right. He was offering to serve you tea and crumpets. Now, if you did something like this it would be fine. If I do something like this it's not."

"That is so not true."

Libby folded her arms over her chest. "Oh yes, it is. I can't do anything right in your eyes."

"That is such a load of crap."

Libby glared at her. Then she started laughing. "I suppose it is, isn't it?"

"Yes," Bernie said as she bent down over Simon Brown. "Are you all right?" she asked him.

He groaned.

Bernie decided that groaning was a good sign. At least he wasn't unconscious. "Do you want us to get a doctor?"

He shook his head and pointed to Libby. "Why'd she hit me?" he asked Bernie.

Libby stepped forward. "You were going to hurt my sister."

"No, I wasn't."

"Then why were you holding a gun on her?"

"You'd be nervous too if someone was stealing bodies out of your cemetery."

Bernie thought his comment had a certain amount of validity to it but decided to remain silent for the moment.

"Do we look like people who would dig up a body?" Libby demanded indignantly.

"How do I know?" Simon replied from the ground. "You might be. After all, I didn't see who did it the first time, did I?"

"I don't know." Bernie extended her hand and helped him up. "That's what we wanted to talk to you about."

"You could have just asked," Simon whined. "I would have told ya if you had."

"That's what my sister was trying to do," Libby put in.

"She didn't say anything to me."

"Well, you didn't give her a chance, did you?"

"Most people would just knock on the door."

"We did," Libby protested. "You didn't answer."

"That's because I was outside taking care of something, not that it's any business of yours."

*Nothing like alienating the person you want to question,* Bernie thought as she intervened before Libby did irreparable damage.

"Why don't we go inside your house and I'll make you a nice cup of tea?" Bernie said in as soothing a voice as she could manage. "Or should we take you to the hospital?"

"I ain't going to no hospital," Simon declared.

"I guess that settles that," Libby said.

And with that Simon started off for his house. Bernie noted that his gait was a little wobbly, but he managed to walk in a straight line, which under the circumstances was a good thing. Simon paused at the front.

"That's a lot of keys," Bernie said as she watched him draw an enormous key chain out of his pocket.

"That's because there are a lot of things I got to keep locked up," Simon said as he opened the door and beckoned for Bernie and Libby to follow him inside.

Bernie looked around. The entranceway

walls were lined with shelves full of Mickey Mouse dolls.

"Been collecting them since I was ten," Simon informed her as he led them into the living room. "You want a Seagram's Seven and Seven or a Budweiser?"

"Wouldn't you like some tea instead?" Libby asked.

"Don't have no tea. Anyway, Seven and Seven's the best thing for getting coshed on the head," he announced.

"I think I'll pass," Bernie said.

The last time she had Seven and Seven she'd been at a fraternity party, had downed three without any dinner, and then spent the rest of the evening in the bathroom throwing up.

"You don't mind if I do?" he asked.

"Not at all," Bernie told him.

She watched as he went to the table in the living room and fixed himself a stiff drink.

"A man needs his comforts," he explained as he raised the glass to his lips and took a long sip. "Sit," he said and indicated the sofa. "Just toss the stuff off onto the floor."

Bernie went over and gingerly pushed a stack of newspapers onto the floor. Libby did the same with a stack of clothes. Bernie looked at Libby. Libby looked back. Finally they both sat.

"So who are you anyway?" Simon asked.

"We're Sean Simmons's daughters," they said in unison.

"Hmm." Simon took another drink and wiped his mouth with the back of his hand. "I knew your mom. Great cook."

"Yes, she was," Libby said.

"She made the best strawberry pie."

"Come to the shop and we'll give you one," Bernie said. At least they were making a little progress.

"I thought you had something to do with Clayton."

Libby opened her mouth to say something, but before she could Bernie cut her off. "Whatever gave you that idea?" she asked.

" 'Cause I saw you with him." Simon leaned forward. "He blames me for what happened, you know."

Bernie leaned forward as well. "Why?"

"Because he's an idiot. How was I to know someone dug old Ms. McDougal up? As far as I can see, no one even knew she was buried."

Now it was Libby's turn to lean forward. "What do you mean?"

"I mean that no one came to her funeral."

"No one?" Bernie repeated.

"No one," Simon told her.

"How sad," Libby observed.

"Happens that way sometimes. I guess she was what you call a recuse . . ."

"A recluse?" Bernie asked.

"That's what I said. A recuse." Simon paused to take another sip of his drink. "No one goes up there . . ."

"There?" Bernie asked for clarification as she shifted her weight. The cushion she was sitting on felt like a bag of pebbles. She didn't even try to guess what it was filled with.

"Where's she buried. Not even the kids. They do their drinkin' and lockin' lips anywhere but there. I mean, there ain't no trees. No benches. No headstones."

Bernie leaned all the way forward. "Can you tell us anything that would help us? Anything at all?"

Simon Brown swung his arm around. "This is a lot of land to keep an eye on. A lot of kids come in here doing heaven knows what. I got my hands full enough. That section that Ms. McDougal was in? I don't go up there much unless I have to."

Bernie remembered the stories she'd heard in high school. "Because it's haunted?"

Simon snorted.

"I'll take that as a no. So you didn't see

anything?"

"That's what I'm saying. That's what I been saying. That's what I would have said if you'd asked me proper instead of hitting me in the head."

"I already said I was sorry," Libby replied.

Simon nodded. "It's true. You did."

"Would you have told us if we did ask you?" Libby asked.

Simon took another gulp of his drink. "There's nothing to tell."

"Nothing? Nothing at all?" Bernie prodded.

"Nope."

"We'd be grateful for anything." And Bernie flashed him her best smile. "Anything at all."

Simon swirled the liquid around in his glass for a moment before he spoke. "Well," he finally said. "Maybe six months ago I came across this couple that was parked down around the bottom of the hill, making out . . . or whatever it is that they call it these days . . . and when they saw me coming they took off. There was something weird about them. But don't ask me what." He tapped his chest. "It was just this feeling I had in the pit of my stomach."

"You didn't recognize them?" Libby asked.

"Nope," Simon said.

"What about the car?" Bernie said.

"What about it?"

"Make? Color? Anything unusual?" Bernie prompted.

"That's it," Simon said. "Don't know much about cars. Never have. Sure you wouldn't have a drink?"

"Positive," Libby said as she got up to go.

Bernie joined her. "Well, that wasn't very helpful, was it?" she said to Libby once they got outside.

"It certainly wasn't," Libby answered as she got in the car.

Bernie started the car up. She slowly backed down the lane and made a left when she got to the place where the road split.

"We should be going to the right," Libby told her.

"This will just take a second."

"Tell me we're not going to Ms. McDougal's grave site."

"Okay. I won't tell you," Bernie said as she negotiated a pothole in the middle of the road.

"I'm serious," Libby said.

"So am I," Bernie retorted.

# CHAPTER 13

Libby glared at her sister as they drove along the outer cemetery. Unfortunately since her sister had her eyes fixed on the road she couldn't see the expression on her face, not that she would have cared anyway.

"You should relax," Bernie told her as she negotiated a particularly tricky turn.

"I am relaxed," Libby protested.

"Five minutes more or less won't make any difference in the scheme of things," Bernie observed.

"It will in my scheme," Libby countered, thinking of everything she still had to do. Like making dough. Like going to Sam's Club. Like ordering the pink sprinkles and little candy hearts they were going to use on their Valentine's Day cookies from the baker's supply house they used. Like making sure Amber cleaned under the counters in the prep area where Googie had spilled half a pound of flour yesterday.

"Well," Bernie continued, "since we're doing this for Marvin I wouldn't think you'd begrudge the extra time."

"It's not the time," Libby fibbed. "It's the place. I told you it gives me the creeps."

"Really?"

"Yes. Really."

"Then why did you tell Marvin we would do this?"

Libby opened her mouth to answer and closed it a second later. She hated when this happened. Why did her sister always get the last word? It wasn't that Libby couldn't think of a reply. It was that she'd think of it tonight. Or two days later. By which point Bernie would have forgotten what the conversation was all about. Which would make Libby even madder. It was time to change the subject.

Libby fished around in her backpack until she found one of the chocolate chip cookies she had baked that morning. She chewed slowly, giving the chocolate time to melt in her mouth. This always calmed her down. What did people do before chocolate? she wondered.

"You know," she said to her sister after a moment had gone by. "I'm not sure I like this brand of chocolate chips. It has a brown sugary aftertaste to it."

"That's because they probably roast the beans too long," Bernie observed. "I noticed that myself. Mrs. Hanson likes them, though."

"Mrs. Hanson likes them because they're organic," Libby said. "Mrs. Hanson likes anything organic. Mrs. Hanson also spins her own yarn and knits her sweaters from it. She's a crunchy."

Bernie nodded. "This is true."

"I wonder if it makes any difference," Libby mused.

"The chocolate being fair trade and organic?"

Libby nodded.

"Well, it certainly does to the people growing it. They don't have to deal with all the pesticides. And more importantly they're being paid a wage. They're not slaves."

"Slaves?" Libby said despite herself.

"Yeah." Bernie rounded another turn. "Despite originating in the Amazon rain forest, something like half to two-thirds of the cacao beans grown in the world are harvested on the Ivory Coast."

"I knew that."

"Did you also know that most of the farms there use child labor? Actually they're slaves, bought and paid for."

Libby shuddered. "That's horrible."

"It is, isn't it?" Bernie agreed. "But it's getting better. Here's a random fact."

Libby groaned.

Bernie ignored her. "I bet you didn't know that the flowers from the cacao tree smell really, really bad. They stink actually."

"The pods we saw at Just Chocolate didn't smell that bad," Libby protested.

"That's because they were dried."

"Fascinating."

"I think so. Here's another interesting factoid. A cacao tree can bear as many as fifty pods a year, and each pod can carry as many as fifty seeds." She slowed down to go around another curve. "I've been thinking . . ."

"Always a dangerous exercise."

"Seriously, Libby. Maybe we should use fair trade chocolate exclusively."

"It's a nice idea," Libby allowed. "If we can find some that tastes better and that we can afford. Afford being the keyword here." Why did she always have to be the practical one? But then, if she wasn't they wouldn't have a business.

"Good enough. I'll look around and see what I can find."

And why did everything have to be so difficult? Libby sat back in her seat and closed her eyes for a second. Suddenly she was very tired. Sometimes the world was just too complicated.

"So what did you think about Simon Brown?" she heard her sister say.

Libby kept her eyes closed. "Aside from the fact he's crazy?"

"Overreactive might be a better word."

"I like crazy."

Bernie gave an impatient snort. "Whatever. I repeat my original question."

Libby pictured him in her mind. "He drinks too much."

"Aside from that."

Libby opened her eyes. "I wonder about the car he saw."

"In what sense?"

"If it was relevant."

"I hope not, because if it is we're out of luck."

"Do you think he's holding anything back?" Libby asked.

"No. Do you?"

"No." Libby looked at her sister. She was tapping her fingernails on the steering wheel. "You know what we need?" she asked her.

"A clue? A witness? Anything?"

"S'mores."

"That would be very helpful. You've finally gone round the bend."

"I mean for the benefit," Libby said impatiently.

"So s'mores are off topic?"

"Off topic" was one of Bernie's new expressions. Personally, Libby found the phrase extremely annoying, but she refrained from sharing her opinion. Instead she said, "Yes. S'mores are off topic. We're looking for something a little bit different, right? Everyone loves s'mores. We could let people make their own."

Bernie bit her lip. "Kind of like a variation on a chocolate fondue."

"I don't see how."

"I meant they're both from the fifties."

As Libby nodded she noticed they were almost at the place where Ms. McDougal's body had been spirited away and replaced with Ted Gorman's. Getting nearer she realized she hadn't been lying to Bernie when she'd told her the place gave her the creeps, because it did. Bernie parked the car on the median next to the road and zipped up her jacket.

"Okay," she told Libby. "Let's go."

"Remind me again why we're doing this," Libby said as they started walking.

"Clues. We're looking for clues."

"There are no clues."

By now they had the grave site in full view.

Bernie rounded on her. "Why are you always so negative?"

"I'm not negative. I'm realistic."

"That's just another word for negative."

"Maybe you'd be" — Libby did the quote thing with her fingers — "*negative* too if you were the one doing the books." She was just about to say something else when she saw a figure rising out of Ms. McDougal's grave.

*This can't be happening,* she thought as she tried to scream. No sounds came out. All she could do was lift her finger and point.

# CHAPTER 14

Sean looked up at his daughters. They looked down at him. He decided they both looked angry. Furious, actually, if he were being accurate. Obviously they didn't regard this little misunderstanding as amusing. *Rose was right,* he thought. *I do have a sick sense of humor.*

But it wasn't his fault that Libby thought he was a ghost rising from the grave. How was he to know they were going to be there? What was that saying? Something about "great minds think alike." He'd ask Bernie but somehow he didn't think this was the time.

"I didn't think I looked that scary," he said as he turned to Marvin. "Right, Marvin?"

"Er. Right," Marvin said, looking as if he'd like to be any place but here.

"Although maybe I do." Sometimes he could bluff Libby out, but he had a feeling this wasn't going to be one of those times.

"I thought I'd stop breathing," Libby cried.

"Good thing you didn't." Dead silence. "It's not as if I did this on purpose," he told her.

"You're not supposed to be here," she said.

Sean could see his oldest child still looked a little pale around the gills.

"You were supposed to be talking to what's-her-name."

"We never decided on that."

"Oh yes, we did." That was Libby. Literal to a fault. "And you." She turned to Marvin. "What were you thinking of, bringing him here?"

Marvin put both his hands up. "Now, Libby," he stammered. "There's nothing wrong with —"

"Don't Libby me."

Looking at Marvin's face, Sean decided to intervene. The guy looked as if he wanted to curl into a ball.

"Give the guy a break," Sean told Libby. After all, what else could he do? He was the one responsible for Marvin being in trouble with his daughter. "He was just doing what I asked him to do."

"He should have known better."

"He's not my keeper," Sean pointed out. "I'm not a child."

This, he decided — as he saw Libby tapping her foot — was not a good thing to say. It left him wide open. But before Libby could reply Marvin jumped in.

"I thought you wanted me to help him," he protested.

"I did," Libby allowed. "But I also expected you to show some common sense," she said turning back to Sean. "You could have gotten hurt getting down there."

"But I didn't."

"But you could have."

"I could also fall off the toilet and crack my head open on the floor. Does that mean I shouldn't go to the bathroom?"

"That's not the same thing," Libby told him. "That's not the same thing at all. And you know it."

"Guys." Everyone turned to Bernie. "Stop."

"I'm not doing anything," Sean pointed out.

"Neither am I," Libby said.

Bernie cut her off. "Remember, you were the one complaining about not having time, so let's not waste ours."

Sean watched Libby's mouth open and close. She was still pissed. Marvin was going to have his work cut out for him. Sean felt guilty, but he reminded himself that Marvin was an adult.

Still, he knew how it felt to be in the doghouse. He'd certainly been in it often enough when he'd been married. He should tell Marvin to bring Libby flowers. Roses. Libby liked the yellow ones. That strategy had always worked with her mom.

"Listen, Libby," he began when Bernie jumped into the grave with him.

"So what do you see?" she asked.

"Nothing. Nothing at all. Unfortunately." That was the worst part, Sean decided. All this arguing about something that had turned out to be a complete waste of time. He gestured around. "Just concrete walls and a dirt floor. Your standard twenty-first-century grave." In the old days, they were just dirt, but now with the new state regs everyone was buried in vaults. He couldn't see any point in it. Ecologically speaking it didn't make any sense. Why preserve something that was just going to decompose anyway?

"Mind if I take a look?" Bernie asked.

Sean shrugged. "Be my guest." He backed up so Bernie could have more room, but the space was pretty tight. He gestured for Marvin to help him up. As he did, it dawned on him that, as with so many things, while getting into the grave had been relatively easy, getting out was going to be much harder.

He was just thinking that he was going to have to stay where he was until his daughters left — no way was he going to let them see him getting helped out of here — when Marvin reappeared with a heavy plank and put it down at the shallow end of the grave.

"Here," he said to Sean. "Walk on this."

*Maybe,* Sean thought as he headed toward it, *I've underestimated this guy after all.*

Marvin reached out and Sean took his hand.

He heard Libby say, "That's not a good idea."

Then Marvin said, "I know what I'm doing."

*You tell her, kid,* Sean thought as he slowly walked up the plank, careful to put one foot in front of the other. The last thing he intended to do was fall off. Not that he was afraid of hurting himself, but if he did something like that he'd never hear the end of it. Never. Even at his eulogy Libby would still be telling the story about the time her dad got into a grave and couldn't get himself out.

Finally he was out.

"Good job," he told Marvin.

Marvin beamed.

*I should compliment the kid more often,* Sean decided. He remembered what Rose had said about some people responding better to praise than criticism.

"Did you at least learn anything?" Libby asked him. She was hugging her jacket to herself. Watching her made Sean realize how cold he was.

Even though it pained him, Sean confessed that he hadn't.

He took a few steps back and his foot hit something. His ankle began to twist. He caught himself before he began to fall.

"You okay?" Marvin asked.

"I'm fine," Sean replied as he looked down at the ground to see what had caused his misstep.

The ground wasn't even. And then he saw what he'd stepped into. Tire tracks. The kind that earthmoving machinery makes. He laughed. Funny how that worked: not noticing something until you were looking for it.

He pointed. "Would a backhoe make those kinds of tracks?"

Marvin followed Sean's hand with his eyes. "They would indeed."

"Do you think they're recent?" Sean

asked him.

Marvin looked uncomfortable. "No way of telling really. There are usually five to seven burials up here a year. These tracks could be from the fall."

"Why don't you call the groundskeeper and find out?" Sean suggested.

Marvin pulled out his cell. "I have his number here," he said, pressing the buttons.

Sean listened while Marvin talked to him.

"He says he doesn't know," he told Sean after hanging up.

"Don't you think that's odd, him not knowing?"

"He drinks a lot. A lot, a lot. Sometimes he doesn't even know what day it is. If you want I can call the head of the office and find out."

Sean nodded. "I'd appreciate that." He scanned the area while Marvin dialed. "You said people don't come up here."

"Not even high school kids," Marvin answered. "At least that's what I've been told."

"So whoever did this could have done it in broad daylight," Sean mused.

Marvin held up a finger while he talked into his cell. A minute later he hung up. "They had three other burials up here since September," he told Sean.

"So the tracks could have come from one of those," Sean said. He pointed toward a small side road that went off at an angle. "They could have come in through there."

"They could have come in through the front gate," Marvin replied. "The maintenance staff is at a low point. Especially in the winter."

Sean jammed his hands in his pockets. "So what does your father think happened?"

Even though Sean had already asked Clayton, he wanted to hear Marvin's version of things.

Marvin shrugged. "He doesn't know. That's the problem. Maybe you should talk to Simon Brown — if you can catch him sober. Maybe there's an off chance that he saw something."

Libby bit her lip. "We already did," she said.

"And what did he tell you?"

"Nothing really."

Sean listened to what Libby had to say.

"You think he might know more than he's telling?" he asked.

Libby paused for a moment while she thought. "Probably not."

"Probably not or definitely not?"

"Er . . ."

Sean took a look at his daughter. He

didn't know if Simon Brown was hiding something, but his daughter definitely was.

"What's going on?" he asked her.

Bernie looked up. Sean noticed she had something in her hand. "She hit him in the head with a frying pan."

"She *what?*"

"You heard me. Libby whacked him with a frying pan."

"You're kidding."

"Do I look like I'm kidding?" Bernie replied.

Libby pouted. "Well, I thought he was going to shoot her."

"He was not," Bernie said.

"What's going on here?" Sean yelled. You sent people out to do a simple thing and they mucked it up. He should just do everything himself. "Now I'm definitely going to talk to him," he said when he'd heard the rest of the story. No one pulled a rifle on one of his girls and got away with it.

"Let it go, Dad," Bernie said, hauling herself out of the grave. "Please."

"All right," Sean grumbled. He'd deal with Brown later.

"What do you think this is?" Bernie asked. "Here in the dirt. These little bumpy things?"

Sean squinted. It all looked like dirt to

him. Then he saw what Bernie was talking about. He took a closer look. "No idea," he said, rolling it around in his fingers. It was dry. "Maybe it's a husk or some kind of shell."

Marvin leaned in to take a closer look. "That might be dried debris from an apple press. There used to be one around here before the cemetery bought the land."

"Oh well," Bernie said as she let the dirt trickle through her fingers.

Libby sighed.

Sean turned to her.

She dug a cookie out of her backpack and ate it. "I just don't understand why anyone would do something like this."

"I'm sure they had a good reason in their own mind." Over the years he'd learned that people could and did rationalize anything they wanted to do into something that they needed to do. The girlfriend or the wife always had it coming. The convenience store owner was just asking to be robbed.

"But what?" Libby asked.

Sean shrugged. "We're not going to know that until we find whoever did this."

"And how are we going to do that?" Libby demanded.

"We'll do what we always do," Sean told her. "We'll work both ends." Another analogy for solving a crime that he'd used with his men was the tangled-up ball of twine. There were two ends to the twine and you worked on both of them. Eventually the knot unraveled. "We'll talk to Ms. McDougal's lone relative. We'll find out everything we can about Ted Gorman," he continued.

"And Marnie and everyone who works for them," Bernie interjected.

Sean smiled. "Exactly. Something will come to light. It always does."

"But why should anyone tell you anything?" Marvin objected. "I know I wouldn't."

"Yes, you would," Sean told him. "You'd talk just to appear not guilty, and lots of times people tell you things without realizing the significance of what they're saying."

"And if that doesn't work," Bernie added, "we'll bring in the big guns and ply them with Libby's cookies. No one can resist those, especially her brownies and lemon bars. And let's not even talk about her rum balls."

Libby laughed. "Especially the rum balls. And if that doesn't work we'll just have Bernie talk them into submission. She can tell them all about the history of chocolate and vanilla . . ."

"And Valentine's Day," Bernie added.

"And Valentine's Day," Libby repeated. "And the history of the universe."

"So you see," Sean told Marvin, "we really do have a plan."

Sean noted that Marvin looked extremely doubtful.

"It'll be fine," Sean reassured him. "Honestly. When have we never not solved something?"

"That's terrible grammar," Bernie objected.

"But true nevertheless." Sean turned back to Marvin. "Listen," he told him. "In my experience everyone makes a mistake sooner or later."

He just hoped it was sooner rather than later.

"Well, let's not lose sight of the important thing," Marvin said.

"And what's that?" Libby asked.

Marvin gave her an incredulous look. "Proving that this mess isn't my father's fault, of course."

"Of course," Sean said. He rubbed his arms. He needed a new parka. "Let's get out of here. It's too cold."

# CHAPTER 15

Bernie leaned back in the driver's seat of the newly repaired van and tried to focus on what she was going to say to Ms. Mc-Dougal's cousin, Eleanor, which was hard to do because she was totally and completely fried.

This was because for the last two days there'd been one calamity after the other at the shop and the house. Something had to be retrograde in the cosmos, Bernie thought, as she twirled her ring around her finger, but then something was always going retrograde. Or maybe it was a full moon. Or both. She'd have to check her charts and see. Recently she was becoming more interested in astrology.

Her mother always used to talk about Murphy's Law. Anything that can go wrong will. Well, Murphy's Law should be renamed the Simmonses' Law. And who was this mythical Murphy anyway and why did he have a law named after him? She'd have to Google it when she got home and find out. Here was another law. Everything always breaks at the same time. Which, come to think of it, was a corollary of the first.

First the phone line in the shop had gone down, which meant no one could call in orders, and more importantly it also meant that their credit card machine was not working. Now, that was really bad because half their orders were paid for by credit card. She'd practically had to have a temper tantrum on the phone to get the phone company to send a repairman out. When he'd finally arrived it had taken him over three hours to find the place where, according to him, a squirrel had eaten the line, although how a squirrel had gotten into the shop's ceiling was beyond her.

Surely they would have heard the varmint. They'd had a squirrel in the walls about ten years ago and you could hear his scratching all night long. Libby thought the house was haunted and refused to sleep in her bed for months. Bernie sighed as she remembered the expression on her mom's face when she'd discovered that Bernie was the one who had planted the idea in Libby's mind in the first place. Oh well.

Next the fax machine had gone. It had

simply stopped working. Bernie had buried it in the garbage can. Then the cooler in the kitchen stopped cooling, which meant that she and Libby had to find space in the other coolers for the contents of the broken one until the repairman came to fix it.

Then Amber had called in sick with the flu, although Libby suspected she just wanted time with her new boyfriend. But no matter what the reason was the result was the same. They were short-staffed at a time when they needed every available hand. For a moment she and Libby had even thought about drafting their dad to help before common sense intervened.

And on top of everything else their sales tax was coming due, the upstairs toilet was leaking, and the construction crew was slated to start replacing the exhaust fan tomorrow. They'd said they'd get there before the shop opened, but Bernie had heard promises like that before. They'd probably get there at the height of the noonday rush.

And then, as if that weren't bad enough, she and Rob had another fight about his being in the bachelor auction. Okay, so the fight wasn't really about the bachelor auction. It was about Rob's generally sucky attitude over the last couple of months. She'd tried to talk to him, but he kept insisting nothing was wrong when it obviously was. Maybe tonight, after they got together for a drink at R.J.'s, she and Rob could have a real talk.

Bernie twirled her ring around her finger and went back to looking at Eleanor McDougal's house. She'd do better to focus on this. At least she might have a chance of success. Clayton kept calling and it would be nice to have something to tell him. That way she wouldn't have to listen to him snort over the phone before he hung up.

She shivered as she got out of the van and walked toward the McDougal house. The guy on the radio had pegged the windchill factor into the single digits and he'd been right. What was that line bad novelists always used? Something about the cold wind cutting through me like a knife? Well, the wind didn't feel like a knife, but it was very, very chilly out. She should have worn gloves. And a scarf. At least she didn't have to walk far. Eleanor McDougal's house faced the street.

The closer she got to the house the more higgledy-piggeldy — now, there was a nice phrase — it looked. The roof was tilting a little bit to the left, while the wall on the right was leaning inward, and the garage was doing a Leaning Tower of Pisa number.

Bernie didn't like the way the three steps groaned as she climbed them to get to the front door, and on top of that they felt suspiciously loose. Usually before she talked to someone she tried to find out a little bit about them, but she hadn't had the time.

"Here we go," Bernie said out loud as she raised her hand and rang the bell.

A moment later the door flew open, revealing a skinny woman with two gray braids hanging down over her shoulders. She was wearing a faded pair of black pants and a shapeless black sweater.

"I don't care what you're selling, I'm not buying," she snarled.

Bernie took a deep breath. "I'm not selling anything. Are you Eleanor McDougal?" Bernie asked.

"Who should I be? The pope?"

The words flew out of Bernie's mouth before she could stop them. "There was supposed to be a female pope."

Suddenly Eleanor McDougal smiled. The smile, Bernie decided, emphasized the lines along her mouth and eyes.

"So rumor says."

"There are pictures in the Vatican that seem to give credence to the assertion."

Eleanor McDougal looked her up and

down. She sniffed. "You read, do you?"

"Certainly. Most people do."

"Would that were so. Now, who did you say you were?"

"I didn't. I'm Bernie Simmons. My sister and I run A Little —"

Eleanor interrupted. "Yes, yes. Horrible name for a store. Too cute for words."

Bernie didn't say anything even though she agreed. The name had been her mother's choice, and now they were stuck with it.

"Cute is never good," Eleanor went on. "Plus, the name is too long."

Bernie extended her hand. Eleanor looked at it but kept her own firmly down by her side.

"I don't believe in shaking hands with people," she informed Bernie. "I don't believe in touching other people. Especially these days. Now, what do you want?"

Bernie took a deep breath and was about to go into the story she'd concocted on the way over when Eleanor said, "Of course I know what you want. You're here to detect. Well, you and your sister are detectives, aren't you? Your father was the former chief of police of Longely, wasn't he?"

"Yes," Bernie managed to get out.

"And no doubt you're trying to find out

what happened to my cousin?"

"How . . ." was all Bernie got out before Eleanor held up her hand.

"If you think you can keep a secret in this town you are very sadly mistaken. Not that I really care what happened to Clara's body. I told that dreadful funeral director as much. It is my belief that people spend way too much time and money on useless funerary rites. As far as I'm concerned we should do what the Tibetans do and leave our corpses in trees for the birds to eat. Not that it will ever happen."

"Thank God," Bernie couldn't help murmuring.

Eleanor glared at her. "There's nothing I can tell you about Clara."

Bernie opened her mouth to speak, but Eleanor beat her to it once again. "But I'll let you come in if you want to. Despite your clothes."

Bernic looked down at what she was wearing. "What's wrong with how I'm dressed?"

Eleanor sniffed again. "Style is a capitalistic notion."

Bernie managed to stop herself from groaning.

"It's true. Have you ever read a book called *The Female Imperative*? It's a treatise on the sexual politics of dress."

Bernie nodded. "By Joanne Mau."

Eleanor's smile grew wider. "Then I say no more."

Personally Bernie had found the book extremely shrill, not to mention badly researched, but she decided this was not the time to mention it. Instead she said, "Can we agree to disagree?"

"I suppose that's possible." Eleanor jerked her head toward the inside. "What are you waiting for? Are you aware of how much heat costs these days?"

"Sorry," Bernie murmured as she stepped inside.

She looked around as she followed Eleanor through her house. The walls of the living room, dining room, and hallway were lined with books. They were stacked everywhere, on the floors, the tables, and the chairs.

Eleanor gestured toward them. "I haven't got around to cataloging these yet."

"How many do you have?" Bernie asked.

Eleanor shrugged. "I've lost count."

"And you've read them all?"

Eleanor laughed. "Not even close. I was a research librarian before I retired. Now I buy and sell books on eBay. By the way, the only things Clara ever read were soap opera digests. She was a complete moron. One year I gave her a very fine copy of *Gibbon's Decline and Fall of the Roman Empire* and I found it six months later underneath a potted plant. There were water stains on the cover, mind you. That was the last time I ever gave her anything."

Bernie felt a pang of sympathy for Clara. Poor lady. "And you find your business profitable?"

"Extremely. Especially biographies and books about food. It's amazing how many people want to read about eating."

"Yes, it is, isn't it," Bernie agreed as she followed Eleanor into the kitchen.

"Right now people want to read about chocolate," Eleanor continued. "Must be because Valentine's Day is coming up."

Bernie glanced around. From the looks of the place she surmised that whatever Eleanor was interested in reading she definitely wasn't interested in cooking. There were books piled on the counters, the kitchen table, and the stove top.

"I use a microwave," Eleanor explained, reading Bernie's expression. "Much more efficient. I don't hold with wasting time. Which brings me back to my cousin. As I said before, there's nothing I can tell you about Clara. Nothing at all."

Bernie leaned against the kitchen counter.

"Do you mind if I ask you some questions anyway?"

Eleanor shrugged. "Obviously I don't. Otherwise you wouldn't be standing here now."

"Did Clara have any friends?"

Eleanor shook her head. "She watched television all day long."

"She must have done something else," Bernie persisted.

"Not to my knowledge."

"When she went out, where did she go?"

"The same places most people do, I imagine."

"What about her family?"

"What about it?"

"Did she have any?"

Eleanor drew herself up. "She and I were the last of our line, and now there's only me. Some people would say that's sad, but I say good riddance to us. It's time to move on and give someone else on the planet some room." She glanced at the clock on the wall. "And now I think it's time you left."

"One more thing," Bernie said.

"Make it quick," Eleanor said.

"Would you mind if I looked through her house?"

Eleanor laughed. "Why would I mind?"

she asked. "Look away to your heart's content. Wait a minute."

Eleanor went over and opened the kitchen cabinet drawer next to the refrigerator and took something out. She walked back to Bernie.

"Here," she said as she put a key in Bernie's hand. "I've had this for twenty years, heaven only knows why. It's about time I got rid of it. This is the key to Clara's front door. And don't bring it back. I don't want it. In fact, don't come back at all. I've said all that I have to say on the subject of Clara McDougal." And with that she escorted Bernie outside.

# CHAPTER 16

Bernie turned the van on and sat back in her seat. She weighed the key sitting in the palm of her hand. It probably wouldn't work after all this time. Surely Clara had changed the lock after twenty years. Not that it really mattered. She could always go through a window if need be. It was not an activity she was unfamiliar with.

And even if the key did work she probably wouldn't find anything of value in Clara's house. The police had probably taken everything of any interest, bagged it, and carted it off to their evidence room when they'd claimed her body. Or possibly not. After all, this wasn't a crime scene she was talking about. Clara had died, as the saying goes, of natural causes. The powers that be could have just left everything the way it was.

And she did need to get back to the shop. She really did. There was dough to be made and pies to be baked. And Tim Conner was coming by with an estimate for the new exhaust fan. Plus, she had to go to the bank and make A Little Taste of Heaven's deposit and get some change. They were running out of dimes and quarters in the shop.

On the other hand, the weather was good. It was thirty degrees and clear. It wasn't snowing or raining or icing, and according to the weather report any or all of those activities would not be starting till later in the evening.

Which meant that the drive up to Clara McDougal's house would be easy. When the weather was bad it was impossible — okay, not impossible — but it was extremely difficult, especially in her van. She should take advantage of the good weather while she could. It probably wasn't going to last for long. It usually didn't this time of year.

Bernie looked at her watch. If she were quick, she could go through the McDougal house and be back at the shop in under two hours. She reached for her cell. She should tell Libby where she was headed.

But if she did that she'd spend ten minutes arguing with Libby about what she was about to do. Possibly even more. These days everything threw Libby for a loop. Nope. It was better to just go ahead and do it. More efficient. And as her dad liked to say, it was always easier to ask for forgiveness than to get permission.

And with that thought Bernie shut off her cell phone. That way there'd be no arguments. Then she put the car into reverse, backed out of Eleanor McDougal's driveway, and headed for Clara McDougal's house. The drive took Bernie longer than expected, but she liked going up the winding road with the view of the Hudson River in the distance. The tankers going downstream looked like little toys from her vantage. The road got rougher as she got closer to the McDougal house, and by the time she arrived it was a mass of ruts and gravel held together by a few pieces of tar.

As Bernie parked her vehicle she wondered what had made Clara live in such a secluded spot. Didn't she like people? Had something happened to her? Then she shrugged. All she knew was that she wouldn't want to live up here.

It's true the view was lovely, but it was so far up in the hills that you couldn't even hear traffic, just the sound of the wind through the pines. Bernie knew she was supposed to find that noise soothing, but she didn't. She found it creepy. That's why she didn't go camping. Too quiet, and quiet made her nervous.

She studied Clara's house before approaching. The word *tidy* came to mind. It was her dad's word, one that she liked. And it fit. The place was tidy, unlike Clara's cousin Eleanor's. In fact, it was as far away from hers as you could get.

The cottage was white with green shutters and an actual white picket fence. The roses in the flower beds next to the house were covered with burlap that was neatly tied in place with twine. Bernie's mom had covered her roses in late fall too, she recalled. Libby had always helped her.

Bernie twisted her ring around her finger. She couldn't help thinking that in the summer this must be a pretty place. She could see why hikers and backpackers would want to stop here before their forays into the woods. She could even picture herself living some place like this on the weekends. Seduced by the view, she shook her head. Who would have thought — usually she was seduced by the Prada window displays.

She saw movement out of the corner of her eye and whirled around. Three deer were hanging out by a stand of trees gazing at her. She could feel herself smiling. She knew some people called them rodents on long legs, but she liked the way they looked. How can you not like Bambi? She took a step and the deer turned and galloped away. She laughed and headed back toward the house. She climbed the two steps, walked across the porch, and put the key in the lock. It fit perfectly.

"Amazing," Bernie said as the door opened.

She stepped inside and looked around.

She was standing in the living room. Again she thought of the place she'd just left with its piles and piles of books. By contrast, this place was bright and cheerful. There was a sofa on the far left. It was flanked by a rocker and a wingback chair with what looked like a coffee table made out of pine planks in the center.

"Okay," Bernie said to the house. "What do you have to tell me?"

Then she felt silly. But it was true — houses did speak about their owners. Spaces talked. You just had to know how to listen. Even her dad said that. She closed her eyes and took a deep breath; opening them again, she looked around the living room.

The furniture looked worn but well cared for. There was a braided rug in the center of the room that Bernie would have bet anything Clara had made herself. Maybe, Bernie thought, Eleanor disliked her cousin so much because she felt inferior to her in some way. Or maybe not. It didn't really matter.

Bernie looked at the pictures hanging on the wall. Most of them were decent water-colors of local scenes. Interesting. But there was nothing on the coffee table. Nothing on the floor, except a stain, which Bernie bet marked where the campers had found her.

"I think I'd prefer clutter," Bernie said out loud. At least that would be something to go through.

*This is going to be a waste of time,* Bernie thought as she headed toward Ms. McDougal's bedroom. The room was just as tidy as the living room. The bed was covered with a white chenille bedspread. Crocheted doilies covered the dresser drawers. The lamps on the nightstand were of cut glass. The place reminded Bernie of her grandmother's bedroom. It even smelled liked it. She wrinkled her nose. Maybe talc and rosewater.

Bernie looked at the picture hanging on the wall over the bed. It was a portrait of the cottage. The signature read *Clara McDougal.* So she was a painter. Bernie bet that if she examined the pictures in the living room they'd sport Clara's McDougal's signature as well.

Even though she knew she wouldn't find

181

anything of interest, Bernie opened the dresser drawers and nightstand. Everything was neatly folded and in place. Evidently Clara had favored pastel-colored shirts and sweaters and white underwear. In the closet Bernie found neatly lined up pairs of jeans and corduroy pants, two pair of sneakers, one pair of clogs, and a pair of sandals.

Bernie sighed as she walked into the dining room. She had half a mind to leave, but as long as she was here she might as well finish the job. Like her dad always said, "If a job is worth doing, it's worth doing right."

The dining room was furnished with two large potted plants — Bernie didn't know what kind — a small round table, a hutch filled with Rosenthal china and crystal, and a pretty light fixture that had to be, by Bernie's estimate, at least one hundred years old. It struck Bernie that the one thing she didn't see in the house was reading material. There were no books, no magazines, no newspapers. There was also no television, radio, or CD player that Bernie could see. Evidently Clara McDougal had lived what used to be called a contemplative life.

*Last room,* Bernie thought as she walked into the kitchen. Libby would love this, she decided as she looked around. All the appliances were from the thirties — from the stove to the sink. And everything looked in working order. Bernie went over and turned on the stove's right burner.

Yup. It worked perfectly. Things like that were worth lots of money down in New York City. Last year, she'd seen one of them for four thousand dollars down in Soho. She drummed her fingers on her thighs while she looked around. The open shelves were lined with staples arranged in order of size and category. Bernie went over and opened the door to the pantry. Neatly labeled Mason jars glistened in front of her eyes.

Again Bernie was reminded of her mom. She used to put up preserves each fall. Bernie had loved watching her mom's eyes focus on the contents of the steaming pots, had loved helping her peel and pick and shell, had loved tasting to make sure everything was just right. But most of all Bernie had loved eating what her mom put up. Each bite reminded her that summer was coming.

One by one she took the jars off the shelves, studied the labels, and replaced them. They were filled with applesauce, pickled beets, strawberry jam, blueberry chutney, dill pickles, bread and butter pickles, pickled green tomatoes, and stewed red tomatoes. A cornucopia of last summer's harvest. Somehow it seemed a shame to leave the jars there. She was sure Clara would have wanted better for them. She decided to get a bag and take them with her. Maybe she could donate them or auction them off at the benefit. Somehow Bernie had a feeling that Clara would like that.

Bernie stepped out of the kitchen and into the little room, the last room in the house. It housed an ancient washing machine and dryer, and a large, oak rolltop desk. A metal sign fixed to the front announced that it was the property of the S&L Railroad Line.

"Okay," Bernie said as she traced the sign with her fingers. She wondered where the line had gone.

The desk looked promising, more promising actually than anything else she'd come upon since she'd entered Clara McDougal's house. She sat down and pushed the top of the desk up. It let out a loud *creak*.

She scanned the interior. There were neat little cubbies, all of them filled with papers or office supplies. Bernie went through the desk quickly. Most of the papers seemed to involve bills, which Clara had evidently paid promptly. She'd either thrown out her junk mail or she didn't get any.

On the bottom of the stack of mail Bernie

came across a letter from Just Chocolate. It read:

Dear Ms. McDougal,
Please accept this box of chocolates with gratitude. We appreciate your long-time patronage and hope we may continue to serve you.

Fondly, Marnie.

*Interesting,* Bernie thought. She looked at the letter more closely. It was computer generated, signature and all. Still, it merited a call. She reached for her cell and turned it back on. When she did she saw that she had a message from Libby. Oh dear. She'd call her after she called Marnie. Then she remembered the chocolates she'd seen in the bowl on the kitchen table. She hadn't paid them any attention, but now that she thought about them she wanted to see what they were.

As she went back into the kitchen she suddenly felt tired. What she needed was some coffee. A coffee with cream and sugar. She could almost taste it on her tongue. But that would have to wait till she got out of here. She went over to the table and picked one of the chocolates out of the bowl. If she'd been paying attention she would have realized when she saw it that it looked like Just Chocolate's coffee almond crunch. She put the candy down, reached for her phone, and dialed Just Chocolate's number.

Marnie answered a moment later. Bernie could hear the sounds of people talking in the background.

"Marnie?" Bernie asked.

"Yes?"

"Did you send Ms. McDougal a complimentary box of chocolates?"

"Yes, we did. We do it twice a year."

"Isn't that a little unusual?"

"Not really. We do that for all our good customers. I find they really appreciate the gesture. It's worth the expense."

"How good a customer was she?"

"She had a standing order. Every month we sold her a box each of coffee almond crunch and hazelnut truffles. The lady had good taste. She said two boxes a month were just right. She had one piece of candy each night after dinner."

"And how long did she have the order for?"

"Let me think." There was a pause on the other end, and then Marnie said, "Maybe four years. Could be five. I'm not sure."

"So you knew her?"

"Never met the lady."

"But you just said she had a standing order."

"Indeed I did. Her order came in over the phone and we mailed it to her. We do that with lots of our customers. Why?"

"No reason," Bernie said. "I just wondered, that's all."

"Does this have anything to do with my husband's . . ." Bernie could hear Marnie's voice break.

"Not really," Bernie confessed. The phrase "grasping at straws" came to her mind, although when she thought about it she couldn't figure out what that phrase actually meant.

"Then you should focus on what's important," Marnie snapped.

"I'm trying," Bernie said.

"Not hard enough from what I can see," Marnie growled. She hung up the phone before Bernie could reply.

"Same to you," Bernie told her even though she had already hung up.

Although maybe Marnie Gorman was right. Maybe this was a total waste of time. She didn't know any more about what happened to Ted Gorman than she did before. She also didn't know any more about Clara McDougal than she did before. Okay. That wasn't strictly true.

She knew a lot more about her actually. She knew she was neat. She knew she was a homemaker. She knew she was an artist, she liked solitude, she was a good cook.

She knew she cooked from scratch. She knew she liked chocolate — but then half of the known universe did. She just didn't know any more about where Clara McDougal had ended up or why than she did before. She sighed and called her father. When he answered she told him what she'd found out.

"So what do you think?" she said.

"I think she was a woman who liked her small comforts," her dad replied.

"Don't we all? I'm on my way home."

"Good thing," Sean replied. "That construction guy is here . . ."

"Tim Conner?"

"Yup. That's the one. And I think your elder sister could use your help. She's been wondering where you were for the last hour or so."

"I'll be home soon," Bernie said.

She took one last look around Clara McDougal's home, gathered up the preserves, and locked the house back up. Somehow it seemed like the right thing to do.

# CHAPTER 17

Sean looked at Clyde as he settled back in the armchair. "Libby doesn't seem in a good mood," he observed.

"She's not," Sean replied. "She doesn't do well with change."

"Do any of us?"

"True. But some of us manage a little better than others."

Clyde grinned. "Guess she takes after her father."

Sean grinned back. "Guess she does."

"Do you think she'd mind bringing me up a piece of her apple pie?" Clyde asked.

"You know she wouldn't." Sean picked up his cell phone and called Libby down below in the shop. "She said she'll be up in a moment," he told Clyde when he got off. "This is a new type she's trying out. Juiced apple."

Clyde grinned. "My grandma used to make a pie like that. You let the apples sit in sugar and cinnamon. Then you pour the juice that they form back in the pie and you bake it."

Sean nodded. "It's delicious with Libby's ice cream."

Clyde rubbed his hands. "I can hardly wait." He sat back in his chair.

"So how are things in Lucy land?" Sean asked.

Actually he was surprised he hadn't had a visit from the police about Ted Gorman by this time. When he was chief, something like the Gorman caper might have upset him a tad. More than a tad actually.

"Things are pretty calm," Clyde told him. "Maybe because Mrs. Lucy has gone to see her sister in Phoenix. Life is always more pleasant when she's gone."

"So I've heard," Sean said. He wheeled his chair over to his bed and picked up his notepad and a pen. "Got any news about Ted Gorman?"

He really would like something useful. He was getting tired explaining to Clayton that he had nothing new to tell him. It was embarrassing.

Clyde rubbed his hands together. "Indeed I do got news."

Sean winced at the grammar but didn't say anything. He was only glad that Bernie wasn't here to correct Clyde's English.

Clyde continued. "Some of which is very interesting."

Sean waited.

"It's worth a pie. Maybe even two."

Sean thought for a moment. "How about banana cream?" He knew Libby had one of those in the freezer.

"Throw in an apple-cranberry crisp and you have yourself a deal."

"Done," Sean said. Libby could whip one of those up in five minutes or less.

Clyde stroked his chin. "Or maybe I should ask for a chocolate-raspberry truffle cake."

"Hey," Sean told him, "you made your deal, now live with it."

"I think you're trying to cheat me," Clyde said. "What I've got could be worth some big bucks."

"Yeah. Like I could ever get anything by you. Come on, buckaroo, give it up."

Clyde made a face. "Buckaroo? You've been reading westerns again?"

"Indeed I have. Now give."

"Okeydokey." Clyde took his notebook out of the breast pocket of his shirt and opened it. "You're going to like this," he said. "You want me to start with the bona fides or go straight to the good stuff?"

"Start with the bona fides," Sean told him.

"Right." Clyde whipped out a pair of reading glasses and put them on.

"When did you get those?" Sean asked.

"From the drugstore."

"I didn't ask where. I asked when."

"About a year ago. Usually I don't wear them. But the print keeps getting smaller and smaller these days."

"It is for me too," Sean admitted.

Clyde nodded.

*He looks like a pelican with those glasses on his face,* Sean thought, *but then, I probably look like a walrus.*

"I'm waiting," he prompted.

Clyde nodded and coughed to clear his throat. Then he began. "Okay, we've got one Theodore Allen Gorman. Thirty-six years of age. Adopted. Father deceased. Mother was living in Brooklyn Heights but currently resides in Schenectady. I have an address if you're interested."

Sean nodded and Clyde passed him a piece of paper.

"Here you go," he said. Then he went on with his recital. "Gorman attended the Allen Steven School for Boys, then went on to CIA." Clyde raised his head. "That's the Culinary Institute of America."

"I figured," Sean said.

"It could have been the other CIA. The

one that does all the government work."

"It could have," Sean agreed. "He just never struck me as the type."

"That's the type they'd be most likely to hire."

Sean snorted. "Can we get on with this?"

"Sure. Gorman studied pastry making. He apprenticed at the Blue Stork in L.A. and the Wild Orchid in San Francisco. Weird names."

"But good places," Sean pointed out. He'd heard about them through Bernie. "Very good places."

"I wouldn't know about that. My wife always wants to eat at places like Chili's."

"Must be tough."

"She's got other good qualities. A sense of taste just isn't one of them."

Sean thought about Rose's sense of taste. It had been impeccable. She'd taught him all about food. It was a gift he'd cherish forever.

Clyde coughed again and consulted his notebook. "Back to the matter at hand. Ted Gorman returned here about fifteen years ago with his wife. They met in high school and continued their relationship on and off until they tied the knot. Our boy worked in a series of restaurants in New York City and here. I'm told many of them are quite notable. Would you like to hear what they are?"

"Not necessary," Sean said.

Clyde readjusted his spectacles. "I don't think so either, but I thought I'd offer. Anyway, he and his wife came up with the money for their shop, money that they borrowed from an uncle who is now deceased. They started a year before that by making candy in their garage and peddling it door to door. Then they rented that spot in the strip mall and they've just gone from there."

Sean nodded while Clyde turned his notebook page. "No kids. Don't know if they couldn't or didn't want to. His and Marnie's business seems to be on the up-and-up. They pay their taxes on time and seem to enjoy a good standing in the community. Give money to the volunteer fire department, the sheriff's charitable fund. Things like that."

"But," Sean said.

"But what?"

Sean rubbed his hands together. "Are you going to get to the good part?"

"This is the good part."

"Does he gamble? Do drugs? Deal drugs? What?"

Clyde took his reading glasses off, folded them up, and put them in the breast pocket of his shirt. "You know Cap, you have such a negative view of people."

"Yes, I do," Sean agreed equably. They'd played this game when he was working. "And so do you. It comes with the job." Boy, did it ever! If he'd ever had any illusions about anything he'd lost them a long time ago. "Now give."

Clyde looked at the cell phone lying near Sean. "And have I heard a phone call asking Libby about the pies?"

"It'll be fine."

"I'd feel better if you called."

"You've become so distrustful."

Clyde smiled. "That's what happens when you get older. You should know."

"Fair enough," Sean said. He picked up the phone and called Libby downstairs. "She's agreed," he said when he hung up. "And she'll be right up with the apple pie and coffee. She apologizes. Things got a little nutty downstairs."

Clyde nodded.

"So." Sean started tapping the side of his wheelchair. "What is it? Drugs? Gambling?"

Clyde shook his head. "Take another guess."

"There's only one thing left. Women."

"Exactly."

"Ted Gorman was fooling around?" Sean

195

couldn't help it. Despite what he'd just said he was shocked. "He and Marnie were supposed to have this great relationship."

"Maybe Ted just needed to supplement it," Clyde commented. "Maybe he got bored."

"I don't believe it," Libby said.

Sean looked up. He'd been so engrossed he hadn't heard Libby coming up the stairs. She came in and set a tray down on the table next to his wheelchair.

"I really don't believe it," she said.

"Well, according to my sources Ted Gorman was stepping out."

"But they were always hugging and kissing," Libby protested.

"Doesn't mean anything," Clyde informed her. "Sometimes the people who seem the most lovey-dovey in public aren't that way in private." He eyed the tray. "Not to change the subject or anything, but your dad said that pie's juiced."

Libby smiled. "It is."

Sean watched as Libby handed Clyde a piece of pie and poured him a cup of coffee, then did the same for him. Clyde took a bite and rolled it around in his mouth before he swallowed.

"This is perfect," he said.

Libby beamed.

"The balance between the crust and the softness of the apples, and the sweet of the sugar, the spice of the cinnamon, and the tart of the apples is flawless."

"Clyde, you've been watching the Cooking Channel again, haven't you?" Sean asked.

Clyde blushed. "Does it show?"

"Is rice white?" Sean retorted.

"Get back to Ted Gorman," Libby instructed. "How do you know?"

"Because one of the cleaning women in the Sleepy Time Motel saw him coming out with a woman right before he wrapped his BMW around a tree."

"What woman?"

Clyde shrugged. "Good question. She didn't get a good look."

Sean put his fork down. "I assume the police know this?"

"Not yet."

"Then how do you?"

"You know what we used to say about hunches?"

"We didn't say anything about hunches because you and I don't believe in them."

"I forgot that."

"Truth, Clyde."

"I heard rumors after Ted wrecked his BMW that there'd been drinking going on and that a girl was involved, but given the circumstances no one ever followed up. Remember, that was when we had that purse snatching and the graffiti going around."

*Like this was a case of the flu,* Sean thought.

"Yeah, it was a regular crime wave," Sean remarked dryly.

"Anyway," Clyde continued, "I figured I'd pursue it a little, and since I know someone who works at the Sleepy Time Motel I decided to start there. What can I say? For once I got lucky."

"You told Lucy yet?"

Clyde shook his head. "I figured I'd give you a couple of days before I do."

"Nice of you," Sean said. He noticed Libby biting her nails. "What's up?" he asked her.

"I just wonder if that was the person who got burned up in the car wreck?" she said.

"Could be," Sean said.

"But then . . ." Libby stopped.

"Then what?" Sean asked.

"Then who put the ring on her finger?" Libby demanded.

"Who do you think?" Sean asked his daughter.

She paused for a moment, then said, "It

had to be Ted Gorman."

Clyde nodded his approval. "The thought had crossed my mind."

"But that means he killed her — that means that he planned this whole thing."

Sean applauded. "Right again."

Libby went back to work on her cuticle. "But then who killed Ted Gorman?"

"Now, that," Sean said, "is the question."

Libby was quiet for a moment. Then she said, "Isn't there any way to identify the girl?"

Clyde ate a piece of his pie. "I checked the files. No reports of missing girls that I can see."

"Maybe someone didn't report her missing," Libby observed.

"Maybe not," Clyde said. "Heaven only knows things like that have happened before. But if that's the case there's nothing I can do. Aside from everything else, what was left of the body was cremated and Marnie scattered the ashes over the Hudson River. So we have nothing."

"That's terrible," Libby said as she put another slice of pie on Clyde's plate.

"Yes, it is," Clyde agreed.

Sean turned to Libby. "Before you get too worked up you should know that Clyde's report might not be true in the first place."

"That's ridiculous," Clyde scoffed.

Sean took a sip of his coffee and put his cup down. "Are you telling me that informants don't lie?"

"No. I'm not telling you that, but this one is telling the truth."

"And how do you know that?"

"Because she owes me big time," Clyde said.

Sean was about to answer when he heard voices, then footsteps coming up the stairs. A few seconds later Clayton stuck his head in the door. Bernie followed.

Sean watched Clayton glance around the door.

"What a nice surprise," Sean said. "To what do we owe this pleasure?"

Clayton sniffed. "I don't think I've ever been up here before."

"I know you haven't," Sean shot back.

"Very cozy," Clayton said. A look of disdain was plastered on his face. "I was driving by and I decided to stop and see what kind of progress you're making."

"We're making some," Sean told him.

"A lot actually," Libby said.

Clayton sneered. "That's not what my son says."

Somehow Sean doubted that was the truth. He leaned forward slightly. "You know," he told Clayton, "my mother had an old saying. Something to the effect that you get what you pay for."

Clayton sniffed. "It works both ways."

"Yes, it does," Sean replied.

The two men glared at each other.

Finally Sean said, "Maybe we'd get more answers if we got a little more publicity. You know, let everyone know what happened at the cemetery. Maybe someone saw something."

Clayton got up. "I don't think that will be necessary," he said and he left the room.

Sean listened to his footsteps going down the stairs and the door to the outside closing.

"That wasn't nice," Libby told him.

"No," Sean agreed. "It wasn't nice. But it was fun."

# CHAPTER 18

Libby looked around R.J.'s. The bar was jammed. She sighed. What were all these people doing here? This was Tuesday.

"The place shouldn't be this packed," she said to Marvin as they wended their way to the other end where Bernie and Rob were sitting.

If she'd known it was going to be this crowded she never would have agreed to come. She really didn't like noisy, crowded places, especially after an extremely busy day.

"It's the dart league," Marvin explained. "Tuesday night is tournament night."

"It's never been tournament night before."

"This is something new."

Libby grunted as she pushed by someone. He turned around. It was Tim Conner.

"Hey," he said. "Fancy meeting you here. You have to quit following me around."

Libby couldn't help smiling. She had to

admit that he did have a nice way about him, even if tomorrow morning he was about to begin replacing their exhaust fan, something that was going to make an incredible mess. How she and the rest of the kitchen crew were going to work around it she had yet to figure out.

It would be nice if they could close down, but that wasn't even close to being possible. But she was going to have to reschedule making the chocolate ruffles for Mrs. Spiegel's chocolate ruffle raspberry cake. She couldn't risk having specks of dust fall into the pan. She'd just have to do the ruffles tonight when she got home.

It was a long and tedious job. First she had to chop the chocolate and melt it. Then she had to heat the cookie sheets and pour the melted chocolate on them. After that she spread the chocolate over the pans and stuck them in the cooler and waited for the chocolate to harden.

Only then could she make the ruffles, which were hard to do. She had to hold the knife blade just so and sweep it in an arc while she gathered the other ends of the chocolate with her free hand, after which they went into the cooler to harden again.

Much as she liked to eat chocolate, she really didn't like cooking with it. It was . . .

what had Bernie called it? Capricious. A drop of water in the pan and all the chocolate could seize up.

Libby sighed again. So much for washing her clothes. That would have to wait until tomorrow. Which was not good. Right now she was down to her old stretched-out black pants and her gray sweater with the frayed cuffs. Bernie called it her street person look, and while the clothes weren't *that* bad, even Libby had to admit they weren't things of beauty. She was hoping that there was something else in her closet when she became aware that Tim Conner was speaking to her.

"Ready for tomorrow?" he asked.

Libby realized she was looking at his chest and averted her eyes. "Not yet. But we will be. How come I've never seen you here before?"

"That's because I'm usually at Dafney's Place."

Dafney's was across town.

"So what are you doing here?"

Tim Conner's smile got bigger. "I'm on Dafney's dart team and we're going to whip everyone's ass."

Someone called his name and he turned and nodded toward them. "See you in the a.m.," he told Libby.

Marvin tugged at her arm as she started walking again.

"Who is that?" he asked.

"My contractor."

Marvin snorted.

"What's the snort supposed to mean?"

"Nothing," Marvin said.

Libby turned and studied his face. *He's jealous,* she thought. The thought gave her a great deal of satisfaction. *Maybe Bernie is wrong,* she decided; *maybe he really doesn't care what I wear.* She started to laugh.

"What are you laughing at?" Marvin asked her.

"Nothing," Libby lied. "Nothing at all."

When they got closer to where Bernie and Rob were seated, Libby could see that the place wasn't as crowded as she thought. Most of the people were jammed up front. She sat down on the bar stool that Bernie had saved for her, while Marvin sat next to her. A moment later Brandon came over to get their order.

"The usual?" he asked them.

"Yes," Libby said. Then she changed her mind. "No. Make mine a kir."

She could see Bernie raising an eyebrow.

"For a change," Libby explained to her sister.

"A kir sounds good to me," she told

Libby. "Make that two," she said to Brandon.

"Two it is." He nodded toward Marvin. "And for you?"

"What is a kir?" he asked.

"White wine and a crème de cassis," Bernie explained.

"It's a girl drink," Rob said.

Bernie turned toward him. "Don't be silly. It's good," she said to Marvin.

"That's okay," Marvin said. "I'm sure it's great, but I'll have a Brooklyn Brown instead."

"Whatever you say," Brandon told him. And he left to get their drinks.

Bernie pushed the bowl of peanuts over in Libby's direction, while Rob took a sip of his beer. Libby decided that he looked slightly annoyed. A moment later Brandon was back with Marvin's beer and Libby's kir.

"Here you go," he said as he set both their drinks down.

Bernie lifted her glass. "A toast," she said. "To friends, food, and time to enjoy them both."

"I'll drink to that," Rob said as he lifted his glass.

Libby and Marvin did the same. Everyone clinked their glasses and drank.

"So how's everything going?" Brandon asked.

Marvin put his glass down. "Can't complain."

"Can you be any more generic?" Brandon commented.

"Not really," Marvin said.

Brandon shrugged and moved away.

"Do you think he knows?" Marvin asked the group.

"Knows what?" Libby asked.

"About . . . the . . . you know . . . the mix-up."

Bernie snickered. "Of course he knows. Brandon knows everything. This place is like Information Central."

"You could have been nicer," Libby told him.

Marvin's face fell. "You're right. I could have been."

Libby felt a stab of guilt. Poor guy. He had his father on his back all the time. He didn't need her as well. She was just about to say as much when she felt a tap on her shoulder. She turned around. Tim Conner was standing there.

"Can I get you guys the next round? Given the amount of money I'm about to extract from you it seems only fair."

Bernie nodded. "I concur," she said.

"Me too," Libby replied. "I thought you were supposed to be playing darts," she added.

"I'm not up yet," he explained as he sat down next to Libby. He nodded to Rob. "Haven't seen you for a while."

"You two know each other?" Bernie asked.

Tim nodded. "He used to do framing for me."

"You mounted pictures?" Libby asked Rob.

"No," Rob said. "Framing as in framing houses."

"He wasn't bad either," Tim said.

"Not bad?" Rob said. "I was great."

Tim took a handful of peanuts from the bowl in front of Libby and popped them in his mouth. "So what have you been up to lately?" he asked Rob.

"I've been busy helping my mom run her business."

Tim nodded.

"Heard you had some trouble," Rob said.

Libby watched Tim frown.

"Not to my knowledge," he replied.

"Heard someone ran off with your back-hoe."

Tim laughed. "Yeah. But they brought it back."

"How can anyone run off with a backhoe?" Libby asked.

"Simple," Tim said. "You put the keys in the ignition and drive it away."

"But how could you get the keys?"

"Easy," Rob replied before Tim could. "People usually keep them on a Peg-Board. All you have to do is reach over and take them."

Tim reached over and took another handful of peanuts. "No dinner," he explained.

"I think you're on," Rob said to him.

Rob looked to the front. "I think you're right." And he got up and walked away.

"I didn't know you did construction," Bernie said to Rob after Tim left.

"For a little while," he said. "But I got tired of being sore every night so I quit."

Libby took another sip of her kir and set the glass down.

"You look sad," Marvin said to her.

"Not sad, just puzzled."

"About what?" Marvin asked.

Libby took another sip of her drink and told Marvin and Rob about what Clyde had told her concerning Marnie.

"I don't believe it," Marvin said. "Not Marnie and Ted Gorman."

"See? That's my reaction too," Libby said.

"So the guy was a player," Rob interjected. "What's so unusual about that?"

Bernie hit him.

"Why'd you do that?" Rob demanded.

"Because of what you said."

Rob rubbed his shoulder. "Most men play around. It's a fact of life, right, Marvin?"

"Er . . ." Marvin said. "Ah . . . not really."

Rob took a sip of his beer. "You're not telling the truth, my man."

"So you're saying that you fool around?" Bernie demanded.

Libby noted there was a dangerous glint in her eye.

"Not at all," Rob said. "I was talking in generalities. You know what that is?"

"Yes. I'm familiar with the term."

Bernie's voice was tinged with ice. Libby decided it was a good time to change the subject. *Redirect* as her father always said.

"I don't know," she said. "I still can't believe it. Ted and Marnie seemed so happy together."

"They probably were," Rob interjected. "Ted just wanted a little variety."

Bernie shot him a dirty look.

"More to the point," she said, "who was the girl?"

Libby shook her head. "I already told you that Clyde didn't know."

Bernie tapped her fingernail against the glass and sighed. "Yeah. I remember."

Marvin leaned forward. "So she wasn't someone local," he said.

"Not necessarily," Bernie replied. "She could just be someone who no one would miss. Like a prostitute or a drug addict . . ."

"Or someone who travels a lot," Libby suggested.

"Or that," Bernie agreed.

"So who would know?" Libby asked.

Bernie thought for a moment. Then she said, "Didn't Clyde say that Ted Gorman's mom was still alive?"

"Yeah. She lives near Albany. But what difference does that make? She wouldn't know."

Bernie twisted her silver and onyx ring around her finger. "You're right. I was just thinking out loud," she explained.

Libby took another sip of her kir. She decided that although she really liked it, she liked chocolate better. She was just about to ask her sister what chocolate she thought would go well with a kir when a new thought popped into her head. "Maybe he wrote to her."

Everyone turned to her.

She explained, "Actually I meant maybe she wrote him a note or something." When she got tired she had a tendency to reverse things.

"Who? Ted's mom?"

"No. The girl."

Rob shot a peanut down the bar. "Not these days. These days everyone uses e-mail. No one uses snail mail."

Bernie smoothed her hair back down with the palm of her hand. "I don't know. Everyone isn't as technologically advanced as you are. Maybe she sent him a card. Or maybe there's something else. Like a receipt from the motel they stayed at."

"He wouldn't keep anything like that," Rob sneered. "He wouldn't be that stupid."

"Well, maybe he was," Bernie countered. "Lots of men are. That's how they get caught."

"None that I know."

Bernie raised an eyebrow. "Really?"

Libby decided that another diversion was called for.

"But where would he keep something like that if it existed?" she asked.

"In his dresser drawers?" Marvin suggested.

"I don't think so," Bernie commented.

"But why not?" Marvin asked.

"Because," Libby said, "most women do the laundry, so they're the ones who put the clothes in drawers."

"So where else would it be?" Marvin said.

"If it exists," Rob said.

"I don't know," Libby confessed.

"How about the garage?" Bernie suggested. "That's guy territory. Most women don't go mucking around in there."

"True." Libby nodded. "We should look."

"Yes, we should," Bernie agreed.

"Why?" Rob asked.

Bernie turned toward him. "Are you serious?"

"Yes, I am," he replied.

"Well, for openers, because it's a lead, and since we don't have anything else, we should, as my dad says, explore every avenue of opportunity."

"I still don't get it."

While Libby listened to Bernie explain things to Rob she realized there was another problem.

"What do we say to Marnie?" she asked. "How are we going to explain why we want to do this?"

The thought made her shudder.

"We don't," Bernie said. "We look around when she's not there."

"That should be easy enough. She's not there most of the time."

"Exactly," Bernie said.

Libby thought Marnie's situation was the disadvantage of having your shop away from your living quarters. At least she and Bernie could go upstairs whenever they had a spare minute or two. The other way they'd never be home at all.

Bernie started tapping her fingers on the table. Then she picked up her cell and dialed.

"Marnie, sorry to bother you this late . . . Oh, it's no problem . . . Good, because I have some ideas for the benefit. I thought if you were free I'd come by the shop and talk to you — that's if you have a moment. Great. How long are you going to be there?" She nodded and hung up. "Okay, guys," she said. "We're in luck. She's going to be there for another hour or so. What do you say?"

Rob picked up his glass, took a big swallow, and put it down. "I say I have better things to do. This is ridiculous."

"What do you have to do that's so important?" Bernie demanded.

"I thought we were supposed to go to the movies," Rob told her.

"We can go tomorrow," Bernie said.

"I'd like to go tonight."

"It's okay," Marvin interjected. "Really. This isn't necessary. We can wait until tomorrow. It'll be fine."

Bernie chewed on the inside of her cheek. "Maybe. Maybe not. But we have an opportunity now. We should take advantage of it. Since we don't have any information, anything we get will be great."

"Why can't you do this some other time?" Rob asked.

"Because Marnie is at the shop now," Bernie said. "We can pick up some DVDs for later and go to the movies tomorrow night."

"Fine." Rob finished his drink, threw a couple of dollars on the bar, and walked out.

"Boy," Libby said to Bernie, "you said you guys weren't getting along, but I hadn't realized it was this bad."

"Neither did I," Bernie said. "I think Venus is retrograde in his sign. I should check his chart."

Libby raised an eyebrow. "Now, that's a new excuse for bad behavior."

Bernie shrugged. "If it's good enough for the ancients it should be good enough for us."

"So were leeches."

"They're making a comeback too."

Marvin leaned in. "This is my fault."

Bernie patted his arm. "Don't be ridiculous. This has nothing to do with you."

"Maybe you should go after Rob," Marvin suggested.

Bernie shook her head. "I don't think so." She smiled. "I think I should visit Marnie while you and Libby should go visit her house."

"What if something goes wrong?" Libby asked.

"That's why God invented cell phones. Just call and tell me you have a kitchen emergency. If you can't get in tell me . . ." Bernie paused for a second. "Say the pantry is locked. And we'll go from there."

# CHAPTER 19

Marvin squinted as he tried to read the street sign. "I think we're lost."

"No, we're not," Libby told him. "This is Woodcrest."

Marvin pushed his glasses back up the bridge of his nose with his finger. "You could be right."

"I know I'm right. Just take a left and go halfway down the block. It's there," Libby said as she pointed to the little white Colonial. "Pull into the driveway."

As Marvin did, Libby noticed with a degree of satisfaction that Marnie's Christmas lights were still up. Of course she and Bernie had just taken theirs down a couple of weeks ago. Still, it was always nice to know that someone was even later than she was.

Marvin stomped on the brake. "Are you sure this is it?"

"Of course I'm sure. This is 1407. It says

it on the mailbox."

"So it does." Marvin lifted his glasses up, looked through them, and put them back down. "Maybe I need to get my prescription checked."

"Well, it wouldn't hurt." And with that Libby reached into her backpack, took out two of her butterscotch cashew cookies, and handed one to Marvin.

He put his car in park and took a bite. "These are great."

"Thanks. I think so too."

In her humble opinion this cookie was as close to perfection as you could get. It balanced the sweet against the salty and the crunch against the soft crust. Of course, when she'd said as much to Bernie, Bernie had replied that the Muslims believed that only Allah could be perfect. Everything that was human has to have some imperfections. Maybe so. But if this cookie had imperfections she couldn't see what they were.

As Libby took another bite of her cookie she decided Marnie's house was the smallest and plainest one on the block. This area of town was fairly ritzy. Most of the other houses in the area were made out of stone, brick, or stucco and had things like verandas, slate roofs, and inground pools attached to them. Libby was trying to estimate how much Marnie's house was worth when Marvin turned toward her.

"Do you think this is safe?" he asked.

"Bernie will call if there's a problem."

Marvin pulled at the collar of his turtleneck. "Maybe we shouldn't do this."

*Works for me,* Libby thought.

Bernie should be doing this while she should be talking to Marnie. Her sister was better at this kind of thing. With her luck, she and Marvin would probably get caught. Scratch that. She *knew* she and Marvin would get caught.

Back at R.J.'s it had seemed like a good idea — at least not a bad idea — but now that she was out here . . . well . . . the whole idea made her nervous. Very nervous. She should be at the shop making pastry dough, not thinking about breaking and entering. Marvin cleared his throat and she turned toward him.

"I've changed my mind," he said.

"Hey, I totally understand if you don't want to."

Marvin waited a second before replying. "No," he told her. "I think we have to. After all, this is my father's livelihood we're talking about."

And good riddance to it, Libby wanted to say. But she didn't. Mostly because she remembered what her mother always told her and her sister: "If you can't say anything nice don't say anything at all."

To which Bernie had always replied, "Fine. I'll be quiet." Well, she felt like that now.

Marvin swallowed. "What happens if the neighbors see us?"

"The neighbors can't see us." Libby pointed to the evergreens on either side of the driveway. "Those cedars provide a perfect screen. That's probably why they were planted in the first place."

"But what if they do?" Marvin insisted. "What if they hear us and call the police?"

"Well, we could always say we're dropping off some cookies for her if anyone asks."

"But what if they want to see them?"

Libby gave up. "I guess then we'll get arrested."

Marvin pushed his glasses back up the bridge of his nose again. "That wouldn't be good."

"Not at all. Your father wouldn't be pleased."

Marvin shuddered. "I don't even want to think about that."

"Well, sitting here isn't helping anything," Libby pointed out.

"You're right." Marvin reached over and

turned off the radio.

"Why did you do that?" Libby asked.

Marvin shrugged. "I don't know. It seemed like the right thing to do. No use making more noise than we have to," he observed.

"So we're going?" Libby asked.

Marvin nodded. "We're going."

Libby opened the car door. "You stay here. I'll go."

"Don't be silly. We'll both go. If we're going to get arrested we'll get arrested together."

Libby gave him a hug. "That's the sweetest thing anyone has ever said to me."

Marvin grinned. *Maybe this was worth it,* Libby thought.

"Ready?" Marvin asked.

"Ready," Libby answered.

"Then let's do it."

They got out of Marvin's car and headed toward Marnie's garage. As they approached the house, they stopped. And that's when it hit Libby.

"Drats," she said. "The door is automatic."

Great. Of course it was. All garage doors these days were. She just hadn't thought about it because they didn't have one on their garage. Maybe that was because they didn't have a garage.

Marvin sighed. "I'm a moron," he said. "I don't know why I didn't think of that before. Come on, let's go back to the car. It's warmer in there."

Libby rubbed her hands together when they were inside. "I guess we should go." After all, it wasn't as if they hadn't tried.

Marvin held up his hand. "Wait a minute. Something just occurred to me."

"Like what?"

"Well, this is a long shot but let's see." Marvin reached over and picked his remote door opener off his dashboard.

"Isn't that for your house?"

"Yup."

"So why will that work here?" Libby asked.

Marvin shrugged. "It's a long shot but sometimes things like this work on the same channel." He pressed. Nothing happened. He put it back down. "Guess not this time."

"Okay. So now can we go?" Libby said.

"There could be a button on the door. Usually it's on the inside to keep people from getting locked in, but you never know. I'm going to go check."

Libby cursed silently. "Fine."

She watched Marvin get out of the car. He walked over to the garage and carefully inspected the molding around the garage door opening.

"Nope," he said when he returned. He rubbed his hands together for warmth. "So that leaves us with one last possibility."

"What's that?" Libby asked.

"We drive over to Just Chocolate and borrow the garage door opener from Marnie's car."

Libby stared at him in amazement. This was not the Marvin she knew.

"Let me get this straight. You want to steal Marnie's garage door opener?"

"That's what I just said. Is that a problem?"

"Yes."

"I don't see why. You and Bernie do things like that all the time."

"We most certainly do not."

"Don't you think I can?"

"It's not that . . ."

"Then what is it?" Marvin demanded.

"Nothing," Libby said. It had been a long day and she was too tired to have this discussion. She reached in her backpack for her cell phone.

"Who are you calling?" Marvin asked.

"Bernie," Libby said. "Maybe she can help."

"I hope she's all right," Marvin said as

Libby waited for Bernie to pick up.

"She's talking to Marnie. Why shouldn't she be okay?"

"I meant her and Rob," Marvin said.

Libby rebuttoned her sweater with her free hand. She had to do something about fixing her buttonholes, although Bernie had said she should just throw the thing out. She was probably right, Libby gloomily concluded. She just hated to part with it. She'd had it since ninth grade.

"Yeah," Libby agreed. "They were pretty bad tonight, weren't they?"

"They sure were."

"I wonder what's going on," Marvin mused.

"He's been offered a job in Jersey and I don't think she wants him to take it."

"What kind of job?"

"A drug rep." She was about to tell Marvin more when Bernie picked up.

"So what's up?" Bernie asked. "Another kitchen emergency?"

"You could say that," Libby said. "We're locked out of the pantry."

"That could be a problem," Bernie said.

"Indeed it is. So we've decided to borrow what we need and return it."

"I see," Bernie said. "What if the cabinet is locked as well?"

Cabinet? What the hell was a cabinet? Libby wondered. Okay. Cabinet started with a *c*. Maybe cabinet meant car in Bernie-speak.

"Do you mean Marnie's car?"

"Exactly."

"Then I guess we're out of luck." Libby didn't want to admit she hadn't thought about that possibility.

"No, no," Bernie said. "Let me see what I can do. If that's the case, I'll call you back."

After they hung up, Libby returned her cell to her backpack.

"So what's happening?" Marvin asked.

Libby shook her head. "Ya got me."

# CHAPTER 20

"My sister," Bernie explained to Marnie.
"So I gathered," Marnie said.

"She's always losing her keys."

Marnie grunted. "She should be more careful."

"It's a problem, that's for sure. Especially if they're the office keys."

"I'd say," Marnie said.

"Libby has even gone so far as to suggest we leave the office unlocked."

Marnie frowned. "That's just plain nuts."

"I know. I trust my workers . . ."

"But there are limits," Marnie said.

"My sentiments exactly," Bernie agreed. "After all, why put temptation in someone's way?"

Marnie stifled a yawn and went back to looking at her cookbook. Bernie twisted her ring around her finger. Was Marnie's car door open? And if it was, how the hell was she supposed to get her keys? Well, she didn't need her keys exactly. She just needed the automatic door opener to her garage. Unfortunately they were attached to her keys. And her keys were . . . where? She usually kept hers in her bag. Marnie probably did too.

"Hey, Marnie," she said.

Marnie turned from the cookbook she was consulting. Bernie noticed she had a dab of chocolate on her apron.

"I'm thinking of getting a Saab."

"That's nice," Marnie said. "We've had ours forever."

"Do you think you could show me yours?"

"Now?" Marnie asked. "You want to see it now?"

"Ah . . . yes," Bernie replied.

Marnie didn't say anything. She just looked at her. Why did it have to be now? Bernie began to panic. Then all of a sudden she had it.

"Well," she ad-libbed, "I'm going to look at a used one tomorrow afternoon, and it would be very helpful if I could see yours for comparison purposes."

Marnie sighed.

"If it's too much trouble —" Bernie began.

"No. It's fine." Marnie marked her page in the cookbook. "Let's go." She followed Marnie over to one of the prep tables.

Marnie bent down and reached behind a carton that said *Chocolate,* got her bag out, and put it on top of the table.

"I should get a smaller one of these," she said, fishing around in the purse.

Bernie smiled. "We all should, but if you think yours is bad you should see Libby's."

Marnie laughed. "I know." A moment later she held up her hand and jangled her keys. "Let's go." And she led Bernie out to the back parking lot. "There's the gray ghost," Marnie said, pointing to a gray Saab parked at the far end.

"Why the gray ghost?" Bernie asked.

"I'm not sure. It was Ted's name for it." And Marnie sighed.

Bernie sighed with her. She figured this was as good a time as any to see if Marnie knew about Ted's affair.

"Such a shame," Bernie said.

Marnie raised an eyebrow.

"I mean you got one of the last of the good ones."

"It's true," Marnie said. "I did."

"Most of the guys I've been with . . ." Bernie faked hesitation. "They run around. They drink too much. They cheat and go out with other women. You know, I think that one hurts the most."

"Thank God I don't know about that,"

Marnie told her. "Ted never did any of those things. He never looked at another woman the entire time we were married."

"Most men aren't like that. You were lucky."

"Yes, I was," Marnie agreed.

Was that a note of hesitation in Marnie's voice? Bernie couldn't be sure.

"There'll never be another man like Ted," Marnie said as she clicked the Saab's door open. "Get in," she told Bernie.

For the next minute Bernie listened to Marnie extol the Saab's virtues while she eyed the automatic garage door opener sitting on the dashboard. She'd love to lean over and snatch it, but she didn't dare.

"Don't you think?" Marnie said.

"Oh, absolutely," Bernie agreed even though she didn't have the vaguest idea what Marnie had been talking about because she hadn't been listening.

"Any questions?" Marnie asked.

Bernie shook her head.

"Good. Then let's get back to planning the benefit's menu."

Bernie got out of the Saab, as did Marnie. Marnie locked the car door with her clicker.

"I know it's silly," she told Bernie. "But I'm always afraid someone will steal the car."

"Doesn't seem silly to me," Bernie replied as they hurried back inside. "These days you never know."

"True," Marnie said. She dropped her keys back in her bag and put it back where it had been.

Bernie leaned against one of the prep tables. What she needed was a distraction. But what? Her cell phone rang. She picked it up and looked at it. Libby.

"What?" she said.

"Is the Saab locked?" Libby asked.

"As of the moment yes."

"So what should Marvin and I do?"

"Give me a few minutes." And she clicked off. "Always something," she explained to Marnie.

Marnie didn't even look up. She was going through her cookbooks. "Maybe a German wine to go with an eighty percent dark chocolate? What do you think? Would it be too sweet?"

"Not at all," Bernie said. "Some of them have a great depth of character. I think they're highly underrated myself."

"You're probably right," Marnie replied. She tapped her pencil on her cookbook and turned the page.

Bernie bent down to readjust the strap on her shoe. As she did she noticed a pile of cartons at the other end of the room.

"What are those?" she asked Marnie.

"Nuts. Raisins. Cranberries. Nibs. Peanut oil for frying the nuts. Bolt was supposed to put them away."

Marnie lowered her head down and wrote something on the pad next to her book.

Oil, Bernie thought. When oil spills it makes an incredible mess. She went over to take a look. The cartons didn't look that stable to her. In fact, one of the cartons looked damaged.

She glanced at Marnie. She was still engrossed in what she was doing. Bernie turned so her body shielded her hand and pulled at the flap of one of the cartons. It gave a little. She pulled harder. Now she had an opening. She checked on Marnie again. Marnie was still engrossed with her notes. Bernie worked her fingers through the hole she'd made. She could feel plastic. She tore at it. A trickle of dried cranberries dribbled out. Next Bernie moved over to the jug of oil. She quickly bent down and loosened the cap. Then she tipped it on its side. A slick of oil started spreading on the floor. She gave a small push and several of the cartons fell down.

"Oh my God," she cried. "I'm so sorry. I turned my ankle and went right into the cartons."

Marnie looked up.

Bernie put her hands to her mouth. "I feel terrible."

"What's the matter?"

"One of the oil containers is leaking all over the floor."

"Damn." Marnie sprang out of her chair and hurried over. "I told Bolt to put this stuff away before he left. I told him twice."

"I'm so sorry," Bernie repeated. "Just tell me where the paper towels are and I'll clean everything up."

"It's not your fault," Marnie replied.

"At least let me help you move the cartons before the oil gets under them too."

"Just get me a couple of rolls of towels. They're on the second shelf on the far wall."

When Bernie came back Marnie had moved all the cartons.

"Here," Bernie said as she handed her the towels.

"I'll get the mop," Bernie said.

Marnie grunted. By now she was down on the floor trying to blot up the oil. Bernie walked over to Marnie's bag, reasoning that if Marnie looked up she could always tell her she thought the mop was by the back door.

Bernie looked at Marnie again. She was

facing away from her. Okay, now was the time. She reached down and grabbed the keys out of Marnie's bag. Hiding them in her hand, she quickly walked to the back door. Now came the tricky part, because she didn't know what she'd say if Marnie looked up while she was opening the back door.

She glanced at Marnie one more time. Good. She was still on her hands and knees. Bernie took a deep breath, put her hand on the doorknob, turned it, and pushed oh so gently. The door opened a crack. Bernie pushed very slowly. The door opened a little more. When she had enough space, she put her arm through and clicked the Saab opener. The car lights blinked. She'd done her part, now the rest was up to Libby.

Bernie quietly closed the door, walked over to the prep table, and carefully dropped the keys back in Marnie's bag.

"I'm sorry," Bernie said. "I can't seem to find the mop bucket."

"That's because it's over near the mop sink. And could you do me a favor and get me another roll of towels?"

"No problem," Bernie assured her. "That's the least I can do."

# CHAPTER 21

Marvin and Libby were sitting in Just Chocolate's parking lot.

"There she is," Libby said as the rear door to the shop opened. The lights on the Saab blinked.

"That's it," Marvin said. "Let's go."

He put his car in gear and zoomed over to the Saab. After stopping, he jumped out and grabbed the automatic door opener before getting back in his car and taking off.

"How much time do you think we have?" he asked Libby as he careened out of the strip mall.

"Not a lot," Libby replied.

Marvin accelerated.

"Slow down," Libby cried. "We don't need to get arrested for speeding."

Marvin reluctantly reduced his speed.

"Stop sign!" Libby yelled as they flew through the intersection of Grand and Teall.

"There's never anyone around this time

of night."

Libby closed her eyes. She could hear her father's comment ringing in her ears when he'd taught her to drive and she'd gone through a stop sign. He'd said, "Criminals commit crimes. Running stop signs is a crime. Don't be a criminal."

But somehow she didn't think this was the time to say that to Marvin. Especially since they'd already committed one criminal act and were about to commit another.

"Are you all right?" Marvin asked her when they got back to Marnie's house. "Because you look a little pale."

"I'm fine," Libby lied as her stomach came down from her throat. "Just fine."

She watched as Marvin raised Marnie's opener and pressed the button. "Presto chango," he said as the door began to rise.

Libby got out of the car and hurried inside. Marvin was right behind her. She looked around. The walls were covered with shelves that housed toolboxes, paint cans, garden hoses, axes, car stuff, and heaven knows what else. Where to begin? This could take all day.

Libby turned to Marvin. "If you were going to hide something in here, where would you put it?"

"I'd never hide anything in here."

"But if you were?"

"Gosh, I don't know. That's a good question. Where would you?"

Libby bit the edge of her cuticle. "I don't know. I don't usually hide things."

"Me neither," Marvin said.

"It's too much trouble. Anyway," Libby added, "I'd probably forget where I put it."

Marvin looked around. "In mysteries they're always hiding something under the floorboards."

"Except there are no floorboards. The floor is cement."

Libby studied the interior of the garage again. Her mother always used to say, "Begin at the beginning."

"Okay," she said. "Why don't you take the right side and I'll take the left and we'll meet in the middle?"

Marvin nodded.

Libby rubbed her hands together. "Then let's get to work."

She began at the very edge of the wall. She lifted up the rakes and the shovels. She moved the curls of garden hose. She inspected the bike hanging up from the garage ceiling. She bent down and looked in the cavity of the snowblower. She did the same with the leaf blower.

As she got up off her knees she reflected

that the Gormans had lots of gadgets. She and Bernie just had a shovel and a rake and that was it. She moved on to the toolboxes and the paint cans. There was nothing there. She peered in the cartons sitting on the shelves. Most of them contained old clothes or old books. Garage sale material. By the time she'd gotten to the far wall she was tired and frustrated.

"Any luck?" she asked Marvin, just to have something to say, because obviously if he'd found something he would have told her.

He shook his head.

"Now what?" she asked.

"I guess we go through what's on the far wall."

"There's nothing but more garage sale stuff," she said when she was done. She noticed Marvin looking up at the ceiling. "What are you looking at?" she asked.

"Maybe Ted hid something behind the light up there."

While Libby watched, Marvin dragged the ladder over, climbed up two steps, and looked.

"Nope," he said. He was climbing back down when Libby's cell rang.

"What, Bernie?" Libby said into it.

"Get back here," Bernie whispered. Her

voice was so low Libby could barely hear her. "Get back here now." Then she hung up.

"We gotta go," she told Marvin. "We really gotta go."

"I figured," he said.

They were running out the door when Marvin stopped dead in his tracks.

"Wait," he cried.

"For what?"

"I have a friend who always hid everything in the garbage."

"The garbage?" Libby echoed.

Marvin nodded. "He took the garbage out every week. He figured his wife would never look in the bottom of the garbage can."

"Kind of like hiding something in plain sight."

"Exactly," Marvin said. "Just give me a moment."

"That's all we have."

Libby watched as he hurried over to the garbage cans. She was right behind him. She peered over his shoulder as he opened the lid on the first one. It was empty.

"Try the second," she urged.

"I was just going to."

Libby held her breath as Marvin took the lid off the second can. He pulled the bag of garbage out.

"Anything?" Libby asked.

"Yes," he said. "There is."

He leaned in and pulled out a knotted-up black plastic bag. He started untying the knot.

"What are you doing?" Libby cried. "We have to get out of here."

"One second." Marvin untied the knot, opened the bag, and pulled out a folded-up brown paper bag. Libby watched as he opened that up.

"Anything in there?" she asked.

Marvin pulled out a cigar box. "There certainly is."

"Super," Libby said. She tugged at his sleeve. "Come on. We have to go."

"I know," Marvin said.

They ran out of the garage and jumped into Marvin's car. Marvin pressed the button and Marnie's garage door came down.

"Let's go," he said and they took off.

Bernie watched Marnie putting on her coat. She glanced at her watch. This was not good. It would probably take Marvin and Libby another couple of minutes to get here. She had to delay Marnie somehow.

"I'm so sorry for the mess," she told her.

"It's okay," Marnie assured her. "Those cartons should have been put away."

239

"At least let me pay for the oil."

"There's no need."

Bernie reached for her bag. "I insist. Tell me how much?"

Marnie wound her scarf around her neck. "I don't know. With the cranberries something like twenty bucks."

"Let me write you a check." And Bernie started fishing around in her bag. Anything to buy time.

"You can give me the money tomorrow," Marnie said. "Or even the day after. It really doesn't matter."

"It'll only take a second," Bernie said as she continued to dig. "Otherwise I'll forget."

"Don't worry, I'll remind you," Marnie told her. "Look, I'm so tired my bones are aching. I can hardly stand up. I have to go home." And she went over and clicked off the light. "After you," she said.

Bernie waited outside while Marnie set the alarm and locked the back door. *Please let Libby and Marvin have returned the garage door opener,* she prayed. *Please.*

"Are you parked in front?" Marnie asked.

Bernie nodded.

Out of the corner of her eye she caught sight of Marvin's vehicle.

She put her hand to her mouth. "Just a second," she cried.

Marnie turned toward her. Bernie pretended to look in her bag. "I'm sorry but I forgot my cell."

Marnie shook her head and trudged back toward the store.

"I'm sorry to be such a pain," Bernie told Marnie as Marnie punched in the security code.

Out of the corner of her eye Bernie could see Marvin pull up to the Saab, jump out of his car, yank open the door of the Saab, and lean in. Then he jumped back into his car and backed out. Bernie breathed a sigh of relief.

"I'm sorry," Bernie said again as she followed Marnie into the store. She tried to look contrite. "I don't know what's the matter with me tonight."

"Neither do I," Marnie snapped. "But whatever you have I hope it passes."

Bernie decided that under the circumstances she would have been equally miffed.

# CHAPTER 22

Sean regarded the cigar box Libby had placed before him, then glanced back at Libby, Marvin, and Bernie.

"Nice," he said as he ate a piece of the lemon curd pie Libby had brought up to him a little while ago. "Did you put more lemon zest in?"

"Just a bit," Libby replied.

Sean took a sip of his coffee and set his cup in its saucer. "It works well." Then he cut off another piece of pie and conveyed it to his mouth.

"Would you mind turning on the TV?" he asked Bernie when he was done chewing.

Libby leaned forward.

"Aren't you going to open the cigar box?" she asked.

"No." Sean took a sip of his coffee and readjusted himself in his wheelchair.

"Why not?" Libby wailed.

"Because considering the way you got it

I'm inclined to throw it in the trash. Simply put, by looking at it I'd be condoning the criminal activities you've committed to acquire it."

Bernie rolled her eyes.

"I'm serious," Sean told her. He'd given the same speech to his men in the past. Of course he'd also told them that garbage out in the street was fair game. They'd found some of their best evidence that way. But that was different. Unfortunately, this trash hadn't been on the street.

Marvin put his fork down and wiped his mouth with his napkin.

"Don't be angry with Libby and Bernie."

"I'm not angry, I'm disappointed." Go for the maximum amount of guilt. That was his motto.

"Okay, then don't be disappointed," Marvin said. "This is all my fault."

Sean glared at Marvin until he dropped his eyes. "How is it your fault? Did you make them do this at gunpoint? Did you threaten to kill them if they didn't comply?"

"No . . . no . . . no," Marvin began to stutter.

Libby turned to Marvin. "He's just being sarcastic," she explained. "He does that when he's annoyed. Just ignore it."

"Ignore me," Sean spluttered. "Now

you're going to ignore me on top of everything else?"

"That isn't what I meant and you know it," Libby retorted.

"Well, what did you mean?" Sean said. "Tell me. I insist."

Libby started to hem and haw. Sean immediately felt guilty. Libby never responded well to his sarcasm, a fact his wife had constantly pointed out to him. She called it bullying. But he wasn't bullying, he was just trying to make sure that Libby and Bernie remembered what he was saying. He wanted to make sure they knew it was important. Unfortunately, he never did convince Rose of that.

Bernie put her glass down on top of the magazine she'd been paging through.

"Give me a break," she said to him. "You know you're not going to throw the cigar box out, so why don't you just open it and tell us what you think?"

Sean ate another piece of the tart. "What difference does it make? You've already seen the contents. What could I possibly add to the equation?"

"Your experience," Marvin told him. "You're the only one here who actually knows anything."

"Really?" Sean said.

"Absolutely. I hear that when you were chief of police you solved more crimes than anyone else."

It was true. He had. Not that he was going to admit it. That would be bragging. But Sean decided the kid was definitely growing on him. Despite Marvin's clumsiness and bad driving and his idiot of a father, Marvin was turning out to have some redeeming features. After all, he was the one who had found the cigar box. That earned him some points. Even if the conception was boneheaded in the extreme.

"Thanks," he told Marvin. He looked back at Bernie. "At the very least you should have called me and asked my opinion before trying the stunt you pulled."

"It was my fault," Libby said.

Bernie chimed in. "No. It was mine."

"I'm the one you should be blaming," Marvin told him.

"That's enough," Sean said. "I don't care who's at fault here. It doesn't matter who made the suggestion. What matters is that everyone went along with it."

"Come on, Dad," Libby urged. "Tell us what you think."

"Both of you could have been arrested."

"But we weren't," Bernie said.

Sean fixed his daughters with his guilt-inducing look, a look he'd perfected over the years — a look his wife suggested he patent.

"How would it look if I had to bail you out of jail?" Sean demanded. "Do you know how embarrassing that would be? The local paper would have a field day with that. You'd probably lose business."

"No, we wouldn't," Bernie retorted. "We'd be exceptionally busy. Notoriety sells, as you well know."

Sean did know. Every time the girls had a murder case, A Little Taste of Heaven was packed with people wanting to know the latest. It was a fact of life. People were attracted to the violent. They always wanted to know the gory details. Ask any cop who had to deal with rubberneckers at the scene of a traffic accident.

But he wasn't going to admit that fact to Bernie. He also wasn't going to admit that he was dying to see what was in the cigar box. Not opening it was, to use one of Rose's favorite expressions, cutting off his nose to spite his face. He suspected — no, he knew — that Bernie and Libby suspected as much but had the good manners not to mention it.

Sean ate another piece of his lemon curd tart while his daughters watched. They can wait *a little longer,* he thought as he put his fork down. He took another sip of coffee. Then he turned to Bernie.

"So where's Rob these days?" he asked.

Bernie snorted. "Good question."

"You two have a fight?"

"Can we change the subject?"

"So you did have a fight."

"I don't want to talk about it."

"Was the fight you don't want to talk about a bad one?"

"Dad, stop it," Bernie said.

"If you insist."

"I do."

"Too bad. I liked him."

"I did too."

Sean reached over and picked up the black plastic bag.

"This is the way you found it?" he asked, changing the subject.

"We opened it up, but we put everything back the way we found it," Libby said.

Sean nodded absentmindedly as he opened the bag, took out a crumpled brown paper grocery bag, and set it aside. Then he turned the plastic bag upside down and shook it. Nothing came out. Next he opened the grocery bag and removed a grease-stained paper bag.

"Good camouflage job," he remarked.

He studied it for a moment, then opened it and took out the cigar box. When he was a kid he used one of his father's cigar boxes to keep his treasures in. They'd been typical boy things: an Indian arrowhead, a crystal that he'd found down in a cave in West Virginia, a lump of what he'd later been told was fool's gold, a starfish he'd found on the beach, a musket ball from Gettysburg, a piece of ocean glass, and his prize possession, a small fossilized insect that he'd found apple-picking with his mom.

He'd carefully wrapped up each of his treasures in pieces of flannel that his mother had given him. The box itself had been cheap. His dad had smoked stogies. They were all he could afford, and their smell had worked its way into his soul, not to mention his mom's drapes. But this box was not cheap. It was actually a humidor with a glass top.

"Expensive cigars," he observed. "Cohibas from Cuba."

"I didn't think that kind of thing was allowed into this country," Marvin said.

"They're not," Sean told him. "Not that that means anything. People smuggle them in all the time. At one point some people were getting as much as a thousand dollars a box for them."

"A thousand dollars," Libby echoed. "That's ridiculous."

"I think so too," Sean answered. "But lots of people don't. Especially the people around here."

Most of which, as his father would have said, had more money than sense.

"Have you ever smoked a Cohiba?" Marvin asked.

"Once to see what I was missing, but for the life of me I couldn't figure out what all the fuss was about."

"Do they still cost that much?" Marvin asked.

Sean took a sip of his coffee. "No. The price has come down considerably. Even though there's still an embargo on Cuba, lots of people go down there now." He ran his finger around the edges of the box. "So what does this box tell us?" he asked.

"That Ted Gorman had money?" Libby replied.

Sean nodded. "Or rich friends. What else?"

There was a moment of silence. Then Bernie said, "That he liked his pleasures. That he was willing to spend money on himself."

Sean nodded again. "Very good."

Marvin pushed his glasses up the bridge of his nose. "But how do we know that this cigar box is his?"

"What do you mean?"

"Well, it could be someone else's."

Sean answered, "There is that chance, but after all, you told me you found the box in Ted Gorman's garage, a garage that was locked. Plus, the box was in his trash can and it was wrapped in a plastic bag as well as a brown paper bag. It seems to me as if the odds favor the box belonging to him." Sean looked at Bernie, Libby, and Marvin. "Are we agreed on that?"

"Yes," everyone chorused.

"Okay," Sean said. "Now that we've settled that, let's see what's inside."

Bernie, Libby, and Marvin leaned forward a little while Sean undid the small clasp. That done, he carefully flipped the lid open with the tip of his index finger. He knew that there was no reason to open it like this — this box would never be seeing the inside of the CID lab — but old habits died hard.

He surveyed the contents of the box. It wasn't exactly overflowing with stuff.

"Did you rearrange any of the papers?" he asked Libby.

"No."

"This is the way they were when you opened the box?"

Libby nodded. "I looked through the

papers, but I put everything back in the same order I took them out in."

"So the bottom papers are still on the bottom?"

"That's what I just said," Libby replied.

Sean noted there was a peevish tone to her voice.

"Just making sure," he told her.

Marvin put his plate on the coffee table and leaned a little farther forward. Sean just hoped he wouldn't tip over. He'd done that once before and it hadn't been a pretty sight.

"Why are you asking?" Marvin inquired. "Is it that important?"

"Probably not in this case," Sean replied. "But the order the things are found in the box provide a rough timeline for us." He saw that Marvin looked puzzled. "It makes things easier to put together," he explained. "I just wanted to make sure that I'm reading things correctly."

"Do you want any help?" Bernie asked.

Sean shook his head. He was now totally engrossed with the matter at hand.

The first thing he took out was an envelope addressed to Ted Gorman. Looked like a greeting card. He lifted it up and read the postmark. The envelope had been mailed from Hudsonville, the next town over, on

November 29.

"When did Ted hit the tree?" Sean asked as he pulled the card out of its envelope.

"I'm not sure," Bernie said. "But I can look it up online if you'd like."

"Please," Sean said.

He could do e-mail, but he had more trouble with the Internet and he figured he was too old to learn. Especially if he didn't have to because he had someone like Bernie to do it for him. Instead Sean studied the card while Bernie sat down at the computer.

The card was a bright yellow and had a picture of two golden retriever puppies cuddled in a basket. Sean opened the card.

It said *Come cuddle with me.* Underneath he read *Make that soon.* It was signed *Didi Mullet.* She'd drawn little hearts around her name. The whole thing looked as if it had come from a female between the ages of eighteen and twenty-five.

"Who's Didi Mullet?" Sean asked. "Does anyone know?"

"No," Libby said. "But a Cyna Mullet works at Just Chocolate."

Sean turned the card over. There was nothing on the back. He slipped it back into its envelope and put it on the coffee table in front of him.

"Mullet is an unusual name," he said. "I

wonder if they're related."

"Want me to Google her?" Bernie asked.

"If you wouldn't mind," Sean replied.

"Not at all," she said.

Sean watched her fingers fly over the keyboard. Even when his hands worked properly he could never go that fast. They were too big and clumsy.

"She's not on Google," Bernie told him a moment later. "Let me try Anywho."

Libby got up and watched over her sister's shoulder as she typed.

"Nothing is coming up here either," Bernie said.

"Let's see what Clyde can do." And Sean gave him a call. "Nope," he said after he'd hung up. "It seems as if he and the missus have taken off for a law enforcement convention in Las Vegas."

"How inconsiderate," Bernie remarked.

"Isn't it, though?" Sean said. He'd gone to a lot of them in his day. The seminars were always a waste of time, but they were a good excuse to hang out with the guys.

"It looks as if we're going to have to do this the old-fashioned way," Bernie said.

"And what way is that?" Libby asked.

"I'll ask her."

Libby stifled a yawn. "That should work." And she went back to the seat she'd been sitting in. Bernie did the same.

"By the way," Bernie said as she grabbed a handful of cashews out of the tin on the table, "according to the paper Ted Gorman died on December second. Services were held on the nineteenth."

"Maybe Didi Mullet is the girl who was in the car with Ted Gorman," Marvin mused.

Bernie popped a cashew into her mouth. "If there was a girl, why didn't anyone report her missing?"

"Let's see if we can find her," Sean said as he took a newspaper page out of the box.

The top half of the page had been ripped off and an advertisement for a company that promised to help you find your birth mother had been circled.

Sean tapped the paper with his finger. "If I remember rightly, Clyde said Ted Gorman was adopted. Judging by this, it seems like our boy was looking for his roots."

"We could call the company," Marvin said.

"We could," Sean agreed. "But they probably won't talk to us. To do so would be to risk a lawsuit."

"What if we offered them money?" Marvin asked.

"First of all, Mr. Hardened Criminal, we have no money to offer them, and secondly, you can't just barge into a place like that waving a fistful of dollars around. At best they'll throw you out and at worst, if you're really annoying, they'll call the police and have you arrested."

Marvin chewed on the inside of his cheek. He looked disappointed.

"Are you sure?" he asked Sean.

"I'm positive," Sean replied.

Marvin reached over and ate a crumb of the lemon curd tart off his plate. "So what do we do?"

Sean shifted his weight around. He could never seem to get comfortable. "I'll go talk to Ted's mother."

"But how do you know she'll talk to you?"

"I don't," Sean replied.

"Because," Marvin continued, "she wouldn't talk to her son."

"What makes you say that?" Sean asked.

Marvin waved his hand around. "He was going through an agency."

"Maybe he didn't want his adopted mom to know he was looking for his birth mom. Maybe he was afraid he'd hurt her feelings."

"I suppose," Marvin said doubtfully.

Sean put the advertisement aside and went on to the next item. It was a spiral-bound pocket notebook, the kind you can get in any drug or stationery store in any part of the country. Sean opened it and started going through it. The first two pages were covered with doodles. There was a doodle of a tree, another of a flower, one of a house with smoke coming out of the chimney.

"What do you make of this?" he asked everyone.

"That he doesn't have much artistic ability," Bernie answered.

"Besides that," Sean said.

Bernie shrugged. "I don't know."

"I don't either," Libby said.

"It's about a home," Marvin blurted out.

Sean nodded. "Very good, Marvin. Very good. This guy is looking for his home."

He turned the page. Nothing. He went to the next page. Gorman had written the initials LC and MB and circled them. Possible leads for Gorman's family search? Sean wondered. Maybe. But since he couldn't possibly identify them at this point he moved on to the next page. It was empty. So were the rest of them.

"It doesn't look as if he's gotten very far," Libby observed.

"No, it doesn't," Sean agreed. "I wonder what made him begin." He put the notebook down and went on to a small ziplocked bag full of pills. He opened the bag and spilled a few into the palm of his hand. Percosets. "It looks as if our friend has a prescription pill problem."

"Maybe he has a script for them," Marvin suggested.

"Doubtful," Sean said. "If he had a script they'd be in the medicine cabinet, instead of in a cigar box hidden in a trash can. No, I think we can safely posit that our Mr. Gorman either was given them or he bought them on the street." He put the pills on the table with the other things and took out a leather-bound notebook. This notebook was fancier — the kind people gave as gifts when they didn't know what else to get you. He opened it and began to read the columns of figures.

"Well?" Bernie said.

Sean startled. He'd lost himself in the columns. "I'd say that our man has lost money on commodities."

Bernie got up and looked over her dad's shoulder. "He could be into numerology."

Libby rolled her eyes.

"Well, he could," Bernie insisted. "It's not that weird."

Sean was about to say something else when Bernie's cell rang. She answered it.

"Calm down," she said. "We'll be right over."

Sean noted the grim expression on her face as she snapped her phone shut. "What's going on?" he asked.

"It's Marnie. She's hysterical. She claims Ted's ghost is haunting her house."

"I guess the stress has finally caught up with her. She's flipped out," Libby observed.

"Maybe her husband really has come back," Bernie posited.

"Don't be ridiculous," Sean told his younger daughter.

"You always said to consider all possibilities."

"In this world," Sean told her.

"I was joking," Bernie said.

Marvin leaned forward.

"Well, we do know that something has upset her," he noted.

"She's an Aquarius," Bernie said. "They tend to be a little unstable."

"No more astrology," Libby pleaded. "Please."

"Fine," Bernie huffed.

Sean decided it was time to intervene. He took a deep breath and let it out. "Do you think she knows that someone was in her garage?"

Bernie completed the sentence for him. "And this is just a ruse to get us there? Doubtful."

"One of the neighbors could have described Libby to her," Sean insisted.

"Then why call me?" Bernie asked. "Why not call Libby? She has her cell number as well."

"You're right, you're right," Sean said. He was just getting paranoid in his old age.

Marvin pushed his glasses up the bridge of his nose for what Sean swore was the fifth time in two hours. "One of us should go."

Bernie got up. "Since she called me I guess I'm the one who's elected."

"And no more shenanigans," Sean warned. "Absolutely none. Are we clear?"

"Crystal," Bernie, Libby, and Marvin chorused.

# CHAPTER 23

Bernie tried to keep her thoughts focused on Marnie as she pulled up in front of her house, but it was hard because she was thinking about Rob. She'd been planning on calling him, and now it would be too late. Or maybe not. She glanced at her watch. It was a little after eleven. If she wrapped this up quickly she could still call him. They really had to talk about the move and other stuff. Why did things with guys always get tense around the holidays? Especially Valentine's Day? Things used to be so much simpler when she was younger.

As Bernie pulled into the driveway, the door to Marnie's house opened, and Marnie rushed out.

Bernie opened her window. Marnie stuck her head in the car.

"Thank God you're here," she cried. "I don't know what I'm going to do."

"You're going to get run over if you don't

move. Let me park and you can tell me what's going on," Bernie suggested. God, she *so* did not want to do this.

"Here," she said when she got out. And she handed Marnie one of Libby's chocolate chip muffins. "It's fresh baked."

Marnie stared at it. "Why are you giving me this?"

"It's a present from Libby."

Marnie furrowed her brows in disbelief.

"She thought you'd like it," Bernie explained. "Did you know that carbs have a calming effect on people?"

"No, I didn't, but I think I'd prefer a Xanax," Marnie replied.

"Well," Bernie answered, "this is the best I can do."

"I have something to confess," Marnie told Bernie as she led her toward the house. "But you have to promise you won't tell anyone this."

"I promise."

"You have to swear."

Bernie put up her hand. "I will."

"I mean it."

"I already said I would," Bernie said. She waited.

They stepped into the house. Marnie closed the door. She leaned toward her. "This is terrible."

"Okay," Bernie said.

Marnie took a deep breath. Then she said, "I really don't like chocolate. Especially dark chocolate. I just like milk chocolate and not very much of that."

Bernie burst out laughing. "That's your secret?"

"It's not funny."

"You're right, it's not," Bernie told her when she'd gotten herself under control. The lady was clearly hysterical. Best to humor her. "I just thought you'd be telling me something more . . . serious."

"This is serious. People wouldn't buy from me if they knew that. Would people buy from you if they found out you lived on protein shakes?"

"Probably not," Bernie admitted.

"Exactly," Marnie said. "Ted was the one who loved chocolate. He was the one who set up the business. I just did the books."

"It must be tough for you now that he's gone," Bernie said, trying to get Marnie back on topic.

"It is," Marnie said. "It is." She sniffed and dabbed at her eyes.

Bernie took a bite of the muffin Libby had given her for Marnie. *Damn,* she thought. *I'm getting like Libby, eating something just because it's there.* This was not good. This was not good at all. She'd just bought a new skirt and the waistband was tight as it was. She put the muffin back in its bag and tightly rolled up the top. Oh, the hell with it. She unrolled the top and pulled the muffin out. She needed something, and this would have to do.

"You want to tell me what's going on?" she asked Marnie after she'd finished it.

Marnie nodded. They were still standing in the hallway. Libby noticed that Marnie was dressed in a pale blue nightgown and matching robe and slippers. Bernie could have sworn the robe was one that had been advertised in the Bendel's Christmas catalog they'd gotten this year.

The robe was 100 percent cashmere and cost 600 dollars, while the slippers were 150 dollars. Or was it 175? In any case they were shot through with silver and gold thread. One thing was for sure — Marnie might be a grieving widow, but she certainly wasn't a poor one.

"So?" Bernie repeated.

Marnie nibbled on her lower lip. It was a mannerism that men would find cute, but Bernie found it extremely annoying. Marnie drew her robe closer and hugged herself. Finally she began to talk.

"I came home right after I left the shop. I

263

was tired. Exhausted really. It had been a hard day."

She paused while Bernie nodded in commiseration.

"I went straight to bed. I didn't even wash my face. I just took off my clothes, put on my nightgown, popped half a Halicon —"

"Halicon?" Bernie couldn't help crying. "Why are you using that for a sleeping pill? It's such bad news."

Marnie shrugged. "My doctor gave it to me. Anyway, I took that and hit the bed. I must have gone right out and that's when it happened." She stopped.

"What happened?" Bernie asked.

"Ted."

Bernie waited.

Marnie nibbled on her lower lip some more. She swallowed. Nothing like building the suspense, Bernie thought uncharitably.

"What about Ted?" Bernie asked again.

"He was standing at the foot of my bed. He was telling me things I had to do for the benefit — just like he used to. It was awful." And Marnie burst into tears.

"What? Ted's advice?" Bernie asked.

Marnie glared at her.

"Sorry," Bernie said. "Why was it so awful?"

Marnie scowled. "Because it was."

Bernie pinned back an errant strand of hair before replying. "Marnie, Ted is dead, I saw him. Unfortunately. He's not going anywhere. You can trust me on this."

"Then his spirit is visiting me," Marnie wailed.

"In that case maybe you should hire an exorcist," Bernie suggested half seriously.

It couldn't hurt. She'd had a friend who had held an exorcism in her apartment in Venice Beach, and she swore it worked. Apparently the spirit of the cat that had lived there before was vanquished. When you came right down to it, who knew?

Marnie wiped her cheeks with the backs of her hand. "That's not funny."

"I'm not being funny. Spirits are out of my range of experience. Libby's too. Sometimes you get these really weird dreams when you take Halicon. Actually, more like hallucinations. It's happened to lots of people. They did a program on it on TV. You should use something else."

In her humble opinion if you were going to use drugs, at least use the right ones.

"Those kinds of things you're talking about have never happened to me," Marnie insisted.

"Okay. Fair enough. But I don't understand what you want me to do," Bernie said.

She was trying to sound warm and supportive, but she knew she was failing. Actually she wanted to strangle Marnie. She needed to talk to Rob, not deal with a woman in the midst of a major meltdown. Was that too much to ask?

Marnie looked down at the floor, then back up at Libby. "I don't know what I want you to do. I don't know if there's anything you can do. All I do know is that I felt scared and you were the only person I could think of to call. I'm sorry. Maybe you should go home. This is ridiculous. I'm an adult. I should be able to cope. I'm really sorry to have bothered you. I know you have better things to do."

Now Bernie felt awful. The woman was good at guilt. She'd give her that. She was almost on a par with her dad. Not quite, but almost.

Bernie sighed. "As long as I'm here," she told Marnie, "I might as well take a quick look around." Not that she expected to see anything.

Marnie's smile lit up her face.

"Oh, would you?" she cried.

"Of course," Bernie replied.

Marnie turned and led her up the stairs to her bedroom.

"Excuse the mess," she said when she

266

reached the door.

She stepped inside. Bernie followed.

"See?" Marnie pointed to the foot of the bed. "I opened my eyes and he was standing there. It was terrible. I screamed and he was gone."

"Maybe you woke yourself up," Bernie said as she took a look around.

Far from being messy, the room was pristine. The bed looked slightly rumpled. Bernie recognized the sheets and duvet from an Italian linen store on Madison Avenue. A fashion magazine lay on one of the pillows. These were art deco lamps on both the nightstands. Marnie's side of the bed had an alarm clock and a box of tissues and that was it. Bernie tried not to think of her bedroom with her pile of clothes in one corner and her pile of books in the other.

"What do you think?" Marnie said.

Bernie shook her head. What could she think? Marnie had obviously had a bad dream. She rubbed her arms. It was cold in here. Odd, because it was so warm downstairs. Then Bernie noticed the curtains billowing. That could be caused by the heat vent. Or not. She walked over and pulled one of the curtains aside. The window behind it was open about two inches. Marnie came up behind her.

"Do you like to sleep with the window open?" Bernie asked her.

"No. Ted did. But I don't."

Bernie pointed to the window. "Did you open this?"

Marnie shook her head.

"Maybe you did and you don't remember."

"Of course I'd remember if I did," Marnie said. She drew her robe tighter around her and rubbed her arms. "I'm not crazy. Close it please. It's cold in here. What are you doing?" she cried as Bernie opened the window all the way instead.

"Checking something out." Bernie leaned out over the sill.

There was a trellis along the side of the house. It was fairly far-fetched, but conceivably someone with an athletic bent could have climbed up it, opened the window, and come inside.

But these were storm windows and Bernie knew from experience that they would be extremely difficult to open from the outside. Not to mention the fact that two inches would hardly be enough to let someone in or out — unless they were shaped like a pancake. No. The simplest explanation was that Marnie had opened the window and forgotten about it. Or she could have done it in her sleep. Halicon made people do strange things. Bernie shut the window and walked back over to the bed.

"What now?" Marnie asked her.

Bernie grunted. For lack of anything better to do she said to Marnie, "Show me where Ted was standing when you woke up."

"Here," Marnie said. She waved her arms around.

"Where exactly is here?"

Marnie went over and stood at the foot of the bed. She was right in the center, Bernie noted.

Marnie pointed to the floor. "He was standing right here."

Bernie moved next to her.

"What was he doing?" she asked.

"Nothing. He was just standing there."

"I thought you said he was talking to you."

Marnie bit her lip again. "He did. But that came after."

"I see." Bernie twisted her silver and onyx ring around her finger. "You know what I think, I think you should make yourself a hot toddy and go to sleep."

"So you don't believe me?" Marnie cried. "You think I'm lying?"

"No, no. It's just that sometimes when people are very upset they see things . . ." How to put this diplomatically, Bernie wondered. ". . . that aren't there."

*That's me,* Bernie thought. *The soul of tact.* But it was true.

Bernie was about to make another comment when she caught a glimpse of something nestled in the loops of the powder-blue shag carpet. She leaned over and picked it up. It was a badge, the kind you get when you go to a convention. It said *Welcome to Chocolate Land.* Below this, Ted Gorman's name was printed in big block letters.

"Oh my God," Marnie gasped.

"What?" Bernie asked.

"That's Ted's pin. He got it when he went to the convention in Hershey. He was given a plaque for best increased sales for a small chocolate store. It's hanging on the wall of the shop office. He was here."

"He wasn't here."

"Then how did the pin get at the foot of the bed?"

"It must have been there all along. You just didn't see it."

"My cleaning lady would have found it." Marnie crossed her arms over her chest. "I told you Ted was here."

"He wasn't, but maybe someone else was. Someone who wants to scare you."

"Who would want to scare me?"

"I was hoping you'd know."

"Well, I don't."

Bernie gave up. "Do you have an alarm system?"

Marnie nodded. "Ted insisted on getting one, but it's broken and I haven't gotten around to getting it fixed."

"Well, now might be a good time to do it."

"I still think it was Ted's spirit."

Bernie held up the badge. "Spirits don't go dropping things like this on floors. When did you see this last?"

"I don't remember." Marnie chewed on her lower lip. "I wonder if Ted is mad at me because I took Cyna off making the love knots and put her on dipping caramels. He always hated when I switched people around. He said it disrupted the rhythm."

"Then he's probably angry," Bernie said.

"Do you think so?"

"Absolutely." She was too tired to argue anymore.

# CHAPTER 24

The words *annoying, irritating,* and just plain *stupid* came into Bernie's mind as she drove away from Marnie's house. Then she decided she was being unkind. And unfair. The woman had suffered a devastating loss. Clearly she was still in shock and unable to think clearly. And waking up to find your dead husband giving you instructions from the foot of your bed probably didn't help any.

Although she had to say that sometimes she wished her mom were standing at the foot of her bed giving her advice. After she'd died, Bernie had dreamt about her often, but over time those dreams had grown less and less frequent. Now she barely had them at all. It was sad really. The Buddhists say that the soul of a person hangs around for three days after death before going off to become someone else. She wondered who her mom was now. She hoped she'd have a nice life.

Bernie shook her head to clear it. She had to be more tired than she thought. As she slowed for a stop sign she decided the real questions she should be concerning herself with were: Who had Marnie pissed off and why?

Because whoever did this — assuming someone really did — had gone to considerable lengths. This was not a casual act. It had required planning and forethought. The fact that the unknown person had used Ted Gorman's badge suggested that he'd been in a position to get it, which in turn meant that he had access to his things.

Where was the badge kept? At home? At the shop? Bernie cursed herself for not asking that question. She almost picked up the phone to call Marnie and ask her, but decided against it. She just couldn't face talking to her right now. Bernie drummed her fingers on the dashboard while she thought.

Who would dislike Marnie enough to do something like this to her? One of her employees? Someone she owed money to? A relative? Did she have any relatives? Maybe Clyde could answer that question.

Or was this whole line of thought ridiculous? Was she conjuring something up where nothing existed? Probably. She had to admit she did have a tendency to do that. What were the odds of someone climbing in the window just to stand at the foot of Marnie's bed? Small at best. Usually people who did things like that had rape or robbery in mind. Maybe she and Libby should just stick to investigating the stuff they'd found in Ted Gorman's cigar box. She didn't know. But her dad would.

Bernie kept one hand on the wheel while she dug into her bag for her cell. When she got it, she called her father and told him what she'd found out.

"Interesting," he said.

"So what do you think?" Bernie asked just as a deer bounded across the road. She screeched to a stop.

"What was that?" her dad asked.

"Nothing," Bernie lied.

"It didn't sound like nothing to me."

"I'm fine." Which was the truth.

"So what was it?"

"A deer," Bernie admitted.

"Are you taking the back roads?"

Bernie admitted she was.

"I seem to remember that just this morn-ing I said —"

Bernie finished the sentence for him. "You said to keep on the main roads because there are deer all over the place."

"And consequently there have been a fair number of accidents."

"Dad, I'm watching." Well, she would be now.

"Keep watching. Where there's one, there are usually more. They're herd animals. You know what herd means."

"Dad, please. I will," Bernie promised.

"As to what you found tonight," her father continued, "I don't think it would hurt to talk to a couple of people and see if they know anything about Marnie. Maybe this is nothing or maybe it's something. It's probably nothing, but it's always good to have more information, even if you do have to speak to Bree Nottingham to get it."

"Dad," Bernie moaned.

While Bree was an extremely unpleasant person, as the social arbiter of Longely she knew everyone's business.

"Can you think of a better source?"

"Uh . . ."

"When you take on a job you do all of it, not just the parts you like," her dad told her.

"Don't steamroller me."

"I'm not. I'm just pointing out the obvious. In fact, why don't you do it now and get it out of the way?"

"It's late."

"Not for Bree. She never goes to sleep before one o'clock. And by the way, did you look outside Marnie's house to see if you could find any footprints around the trellis?"

Of course she hadn't.

"It's dark out. I don't think I can see anything now."

"Don't you have a flashlight?"

"Uh. No."

"What happened to it?"

"I used it to go down to the basement."

"You should always have one in the vehicle."

"I know, Dad. I'll get one first thing in the morning."

Bernie heard her dad sigh.

"So, are you coming home?" he asked.

"I'm going to Rob's for a little while." She hadn't even known she was going until after she'd said it.

"Don't be too late." And with that her dad had hung up.

Bernie slowed down as another deer crossed the road. It was amazing but her father was usually right. Okay, he was almost always right. She reached for her cell again and punched in Rob's number. No answer. She left a voice message.

Maybe he was asleep. He tended to do that sometimes — fall asleep on the sofa while he was watching TV. Especially old movies. She was so near his house, she decided to drive by and see if his car was in the driveway and if the lights were on in his house. If they weren't she'd turn around and go home.

In the meantime she decided to call Bree. Her dad was right about that too — better to get it over with. If she was lucky she could just leave voice mail. But Bree answered on the second ring.

"Oh dear," she said when she heard Bernie's voice, "I've been wondering how the preparations for the benefit are going."

"They're going," Bernie said.

"I suppose you've called for my recipe for spiced chocolate nuts."

"How did you guess?" Bernie lied. Those things tasted vile.

"Good, because my friends have been asking. I'll just run the recipe down to your sister tomorrow morning."

"Libby will be so pleased," Bernie told her. She could just hear Libby groaning.

"So how is poor Marnie doing?"

"As well as can be expected."

The nice thing about Bree, Bernie reflected, was that you could always count on her to gossip.

"I don't know how she keeps going."

"She seems a bit . . . unstrung."

"Unstrung?"

"Well, she says she's seeing Ted's ghost."

"Oh dear." Bree sighed. "I was afraid something like this would happen."

And Bree was off and running. But all Bernie learned was that Marnie was bulimic and had had a boob job. By the time she and Bree finished talking she had reached Rob's house. The lights were on. And there was another car in his driveway.

A red BMW.

Sarah Wadley's BMW, to be precise.

Bernie recognized it because Sarah Wadley came into the shop every morning and bought two cranberry scones and an extra-large coffee with cream and two sugars before she caught the 7:35 down to the city. Sarah Wadley of the ill-fitting pantsuits, the sensible orthopedic shoes, and the frizzy hair.

Obviously Rob had found something else to occupy himself with this evening. Bernie stopped her car right behind the BMW, put it in park, and got out. She marched up to the front door and rang Rob's bell. She could hardly wait to see his face.

A moment later Rob answered the door.

Bernie had the intense satisfaction of seeing him go pale.

"Aren't you going to invite me in?" she asked.

Rob started to stutter.

"Don't you want me to meet your company?" she asked him.

"Sarah just . . ." Rob stammered.

"Came to show you how to bake cookies?" Bernie asked. "Wait. I know. She's helping fix your plumbing."

"No . . . She . . ."

Bernie held up her hand. "I don't want to hear it."

"But —"

"No buts. No ands. No ifs. We're done."

"Hey," Rob said. "Sarah and I were just having fun."

"Fun?" Bernie said. "You call what you were doing fun?"

Rob shrugged. "We are what we are."

"What the hell is that supposed to mean?"

"Exactly what I said."

"You are such an ass."

Bernie whirled around and strode toward her car. When she got behind the wheel she thought of backing into Sarah Wadley's car. The satisfaction would be intense, but so would the penalties. Instead she took a shortcut over Rob's lawn and drove off.

Halfway to her house she decided she didn't feel as bad as she thought she would. Maybe she'd feel horrible tomorrow, but tonight she felt okay. Maybe she was getting better at this breaking-up thing. Heaven only knows, she'd had enough experience by now. When she got to Ash Street she made a right instead of a left.

"I should go home," Bernie said out loud. The problem was she didn't feel like it.

She didn't want to tell Libby or her dad what happened. She just wasn't ready. She decided to have a drink at R.J.'s first. Then she'd go home. If she were lucky, by that time everyone would be asleep.

# CHAPTER 25

Bernie looked around R.J.'s when she walked in. Twelve thirty on a week night and the place was dead. Which suited her just fine. The quieter the better, as far as she was concerned. There were five people sitting at the bar, one of whom she recognized. That would be Bolt, the cute guy who worked for Marnie as a candy dipper. The other four guys, including the one Bolt was sitting with, she didn't recognize at all.

Bolt. Normally she wasn't good with names, but she certainly couldn't forget this one. How could anyone? Maybe his parents thought he was going to be a movie star when they named him. Either that or a hardware store owner.

Bernie grinned. She was going to have to talk to him anyway. What was her father always saying about there being no time like the present? Talk about serendipity. A word she was particularly fond of since fortunate circumstances so rarely happened to her. Although the circumstances weren't ideal. Well, not ideal in the sense that she usually had some shtick worked out. But what the hell? Time to give it a try.

Bolt nodded at her as she passed by him.

"How's it going?" he asked her.

Good. He'd made the first move. Bernie put a smile on her face.

"It's going," she told him.

"Marnie okay?"

Bernie raised an eyebrow. *Now, why should he be asking me that?* she wondered.

Bolt took a sip of his beer and put his glass down.

"She said she was going to call you," he replied to Bernie's unspoken question.

"So she called you first?" That was somewhat strange, Bernie decided.

Bolt shrugged. "It would appear so. She does that sometimes. Maybe because I used to do handyman stuff around her place she thinks of me as helpful."

"And are you?"

"When I can be."

"Did she say what she wanted?" Had Marnie mentioned Ted Gorman to Bolt?

Bolt shrugged again. "She said she saw something."

"Did she say what?"

"What are you writing? A book?"

"Yeah. A mystery."

"Ha. Ha. No, she didn't say what she saw. But she's always seeing things. Mostly they turn out to be dogs or stray cats. Last week it was someone walking around her backyard."

"Was there someone?" Bernie asked. Maybe they were checking out the trellis.

"I don't know. I told her to call the police. But she didn't."

"Why not?"

"She said that by the time the cops got there the man would be gone. Everything's okay, though?"

"Everything is fine," Bernie told him.

"Good," Bolt said. "Because I'd hate for anything to happen to her. She's a nice lady and she's been through a lot. Her husband becomes a crispy critter, she buries him, and he turns up in someone else's grave. That really sucks."

"You know about that?"

"Of course. She told me. Creepy stuff. If you're buried you should stay buried."

"I've always thought so," Bernie said.

Bolt took a sip of his beer. "She should get a dog."

"Or get her alarm system fixed."

"Dogs are better. You can always circumvent an alarm system."

"You sound as if you know."

Bolt grinned. "I won't deny I committed a few youthful indiscretions."

"Me too," Bernie said.

Bolt leered at her. "But I bet yours were different from mine."

The guy was coming on to her. Ordinarily she wouldn't mind, but she wasn't in the mood right now. Bernie steered the conversation back to Marnie. "So how is it working at the shop since Ted died?"

Bolt shrugged again. "Intense. Marn . . . I mean Marnie gets a little wound up. She's really uptight about the benefit, that I can tell you."

"Well, yes." Bernie realized she was twisting her ring around her finger and stopped. "Five hundred people is a lot. Libby and I are going nuts too and the thing isn't even at our place."

Bolt's friend coughed and pointed at his watch.

"Guess that's my sign to leave. Gotta go with my ride," Bolt told Bernie. He leaned over and took her hand in both of his. "Anything I can help you with — and I mean anything — give me a call."

Bernie pulled her hand out from his. "Definitely." She wouldn't even call him to empty her garbage. He winked at her, drew a business card out of his wallet, and pressed it into her hand. "I'll be waiting to hear from you." Then he got up, drained his glass, and sauntered out the door.

Bernie walked over to the far side of the bar. Brandon finished wiping a beer glass and wandered over to where she was sitting.

"I noticed you got the full Bolt treatment," Brandon observed.

"I've never seen him in here before," she said.

"Oh, he comes in this time of night once or twice a month with his pal. Usually he has a couple of females draped over him. He's quite the ladies' man."

"Not to me." Bernie took the card Bolt had just given her and handed it to Brandon. "Do me a favor and throw this in the trash."

"With pleasure. So what can I get for you?"

"A white wine. No, make that a vodka martini with Gray Goose."

Brandon bowed. "My lady has only to ask. One Gray Goose martini coming up."

A moment later Brandon was back with it. "So what gives?" he asked as he put the drink down in front of Bernie.

She took a sip. "Nothing gives." She put

the glass back down and traced the rim with her finger.

"You don't look like nothing gives."

"Leave it alone, Brandon."

"I can do that."

"Don't sulk."

"I'm not sulking."

"Have you heard anything about Marnie? Marnie Gorman?"

"First you brush me off and now you want information?"

"Come on, Brandon. Please."

"Yup. That's me. Good ole Brandon the white knight. Is that why you're here? To ask me about Marnie?"

"Yes."

"You're lying."

"No, I'm not."

"You furrow your forehead when you lie. Your forehead is furrowed. Ergo, you are not telling the truth."

"Really?" Bernie asked. No one had ever told her that before. No wonder she always lost at poker.

"Really. Hold it a minute. I'll be right back." Brandon went to wait on the guy with the bad hair plug job sitting at the other end of the bar.

Bernie took another sip of her martini — well, maybe it was more like a gulp. Then she remembered she hadn't eaten dinner. The hell with it, she thought, and she downed the rest of it.

"Hey, take it easy," Brandon said when he came back.

"You take it easy. I want another one."

"Fine. But I'm driving you home."

Bernie nodded. That was probably a good idea.

"I caught Rob with Sarah Wadley," she blurted out when Brandon came back with her second martini. And then she told him what had happened.

"Maybe it wasn't what you think it was."

"What else could it be?"

Brandon scratched behind his ear. "You should go ask him."

Bernie thought about that for a moment. Maybe she should. Maybe Brandon was right.

"Good idea." She began to get off the stool.

"Where are you going?" Brandon asked.

"To do what you suggested."

"I don't think so," Brandon said.

Then, before she could do anything, he reached over and grabbed her bag off the counter.

"Give that back," Bernie cried as Brandon started rummaging through it.

He laughed and kept going.

"I could have you arrested for that."

As Bernie watched, Brandon took her keys out of her bag and dangled them in front of her face. "Arrest away."

"That is so unfair."

Brandon put her bag back on the counter. "If you'd like we can drive by Rob's house after I'm done."

"But that'll be two o'clock in the morning," Bernie wailed.

"It'll be fifteen minutes. Scooter is coming in and closing tonight."

Bernie nodded. What else could she say? She asked Brandon to bring her another drink. He brought her a candy bar instead. Snickers and martinis. Not a good combination, she reflected as she bit into it. Not something they'd feature at the benefit. She ate it anyway. She was surprised at how hungry she was.

# CHAPTER 26

Bernie settled back in the seat of Brandon's Nissan. His car was clean, unlike hers and Libby's. They should really take it in and get it detailed. In their spare time. As if they had so much of it.

"Are you sure you're going to be all right?" Brandon asked.

"Definitely," Bernie replied.

She should have stuck with one martini. Two was excessive. Three would be a disaster. She knew this. She just could never remember until it was too late.

"I didn't know Rob lived this far out," Brandon said.

Bernie closed her eyes for a minute. "He moved recently. He said he likes the quiet."

Brandon stopped.

Bernie opened one eye. "What's up?"

"Left or right?"

"Left." Bernie closed her eyes again. She felt better that way.

What was she going to say to Rob? She certainly wasn't going to apologize. Ask for an explanation? It seemed a little late for that. But Brandon was right. This would clarify things. And speaking of clarifying. Her mind went back to what Bolt had said. Was someone really wandering around Marnie's house? The more Bernie thought about it, the more unlikely the scenario she'd devised seemed.

It was way too elaborate. Why go to that much trouble when you could do something so much simpler and still scare Marnie? The more likely case was that the pin from the chocolate convention was under the bed and the maid had missed it when she was cleaning. And as for the opened window — Marnie had probably opened it herself.

Given her state and the meds she was taking, it was amazing she was walking around at all, let alone remembering everything that she'd done. Bernie rubbed her forehead. She felt as if she was coming down with something.

Tomorrow morning she'd go back to Marnie's house and see if she could find footprints around the trellis, or some evidence that someone had been there. Maybe she'd do that after she talked to Cyna Mullet. If she remembered correctly, Cyna lived about five minutes away from Marnie Gorman.

Suddenly Bernie realized that they'd stopped. She opened her eyes. They were in front of Rob's house.

"That was quick," she said.

"You passed out."

"No, I didn't. I was thinking."

"If that's what you want to think go ahead." Brandon pointed to Rob's house.

Bernie noticed that the lights were off and the driveway was empty.

"It looks like he left," Brandon noted.

Bernie straightened up. She didn't know whether she was relieved or not.

Brandon stifled a yawn. "So I guess it's time to take you home."

Bernie put a hand on his arm. "Do you have a flashlight?"

"In the glove compartment. Why?"

"Wouldn't you like to have an adventure?"

Brandon laughed. "I remember some of your adventures from high school. I think I'm too old to be running from the cops."

"I'm not thinking of that kind of adventure."

"Then what?"

"Well, the McDougal house is right up the road," Bernie said.

She looked at Brandon, who was leaning

back in his seat with his arms folded across his chest. He didn't look very enthusiastic.

"I'd like to go back inside," Bernie explained. She had a hunch she'd like to check out.

"You can do that tomorrow."

"Yes, but I'd have to come all the way back up. And since we're almost there . . . Please, Brandon."

Brandon sighed. "You know I could never resist you."

"Yes, you could. You did. How come we never got together?"

Even though it was dark, Bernie could have sworn she could see Brandon blush. "You made me nervous, and by the time I decided to ask you out, you were going with George, and he and I were both on the football team . . ." Brandon's voice trailed off. Then he said, "Okay. The McDougal household it is, but after this it's home."

"Thank you."

"I just hope I don't regret it," Brandon said as he stepped on the gas. "I still remember when you talked me into going to that field party and the cops came and we climbed that tree and got stuck there for hours while they rounded everyone else up. I thought we'd never get down."

"Come on. Admit it, it was exciting."

"Okay, it was exciting."

Bernie smiled.

"God," Brandon groused as the road got worse. "I hope I don't tear my undercarriage. This car is too low for this road."

"It'll be fine," Bernie reassured him.

"I forgot how bad this road is," Brandon muttered.

"Me too," Bernie said.

Brandon threw her a look. "No, you didn't. You just don't care about my car."

"I care about your car. I just forgot how low it is. Why don't you get something higher?"

"Because I like this one. I like the way it handles. Plus, I got a great deal."

"You could afford a new car if you wanted."

"Nope. I believe you should never pay more than fifteen hundred dollars for a vehicle."

"You used to say five hundred."

"I'm a victim of rising expectations," Brandon said as they bumped up the road to the McDougal house.

Once they rounded the last curve the house came into view. It was sitting by itself away from the trees.

"I haven't been here since . . ." Brandon paused. "Since I can't remember when."

"Did you know Ms. McDougal?" Bernie asked him.

Brandon shook his head.

"Evidently, most people didn't," Bernie told him. "I guess she was a hermit. Well, not exactly. Antisocial would probably be a better word. Do you realize that the word *hermit* comes from the Greek and means living in the desert and that the root of that word means desolate?"

"Please, Bernie. Enough."

"The trouble with you is that you don't like words."

"And the trouble with you is that you like them too much," Brandon replied as he pulled off the road and headed toward the cords of wood stacked directly in front of them.

"Where are you going?" Bernie cried.

"I'm pulling in behind the wood."

"But why?" Bernie wailed.

Brandon backed the car in so it was facing the road and turned the motor off before responding. Then he held up his hand and ticked the reasons off on his fingers.

"Number one: I don't want to rip my muffler off going up the road to the house. The road is too steep and my car is too low. And number two: This way no one can see us."

"You're paranoid. There's no one around."

"Just because I'm paranoid doesn't mean I'm wrong. Someone could come up."

Bernie couldn't think of an answer to that, so she pointed to her feet instead. "Look at my shoes."

Brandon looked. "You should have worn more appropriate ones."

"I didn't think I'd be hiking."

"You'll manage," Brandon said as he grabbed a flashlight out of the glove compartment and got out of the Nissan. "You always do."

"Now I remember," Bernie said as she levered her way out of the Nissan. "You were mean in high school."

"I still am," Brandon told her.

She opened her mouth to reply, but the wind took her breath away. It slapped her in the face and she had to blink her eyes to keep them from tearing. This was not a good idea, she decided. Next time she was going to stick to white wine. No. The next time she was going to stick to brownies. God, she couldn't believe how steep this road was. Her ankles were killing her. And the fact that she was doing this in the dark — because Brandon refused to turn on the flashlight — was making this walk particularly difficult. He'd said, "I'll turn it on when we get to the house. You'll be able to see it for miles out here."

Like anyone would care.

"Hey," she called to Brandon, who was in front of her. "Wait for me."

"Then hurry up," he told her. "It's freezing."

"Tell me about it. I feel like a Popsicle."

She was puffing by the time they got to the McDougal house. "I've got to go back to the gym." The problem was she didn't have the time.

"Yeah, I say that too," Brandon cracked as he stopped in front of the house. "Now what?" he asked.

Bernie hiccupped. "Now you give me the flashlight and I go inside."

"I keep the flashlight and we both go inside," Brandon said firmly.

"Okay." Truth be told she really wasn't in the mood to argue. Her head was starting to hurt. Maybe it was the cold. Maybe it was the alcohol. She didn't know and she didn't care. Bernie stumbled twice as she walked toward the door.

"Brandon, hold the flashlight steady."

"I am," he protested. "You're the one who's wobbling."

When they got to the door Bernie turned the knob. Nothing. The door stayed where it was. Great. She was positive she'd left it unlocked the last time she'd been here. Obviously, she'd been wrong.

Brandon stamped his feet and rubbed his hands together. "Come on. Let's get out of here. It's cold."

"In a sec. I want to see something." She hadn't come all this way for nothing.

Bernie yanked the flashlight out of Brandon's hand and marched off to the side of the cottage.

"Hey," he cried. "Give that back."

"I will." She flicked the light on and peered in through the cottage window. And that's when Bernie saw it. "Look," she said, pointing into the cottage.

Brandon looked inside. "So? All I see is a cot and a sleeping bag."

"Exactly. They weren't here before."

"So someone is camping out here."

"Obviously," Bernie said.

She handed Brandon the flashlight, took a couple of steps back, and scanned the ground for a rock. When she found the size she was looking for she picked it up and weighed it in her hand.

"Whoa there, little lady." Brandon grabbed her wrist. "Don't tell me you're going to do what I think you are."

"Then I won't tell you," Bernie said.

Brandon took the rock out of her hand and dropped it back on the ground.

"We are not breaking in," he said firmly.

"Chicken," Bernie said.

"No. *Smart.* Breaking and entering is a felony. On the other hand, trespassing is an appearance ticket. Not to mention the fact that what you want to do is totally unnecessary."

"But I want to get in."

Brandon let go of her wrist. "Then look and learn."

He walked around to the front. Bernie trotted behind him. When Brandon got to the front door he took out his wallet and extracted a credit card. "See?"

"I see," Bernie said.

She watched as Brandon inserted the credit card in the space between the door and the lock and made a sharp upward motion. Then he twisted the doorknob and pushed. The door opened.

"Voila," he said and bowed.

Bernie clapped. She took a step forward. "Now if you don't mind."

Brandon held up his hand. Bernie stopped.

"Listen." Brandon cupped his hand behind his ear. "Did you hear someone cry for help inside?"

"No!"

Brandon sighed in exasperation. "It was a rhetorical question."

"Oh, I get it," Bernie cried.

"Good," Brandon said. "Let me start again. Did you hear someone cry for help inside the cottage?" He went into a higher pitched voice. "Why, yes. I did hear someone." And he pushed the door open and went inside.

"Where did you learn how to do the credit card trick?" Bernie asked as she joined him.

"And give away all my secrets? I don't think so."

Bernie looked around. When she'd been in here last the cottage was neat as the proverbial pin — although why pins were neat was a mystery to her.

"Let's do this fast," Brandon told her. "Because if anything happens to you, your father will kill me."

"So don't let it happen," Bernie said as she picked up a fleece that was lying on the sofa. It looked like a men's large.

She put it down and moved on. There was a pile of clothes on the coffee table. She picked the items up one by one. They consisted of a man's pants, shirts, and underwear. She started to go through the pants' pockets.

"What do you expect to find?" Brandon asked.

"I don't have a clue." Bernie kept turning out pockets. There was nothing in the first pair of jeans, candy wrappers in the second, candy wrappers in the third.

"Guess the guy has a sweet tooth," Brandon observed.

"Guess so," Bernie said as she started on the last pair. She pulled out the pocket. Two crumpled pieces of paper fell to the floor.

Bernie picked them up and smoothed them out.

"What are they?" Brandon asked.

Bernie showed the papers to him. "One has some numbers and a date scribbled on the corner, while the second is a recipt from a camping goods store for a lantern and a sleeping bag."

"Probably that one," Brandon said, pointing to the one lying on the cot in the corner.

Bernie nodded, but she wasn't looking at the sleeping bag, she was looking at the two slips of paper. If they meant anything she didn't know what it was. *Maybe Brandon is right,* she thought. *Maybe this is a waste of time. These belong to some poor camper who's crashing here.* She stuffed them in her pocket anyway. It had been her experience that you can never tell when something is going to turn out to be important.

Bernie put everything back the way she found it and walked over to the sleeping bag and cot. They looked like every sleeping bag and cot she'd ever seen. She unzipped the sleeping bag just to make sure nothing was inside it. She straightened up and wandered into the bedroom. At least this room was untouched. Next Bernie went into the kitchen. Whoever was living here had a fondness for Cheerios. Three boxes sat on the counter. She was about to open the cabinets when Brandon tugged her jacket sleeve.

"I hear something," he said.

"It's the wind."

"No. It's something else. We gotta go. We gotta go now." Before Bernie could answer, Brandon grabbed her by the wrist and started pulling her out the door. He stopped to shut it and continued on. "Come on," he urged as he guided her toward the woodpile.

Bernie could hear the noise now too. "It sounds like a car," she said.

"It is a car."

The noise was getting louder.

When they got to the woodpile Brandon went behind it and hunkered down. "Get down," he whispered.

"I am," Bernie told him as she squatted

beside him. The noise was getting louder. Bernie raised her head.

"What are you doing?" Brandon hissed.

"Trying to see who's driving the car."

"They might see you," Brandon said.

"Let them. We have a right to be up here," Bernie hissed back.

"Maybe we do. But at two o'clock in the morning people are apt to be less than understanding. I don't want to tangle with whoever is driving the car or with the police."

Bernie lowered her head and crept around the side of the woodpile. The car was going by them, but it was too dark to see who the driver was. She was thinking that maybe she could creep back up to the cottage and look in the window when Brandon started dragging her toward the Nissan.

"Let's go," he said.

"Can't we —" Bernie whispered.

"No, we can't."

"You don't know what I was going to say," Bernie objected.

"Whatever it is, the answer is still no." Brandon unlocked the door of the Nissan and pushed Bernie in, before scrambling in himself. Bernie watched as he started the car. Then he put it in gear and started toward the road.

"Aren't you going to turn on the lights?"

"When we get to the road."

Everything seemed to be rushing at her. Bernie decided it would be better not to look at the road. Instead she turned and stared out the back window until she couldn't see the McDougal place anymore.

She started to laugh.

"That was fun," she said to Brandon.

"And it'll be even more fun if I can keep this car on the road."

"I'm not worried," Bernie told him.

"I'm glad someone isn't," Brandon retorted.

"You're very good with vehicles. Always were, always will be."

And with that Bernie leaned her head against the seat and closed her eyes. It had been a long day and she was suddenly very, very tired.

"You know," Brandon said to her, "I don't know if it makes any difference but I never liked Rob anyway."

Bernie opened one eye. "Why not?"

"He's too full of himself."

"Maybe you're right," Bernie said. Then she closed her eyes again.

It was comforting to hear Brandon say that, she decided. He really was a good friend to her. And that was the last thought she had until Brandon was shaking her.

She opened her eyes. They were at her house. She managed to get her key in the lock and walk upstairs in what she considered to be a quiet manner. Evidently it wasn't quiet enough, because Libby was waiting for her at the top of the stairs.

"Where have you been?" she demanded. "I was worried."

Bernie rubbed her head. This was not what she needed now. "You should have called my cell."

"I tried. I think it's off."

Bernie took a look. So it was.

Libby retied her terry cloth robe, the robe she'd had since high school.

"That robe could be in the Smithsonian, you know," Bernie told her.

Libby ignored her comment.

"Then I tried calling Rob," she continued, "and he didn't answer."

"I'm not surprised." And Bernie explained.

Libby's face fell. "But that's terrible."

"Well, it's not great," Bernie allowed before stumbling off to bed. She really needed some sleep.

# CHAPTER 27

Libby sniffed appreciatively at the cup. Sumatra. And the beans had been roasted yesterday and ground this morning. It made such a difference. She was thinking that maybe they should invest in a coffee roaster when Bernie came down the stairs.

She clapped her hands. "Come on. Let's go. Chop, chop. You're going to be late."

Libby put her coffee cup down on the prep table. "Don't *chop, chop* me, Bernie. Why do I have to talk to Cyna Mullet?"

"Because we drew straws last night and you lost."

"I only did that because you were so upset about Rob."

"A deal is a deal."

"I didn't think you were serious."

"Well, I was. We have to get this thing resolved."

Libby knew as much. She'd gotten a very unpleasant phone call late last night from

Clayton demanding to know the progress they were making. Fortunately, Marvin had gone by then. He hated when his dad got like that.

"But it's seven thirty in the morning," Libby objected. "No one talks to anyone at seven thirty in the morning."

"This is perfect. She'll be off-guard."

"She'll be annoyed. I know I would be."

"So bring her a thermos of your coffee and two of your cranberry-orange muffins. Everybody loves those."

"And that's supposed to keep her from slamming the door in my face?"

"It might. If she opens the door in the first place."

"Bernie, you're giving me a headache."

"Good. Then we can both have one."

"Yeah, but mine didn't come from two martinis."

Bernie waved her hand in Libby's direction. "Pish-tush."

"I wish you'd stop making up words."

"I'm not making up words. It's an English expression. Anyway," Bernie went on, "you were the one complaining that you couldn't talk to her during the day. You were the one who said you had too much to do."

Which was true, Libby admitted to herself. But still.

"How do you know she's home?" she asked, hoping to find a loophole.

"Because I just called her and she answered."

"She's probably going straight off to work."

"Marnie told me no one gets to Just Chocolate till nine."

"Bernie, I think this is ridiculous."

"When else can we talk to her? It certainly can't be during the day when she's at the shop. I don't want to have to explain to Marnie."

Libby bit at her cuticle. "Maybe she already knows."

"Maybe she does, but we can't assume that."

"How about at night?"

"Possible. But we know she's home now. We don't know what she does after work. She could be taking archery lessons or learning ancient Greek for all we know."

Libby sighed. "Fine. You win. But if I strike out you have to talk to her this evening."

"You won't," Bernie said. "But you got yourself a deal."

Libby chugged the rest of her coffee down and went to get a thermos so she could fill it with coffee for Cyna. Or maybe hot chocolate. She'd gotten some new cocoa mix with cinnamon and chilies that was really excellent. No, she decided, coffee was better. Given where she worked, Cyna probably had her fill of chocolate.

Anyway, the coffee would be quicker. It was already made, and the sooner she got started the sooner she'd be back. The construction guys were scheduled to start sometime this morning, and she wanted to be here when they arrived.

"Hey, Libby," Bernie called as she headed out the door.

"What?"

"Your hem is down on the left leg of your pants."

"Thanks for sharing."

"Okay, go ahead and trip."

Although her mother would have killed her she decided to fix it with Scotch tape.

Libby stopped in front of the place where Cyna Mullet lived. It was a run-down two-story house, which somebody had painted bright purple. Or maybe it was maroon. Bernie would know. As she studied the color Libby wondered what Bernie would say about it. Probably nothing good.

*Okay, Libby, here we go,* she said to herself. She grabbed the thermos of coffee, the muffins, and the homemade maple spread and walked to the house and up the stairs, which she noted were slippery with unshoveled snow. The mailbox said that Cyna Mullet lived in apartment A, which was on the first floor.

She rang the bell. A few seconds later someone called out, "Who is it?"

"It's Libby Simmons. I'd like to talk to you."

"I don't know any Libby Simmons."

"I'm Bernie Simmons's sister."

"Ah. The fashion plate," came the voice from the other side of the door.

Somehow Libby didn't think she meant that comment in a good way. "This will only take a second."

"I'm busy. My hamster is sick."

"Oh dear," Libby said. "Poor thing."

"You like hamsters?" came the voice through the door.

"I used to have them."

"Most people think they're rats."

"They're not. And anyway, rats get a really bum rap. They're extremely smart, as well as family-oriented."

"Do you know about hamsters?"

"A little," Libby said, which was true.

The door swung open. Cyna was standing inside. She had on a long-sleeved T-shirt, striped pajamas, and a bathrobe that looked like an old Indian blanket. *And Bernie thinks my robe is bad,* Libby reflected. *She should see Cyna's.* Tucked in the breast pocket of Cyna's robe was the sick hamster.

Cyna pointed to the thermos of coffee Libby was holding. "What's that?"

"Coffee."

"Never drink the stuff," Cyna said. "It's poison."

*Guess I should have gone for the hot chocolate,* Libby thought.

"Then how about a muffin?"

"Is it made with butter?"

"Yes."

"Sorry. I'm strictly vegan. I don't eat anything made with animal products. Do you really know about hamsters?"

"A little. We used to have them when I was a kid."

"Well, Harry isn't feeling well."

"Who is Harry?"

"The hamster, of course."

"Of course."

Cyna reached up and stroked the hamster's nose. "He was fine last night, but when I gave him some sunflower seeds this morning he wouldn't take them. I think he has a cold. His nose is running."

Libby reached up and touched it. It was

wet. Not a good sign.

"I'd take him to the vet, but I don't have the money."

"He'll probably be all right," Libby told her.

"But what if he's not?"

Libby decided it was better to ignore the question.

"Why don't we get him out of the draft?" she suggested instead.

"Good idea," Cyna said.

She turned and walked down the hall. Libby followed.

"Do you have a shoe box and some dry shredded newspaper?" Libby asked. "Maybe you can put Harry in there to keep him warm."

"How come you know so much about this stuff?" Cyna said when they reached the kitchen.

The room was painted black with thin yellow stripes spaced about an inch and a half apart. Libby felt her head beginning to spin.

"My mom used to do this when one of our hamsters got sick," Libby replied while she put the thermos and muffins down on the black lacquered table.

"Did you have a lot of them?"

"Five," Libby said. "Although not all at once." And she ticked them off on her fingers. "There was Goofy and Gumby, Golly, Givens, and Horace. My dad picked Horace."

Libby bit at her cuticle. She was supposed to be finding out about Didi Mullet, and instead she was helping treat a sick hamster. Jeez. She shook her head in disgust at herself. Bernie would never get into something like this.

"Do you have an antibiotic around the house?"

Cyna looked blank.

"You know, that liquid pink stuff." The name eluded her for a moment and then she had it. "Amoxicillin."

Cyna nodded. "From my last bout of strep throat. Are you going to give it to him?"

"I'm going to try," Libby told her.

"It's in the medicine cabinet in the bathroom."

Libby nodded and started out the door.

"To the left," Cyna called out as Libby went right. "It's the second door on your left. You can't miss it."

Cyna was right. You couldn't miss it. Mostly because it was bright orange. The kind of orange that pulsed. Libby wondered who had picked the colors out for the flat as she walked inside. Somehow she thought it was Cyna. She opened the medicine cabinet. The amoxicillin was on the bottom shelf.

The prescription on the bottle was made out to a Cyna D. Mullet. Interesting, although Bernie would say it was suggestive. Could Didi be Cyna's middle name? Was she the one who's been riding around with Ted and doing who knows what? Well, Libby knew what. There was only one way to find out. Ask. She took a deep breath and let it out. *Bernie wouldn't have any trouble doing this,* she told herself. Neither should she.

"Did you find it?" Cyna yelled from the kitchen.

"Yup," Libby yelled back. Whether she liked it or not it was showtime.

She came out of the bathroom with the bottle in her hand and went into the kitchen. In Libby's absence Cyna had filled a shoe box with shredded paper and put Harry in it. She'd also rigged up a lamp so Harry could have some heat. Libby went and stood across from her.

"Didi, do you happen to have an eyedropper on you?"

"No," Cyna said. Then she caught herself and said, "That isn't my name."

Libby pointed to the medicine bottle. "It's your middle initial. See it says it right on the bottle. D for Didi."

"It could also be Diana or . . . or Debbie . . . or Dolores."

"It could be, but it isn't." The look on Cyna's face told her that. "How many Mullets are in the phone book?" Libby asked.

"I don't know. One or two."

"None. I looked it up before I came."

"Okay, okay, okay. So my middle name is Didi, big deal."

"Well, it is a big deal. I found a card in Ted Gorman's garage written by a Didi Mullet."

*I hope she doesn't ask me what I was doing in the garage,* Libby thought, but she didn't. Instead she said, "What note? I didn't write any note."

"Actually, it was a yellow greeting card with a picture of two golden retriever puppies cuddled in a basket on the cover. The one where you wrote 'make it soon.' The one that you signed with little hearts."

Cyna didn't say anything.

Libby tried again. "Why did you use your middle name instead of your given one?"

Cyna reached down and stroked Harry the Hamster's back with the tip of her finger.

"Come on, Cyna," Libby said. "We have the card you sent Ted."

Cyna scowled. "So what?"

"You were going out with him, weren't you?" Libby guessed.

Cyna took a step back and studied Libby.

"Marnie sent you, didn't she?" Cyna finally said.

Libby shook her head. "Marnie doesn't know I'm here."

"She hates me, you know. Because I'm young and she's not. She jealous because she's pruning out."

Somehow Libby didn't think so, but she let that pass. "Were you in the car the night it crashed?"

"If I had been I wouldn't be here, would I?"

"If you arranged the crash you might."

Cyna snorted. "Don't be daft. I don't kill mosquitoes, let alone people."

"But someone saw Ted in the car with a girl the night he died. I'm betting that girl is you."

"Doubtful. I was at my art class. You can check if you want to."

"I want to."

Cyna gave her a number. "Joe will tell you."

"Let's see." And Libby dialed the number.

A moment later a man's voice answered, "This is the School of Conceptual Art. How may I help you?"

"I'd like to speak to Joe."

"This is Joe."

Libby explained what she wanted. "You were right," she said to Cyna when she got off the phone.

"Of course I'm right." She stroked Harry's head. "So are you going to give him the medicine or what?"

Libby dabbed a tiny bit on the tip of her finger and held it out to Harry. He sniffed, then licked it off her finger.

"You should do this in the evening when you come home from work and in the morning when you get up. Keep it up for seven days," Libby said. "Hopefully he should get better."

Cyna nodded. Libby went back to the subject at hand.

"So why did you take up with Ted?" she asked.

"I told you I didn't."

"Would you like me to give the card to the police?"

Cyna looked alarmed. "You wouldn't."

Libby did her tough guy imitation. "Try me."

Cyna threw up her hands. "Fine, fine, fine. I was bored and he was interested. Happy now?"

"Yes, I am. It was as simple as that?"

"I liked his car. It was cool riding around in it."

"Do you know if he was going out with anyone else?" Libby asked.

"He wouldn't tell me, would he?"

"I suppose not."

Cyna tightened the belt on her bathrobe.

Libby bit her lip. She felt like they were at a standstill.

"Can you tell me anything that would help me?" she asked. "Anything at all?"

"Like what?" Cyna asked.

Libby thought about what they'd found in the bag buried in the trash. "Like who he got his drugs from. Like was he looking for his birth mother? Feel free to add to the list."

"I don't know about any of that," Cyna answered, but Libby could tell from the expression on her face that she did.

"I know you do," Libby answered in what she hoped was a scary voice.

Evidently, Libby decided, it wasn't scary enough, because Cyna just stood there twisting the end of her belt around.

"Come on," Libby urged. "Please. I don't want to get you in trouble. I just need to know."

Cyna looked at her. "You won't tell anyone this came from me?"

Libby held up her hand. "I swear."

"Well, he did lots of pills and I'm not sure where he got them, but I do know he was supposed to be getting some E that night from Bolt."

"Bolt?" Libby couldn't keep the surprise out of her voice.

"Yeah, Bolt. Mr. Gift From the Gods himself."

"I guess you don't like him very much."

"What's to like? He's a putz. I hope you tell the authorities and have him arrested."

"Can I ask you one last question?"

Cyna looked at the clock. "Make it quick. I have to get ready to go to work."

"Why did you sign your note to Ted Didi? Why not use your real name?"

Cyna grimaced. "If you had a name like Cyna would you use it? My mother must have been coked up — and I don't mean from soda — when she chose it. She told me she liked things from the Orient. How weird is that?"

"Well," Libby began, wondering how she could frame what she was going to say tactfully, but she didn't have to bother because Cyna didn't let her get started.

"Exactly," Cyna said. "It's a stupid name. I like Didi. That's the name I go by. Everyone calls me that. Except for Marnie, of course. She calls me Cyna because she knows I hate it."

# CHAPTER 28

Bernie looked down at her shirt. It was black with tasteful applications of flour across her chest. Wonderful. Why did she continue to wear black? Especially her black Bebe shirt. By now she should know better.

Or at the very least she should remember to put on an apron. Or more to the point she should tell Googie to move the soda. He'd stacked it too near the mixer — again — and every time someone turned on the machine, flour splashed out onto the bottles. Some of the bottles looked as if they'd been chalked. She was glad the kid was in love, but it would be nice if he'd stay focused at the shop for a change.

Oh well. Bernie dusted herself off and went back to clearing the prep table. She figured the more she could put away, the less cleaning they'd have to do when Conner and his crew got done. Even though they were just moving ceiling tiles, dirt still managed to rain down on everything. She was just putting mixing bowls in a carton when her cell rang. She picked it up and looked at it. Libby.

"So how did it go?" she asked.

Libby told her.

One problem solved, Bernie thought as she listened to Libby's recital of her conversation with Cyna. At least now they knew who Didi Mullet was. Libby continued talking, although now Bernie was having trouble hearing her. The connection had gone bad.

"Did you say Bolt?" Bernie asked.

Libby admitted she had.

"Interesting," Bernie said to herself as Libby clicked off. "Very interesting indeed."

Now they knew where Ted Gorman was getting some, if not all, of his drugs. They were making progress, even if it was slow progress, which was better than no progress at all. Not that Marvin's father would agree with that assessment. He wanted things solved and he wanted them solved ASAP, as he had made clear on the phone this morning.

Bernie tapped her cell against her teeth, realized what she was doing, and stopped. And she thought Amber and Googie were prone to drama. She would never say that again.

The more relevant question was: Where did Bolt fit into this equation? Was he a dealer? Was he just getting E as a favor to Ted? And with whom was Ted planning to use it? Was he going to a rave? Was he planning on having a private party? Instead of the possibilities narrowing they were increasing. Bernie turned her ring around on her finger. She really had to talk to him. The question was, when?

"What's up?" Tim Conner asked.

Bernie jumped. She'd been so intent on her thoughts she hadn't heard him come up. "Not much. Just waiting for you to get started."

She hoped Conner's construction crew was as fast as rumored, because until they finished, the kitchen was as good as closed. She'd given them coffee and scones when they'd come in, and now it was time for them to do their thing and leave.

"I thought I heard you mention Bolt," Conner said.

Bernie perked up. "You know him?"

"He used to work for me."

"I take it he doesn't anymore?"

"No, sir. Anyone who steals from me I get rid of."

"Seems like a wise move."

Tim Conner nodded. "Must be the same

in your business."

"Pretty much. We've been lucky."

"Well, I haven't."

"Was he dealing?"

Conner shrugged. "I can't really say. He could have been. Let's just say it wouldn't surprise me."

Bernie was going to ask him why when Amber came in. They had a crisis out front. Somehow or other they'd run out of take-out containers, and as far as Amber could see there weren't any in the storeroom.

"I'll look," Bernie told Amber as she hurried off to the storeroom to double-check. Something told her this wasn't going to be a very good day. She was halfway there when Amber came running in with the store phone.

"It's Marnie Gorman," she mouthed.

Bernie reached out her hand and took the receiver.

"You have to come to the store," Marnie sobbed. "You have to come now."

Bernie sighed and asked what the matter was.

"I can't tell you over the phone," Marnie cried.

The word *naturally* almost slipped out of Bernie's mouth, but she managed to catch herself in time. She decided that Marnie gave new meaning to the expression "drama queen."

"Please," Marnie begged.

"I'll be there as soon as Libby comes back," Bernie told her, and then before she could say anything else she hung up and headed to the storeroom.

Fortunately, she managed to find some take-out containers underneath a carton of paper towels. When her cell rang again she ignored it. Her horoscope had said this was a day for practicing calm — never one of her strengths.

Libby was back at the store twenty minutes later. By that time Marnie had called twice more and Bernie was ready to strangle her.

"Do you think I could get away with killing Marnie?" she asked her dad as he got into Marvin's car. They were off to talk to Ted Gorman's mom, and Bernie wished with all her heart that she was going with them instead of driving over to Just Chocolate.

Sean considered the matter for a moment.

"Probably not," he finally said. "But someone else might think they can."

Her dad's words kept racing around in Bernie's head as she drove to Just Chocolate. Was she not taking Marnie as seriously as she should be? Was someone really trying to harm Marnie? Bernie knew it was a real possibility, but somehow she just couldn't get herself to believe it.

Everything that had happened since they'd discovered Ted Gorman's body in Ms. McDougal's grave made no sense whatsoever. Usually there was a common thread that linked things together, but that didn't seem to be the case here. Bernie was still thinking about what the thread could be when she arrived at Just Chocolate.

Marnie must have been on the lookout for her, because the moment she walked through the door, Marnie ran over to her and dragged her into the back. She appeared as if she'd lost weight since Bernie had seen her last, and there were plum-hued circles underneath her eyes.

"Look," she demanded as she dragged Bernie over to one of the chocolate vats. "Just look."

Bernie peeled Marnie's fingers off her upper arm. "What am I looking for?" she asked.

"You'll see," Marnie told her.

And Bernie did. The chocolate in the vat was a lumpy, dark brown mass. All of its luster was gone. As Bernie straightened up she noticed the empty bottle of water sitting on the table next to it. Water and untempered chocolate don't mix. Add even a small drop and the chocolate seizes up and you have to throw it out.

"Are all the other vats like this?"

Marnie shook her head.

Bernie twisted her ring around her finger. "Whose station is this?"

"Bolt's."

"Where is he?"

"He called in sick."

Bernie raised an eyebrow.

"He'd never do anything like this to me," Marnie told her.

"Why not?"

A flush crawled up Marnie's face. She didn't say anything.

Bernie remembered what Brandon had said about Bolt being a ladies' man. Could Marnie be one of his ladies? It was an interesting thought.

"Marnie, can I have his number?"

"Why?"

"Because I want to talk to him, obviously."

"About what?"

Bernie gestured toward the vat. "About this. And other things."

"What other things?"

"I've heard that Bolt supplied E to your husband."

"That's a lie," Marnie cried. Two spots of color appeared on her cheeks. "A terrible lie. Who would say something like that?"

*Like I'm going to tell you,* Bernie thought. She shrugged. "You know how rumors go around."

"Those people should be shot." Marnie's hands fluttered in the air. "He would never, never do anything like that."

"You mean deal drugs?" Bernie asked.

Marnie nodded. "Bolt isn't like that."

Bernie pointed to the vat. "Would he do something like this?"

"Never. He would never do something like this to me. Never."

That was five nevers in the last minute, Bernie observed. What was the line about "methinks the lady doth protest too much"?

"This is all Ted's work," Marnie insisted.

Bernie grunted. Obviously Ted was bored in the afterlife. He needed a project. Like knitting. Or macramé. Or doing crossword puzzles.

"He must hate me," Marnie whispered. "Otherwise why would he be doing this to me?" Marnie looked at Bernie as if she expected her to supply an answer.

Bernie decided to try another tack. She drew herself up and tried to look brisk. "Okay, who has the combination to the shop alarm?"

"No one. Just me and Ted."

"Maybe you forgot to set the alarm," Bernie suggested. Heaven only knows, it had happened to her more than once.

The corners of Marnie's mouth turned down. "No. I didn't."

"Are you sure?"

Marnie folded her arms across her chest. "I never forget to set the alarm. Never."

"Okay, then. Maybe one of the alarm circuits isn't working."

Marnie shook her head. "If they weren't working the alarm company would have called."

Bernie had to admit this was true. "Do you mind if I check anyway?"

"Check away, but I know it's Ted. I'm just sorry you're refusing to see that. And now if you'll excuse me I have things to do."

And with that Marnie went out front.

Bernie sighed. She was glad that someone was sure of something.

She rubbed her head as she tried to imagine what her father would do in this situation. First, he would check the alarm to make sure it hadn't been tampered with, after which he'd take a look outside and see if there was any evidence of someone walking around, an unlikely possibility considering the hardness of the ground. But maybe whoever had done this had dropped something.

After he was done doing that he'd drive over to Marnie's house and examine the dirt by the shrubs next to the trellis to see if he could see any footprints, after which he'd track Bolt down and have a conversation with him. Bernie sighed again. She really needed a shot of espresso after her conversation with Marnie. Or maybe she should just find an exorcist and be done with the whole thing. One thing was clear: One way or another, even if Ted Gorman was dead, he was causing a great deal of trouble.

On the way to the shop's back door Bernie passed by bags of sugar, cartons of nuts, a couple of bags of chocolate nibs, and stacks of chocolate in ten-pound bars. All of it was waiting to be made into candies. She was interested to see that Marnie was using some of the expensive stuff — unblended, first-growth, fair-trade chocolate from South America, as well as some of the blended chocolate. Maybe she and Libby should use some at their shop, Bernie thought. They'd just charge more.

# CHAPTER 29

Sean looked at Marvin. He had both hands on the wheel and his eyes were focused on the road. *Yes,* Sean thought. Under his tutelage Marvin was actually turning out to be a pretty good driver. Or at least a competent one. It was all a matter of patience and repetition. Say something often enough and people begin to catch on. And contrary to what Libby thought, a little yelling didn't hurt. It helped fix things in a person's mind. He knew this from his time as chief. So Marvin had needed a lot of fixing, it just couldn't be helped.

At least now Libby would be safe. Every time Libby had gone out the door with Marvin it had pained Sean to think of his daughter driving around with him, and even though he'd told her of his concerns she'd pooh-poohed them. Not at all untypical for Libby. Oh well. But he'd fixed the problem — he was good at fixing problems. And on the way back he could ask Marvin to stop at a pharmacy so he could get Inez a card. He settled back into his seat, fished out the orange-cranberry muffin Libby had given him for the trip, and began to eat. Of course, Libby had given him a muffin for Marvin as well, in addition to the basket full of baked goods for Ted Gorman's mom, but Sean decided it was better to wait until after they arrived at their destination to give Marvin the muffin. In his opinion, the fewer distractions Marvin had while operating a moving vehicle, the better.

"What are you going to ask Mrs. Gorman?" Marvin asked him.

Sean peeled the paper from half the muffin and deposited it in the brown paper bakery bag.

"I don't know," Sean told him.

"You don't know?" Marvin said.

Sean noticed Marvin's head beginning to turn, so he corrected him at once.

"Eyes front. That's right. I don't know," he told Marvin when he'd resumed watching the road. "I'm hoping that one question will lead to another one. Have you ever shaken a cherry tree to get the fruit at the top?"

Marvin shook his head.

"We used to do that all the time when I

was a kid. We'd shake the tree and we'd get cherries, but we'd get bugs too."

"I don't understand. Why would you want to get bugs?"

"I'm using a metaphor," Sean said.

"Oh."

Sean decided it was better not to say anything. Instead he took another bite of his muffin and closed his eyes. He could think better about his upcoming interview with Mrs. Gorman that way. He hadn't told Marvin that she wasn't expecting him. But he figured first he'd get there and then he'd decide on an approach. He patted the basket Libby had given him. Hopefully the scones, muffins, jams, and maple spread would help. Considering the circumstances, Mrs. Gorman might not want to talk to him, but then again maybe she would.

Sometimes it happened one way, sometimes it happened the other. The only thing Sean knew was that it was impossible to predict the outcome beforehand. He remembered the time he'd had to tell Mrs. Viceroy that her pet frog had died, and had been treated to a two-hour slide show on Buster's development from a spawn, through his tadpole stage, to the bullfrog he'd become. He certainly hoped things didn't go like that. And then he started thinking about nothing much at all.

Sean woke with a start. He didn't remember falling asleep, but that's what he must have done. He was straightening up when he caught sight of the sign, NEW YORK 75 MILES. *New York! Oh my God.*

He turned to Marvin. "You're going the wrong way."

"No, I'm not. You told me Ted's mom lived in Brooklyn."

"I told you she lived in Schenectady."

"No, you didn't."

"Then I told Libby."

"Well, she didn't tell me. You want me to turn around?"

"Of course I want you to turn around," Sean snapped. "You're going the wrong way."

"Fine." Marvin yanked on the wheel.

Sean watched in horror as Marvin cut across four lanes of traffic to get to the exit. Cars honked. Brakes squealed. People screamed obscenities. Marvin remained unfazed. Sean noted that he hadn't even put on his directional signal. He didn't even want to think of all the penalties Marvin had just racked up with that maneuver of his.

Marvin turned toward him.

"You look pale," he observed. "Are you

feeling all right?"

Sean opened his mouth. For once no words came out. He shut it again.

He didn't know what to say, or rather he didn't know how he could say nicely what he wanted to say. The only thing he could do was point to the road. He knew if he said what he wanted to — something involving the words *moron* and *idiot* with a couple of *incompetents* thrown in — Libby would never forgive him.

They finally reached Schenectady an hour and a half later. By then Sean's breathing had returned to normal. As he looked out the window he reflected that the city was like so many of the others around here. It was a factory town that had thrived when G&E was here, but then the factories all relocated to places like Mexico, Indonesia, and China. The city never recovered.

Marvin spoke for the first time since he'd switched lanes. "Ted Gorman's mom never came to his funeral. She said she couldn't travel."

"Maybe she was sick," Sean said. "Maybe she couldn't face it."

"Maybe," Marvin said, but to Sean's ear he didn't sound convinced.

They arrived at Susan Gorman's house ten minutes later. The house was on the outskirts of the city in a neighborhood that to Sean's eyes said *solid working class.* Susan Gorman's house did not appear to be the exception.

It was a small cottage painted a light blue with white trim around the windows and doors. The portico, under which an old Taurus resided, was painted in matching colors. Laurel hedges demarcated the property line. A large bird feeder was placed near a picture window. A coat of birdseed covered the ground around the feeder.

Nothing about the house or the street it was on was remarkable in any way. All the houses looked alike, except that some of them had porches on the left side and some had them on the right.

As he slowly made his way up to the front door Sean reflected that this area was probably one of those subdivisions they built in the fifties. Marvin followed on his heels like some goddamned herding dog.

"You're practically stepping on my feet," Sean groused when he was halfway up the path. "Could you back up a bit and give me a little space?"

Marvin shifted Libby's basket from his left to his right arm. "I just want to make sure I can catch you if you fall," he explained.

"I'm not going to fall and you're not my mother," Sean snapped.

And then he turned and continued toward Sue Gorman's house. That way he didn't have to see the injured look he was sure was on Marvin's face. When he got to the front door he rang the bell.

Two minutes later the door opened a sliver. A crescendo of voices, hoots, tweets, and cackles poured out into the street.

A hoarse voice asked, "Who is it?"

As Sean said, "Susan Gorman?" he remembered Rose had always remarked that he had a bad habit of answering a question with a question.

"You can't come in. I'm busy cleaning."

Sean motioned for Marvin to give him the basket.

"Here," he said, holding it out in front of him. "Please accept this as a small token for your loss."

The door opened a little wider. The noise was deafening.

"You're not the code enforcement officer?" the woman asked.

"No. I'm Sean Simmons and this is Marvin Hanson. We just want to talk to you about your son."

"And you're not from the ASPCA?"

"Not the last time I checked."

The door opened wider. The woman stuck her head out. Hanks of her hair stood straight up. Just like she had wires in it, Sean thought. Suspiciously she looked to the right and then to the left; then she motioned Sean and Marvin in.

"Quick," she said as they stepped inside. "I don't want them to come inside."

"Them?" Sean asked.

Instead of answering she grabbed the basket from Sean and started rummaging through it.

"Do you have any cranberry scones?" she asked him.

Sean looked at Marvin. "Do we?"

Marvin nodded.

"Good. Oscar will like that," she informed him. "Next time bring some date muffins. He really loves those."

"Who is Oscar?" Sean said as he looked around. He felt like sticking his fingers in his ears to block out the noise.

"My African gray," Susan Gorman said.

"That's a parrot," Marvin explained to Sean.

"I'm impressed," Sean told him.

"My mom used to have one before my dad made her get rid of it," Marvin explained. He turned to Susan Gorman. "Are you having trouble with the city?"

Her eyes widened. Sean watched while Susan tugged at the collar of her sweatshirt.

"How do you know?"

"Just a guess."

"They want to take my birds." Her eyes began to mist over. "But they're my babies. I've had some of them for twenty years."

"How many do you have?" Sean asked.

"Four or five hundred. Most of them are parrots, but I have love birds, parakeets, and canaries as well."

*Great,* Sean thought. They were interviewing the bird lady. He could feel his throat start to contract. He was allergic to birds. Had been ever since he was thirteen and a half years old and he'd been attacked by a crow. He really wanted to get out of here as soon as possible.

He cleared his throat. "I'm very sorry about the death of your son, Ted."

"Oscar never liked him," Sue Gorman told Sean and Marvin. "Never."

"Did Ted like Oscar?" Sean asked.

She shook her head. "He never liked Oscar or Joey or Seth. He never liked any of the birds. When he left he told me he wouldn't come back if the birds were here. But what could I do? They were my children too."

"When was the last time you saw him?"

Sean asked.

A vacant look crossed Sue's face. "They visited a while ago. A long while."

Sean leaned forward a little. "What do you mean they?"

Sue shook her head. "He and his shadow. He's a Gemini. That's bad. A Gemini is a trickster, you know."

"I didn't," Sean replied, although Bernie probably would.

Sue bobbed her head up and down. "Oh yes. Always have been. Look what happened to Castor and Pollux."

*Please, no astrology,* Sean thought. *Not now.* He sneezed. He could feel his sinuses begin to fill up. He had to get out of here before he stopped breathing.

"When did you adopt Ted?" he asked, hoping to get an answer that made sense.

Sue gave him another vacant look. "His mother dropped him off in a balloon. But when Oscar came it was too much. Good and evil are hard to balance."

Sean sneezed again. His head felt as if it were in a vise. "Do you remember the name of the adoption agency?"

Sue took a scone out of the basket and crumpled it on the floor. "It was through a lawyer. Roland . . . Rufus . . . Riley . . . Riley Watson. I told him I didn't like Ted's shadow. I told him but he didn't listen to me."

"Thank you for your help," Sean said and turned and headed for the door. Once he got outside he took several breaths of fresh air.

"Wow," Marvin said when they were sitting back in his car. "Now, that's someone who needs to be on serious meds."

"No wonder Ted Gorman went looking for his birth mother," Sean commented.

"Do you think she was always like that?"

Sean shook his head. "No. She was probably fine. Or at least functional when she adopted Ted."

Marvin started the car. "Back to Longely?"

Sean sneezed again. "First let's see if there's a Riley Watson in town."

"What makes you think he's here?"

"Just a hunch." Sean sneezed again. "But first let's stop at a drugstore. I need to get an antihistamine."

And a card.

Valentine's Day was coming up.

He should probably get something for Bernie and Libby while he was at it. Maybe a chocolate kiss. As much as his daughters were into the fancy stuff, deep down in their hearts they still liked good old Hershey's.

In the meantime he'd call Bernie and find out who the hell Castor and Pollux were. Not that the answer would shed any light on the problem at hand — he was positive of that — but if he didn't find out it was going to bother him for the rest of the day.

As he reached for his cell, he decided that of all the modern inventions, he liked this one the best. But before he did anything he'd call 411 and see if they had a listing for a Riley Watson in Schenectady, Albany, or Troy.

# CHAPTER 30

Bernie had just gotten into Brandon's Nissan when her cell phone went off.

"My dad," she mouthed to Brandon as she answered it.

He nodded.

"Who are Castor and Pollux?" she repeated.

"That's what I just said," Sean replied.

"They're the main stars in the Gemini constellation. Why?"

Instead of answering, she heard her dad yell, "No, no, Marvin, take a left. I said left. A hard left."

Bernie moved her cell away from her ear.

"I think I lost a couple of hearing decibels," she told her dad.

"Sorry," he replied.

They chatted for a few more minutes and then he hung up.

She was really glad she wasn't driving with her dad, she thought as she turned to

Brandon. He was bad in a car before, but since he'd gotten sick he'd become even worse.

"My dad says hello," she said to Brandon.

"He's a good guy," Brandon observed.

"Yes, he is. I have a question for you."

"Shoot."

"When were you born?"

"August. I'm a Leo."

"We're not compatible."

"You told me that in high school," Brandon reminded her.

Bernie laughed. "So I did. It's nice to know some things never change."

"Isn't it, though? Are you ready to tackle Bolt?"

Bernie nodded. "I certainly am."

"Then buckle up and let's go."

Brandon threw the car in gear and they were off.

Bernie took a look at him. He was focused on the road.

"Heard from Rob?" he asked as they took a left onto Ash.

"Nope."

"For what it's worth you're better off."

"You said that before."

"I just want to emphasize the point."

"You have."

Brandon reached over and turned on the

radio. Country and western came floating out.

"Country and western?" Bernie asked.

"I like it."

Brandon stopped at the stop sign. Little flakes of snow came trickling down. He cleared his throat.

"Rob's a player," he told her.

"I already saw that."

"No. He has another steady."

Bernie felt her stomach begin to knot. "How do you know?"

"Please. I'm a bartender. The girlfriend of the girl he's seeing comes into R.J.'s all the time. Candy's a stripper. She works at Dream Girls."

Somehow Bernie wasn't surprised. She wanted to be, but she wasn't. "Brandon, why didn't you tell me before?"

Brandon shrugged. "I figured it wasn't my business."

"How was it not your business?"

"It just wasn't."

"That's guy logic." Bernie put her hands over her face. "I think I'm going to take a vow of chastity."

Brandon smiled at her. "Now, that would be a real shame."

Instead of answering Bernie sat back in her seat and closed her eyes.

"Are you okay?" Brandon asked.

"Sure. I'm great."

"Hey," Brandon said. "You're with me. You're riding in my Nissan. You're out of the shop. What could be so bad?"

Even though she didn't want to, Bernie could feel the corners of her mouth turning up. In high school Brandon was the one who could always make her smile.

"That's better," he said.

And it was. She hadn't planned on having Brandon come along, but he'd stopped when she was scanning the shrubbery around Marnie's house for footprints — what a waste of time that had been. One thing had led to another and here they were. Anyway, she'd figured she could always use another person around when she was talking to Bolt, and the fact that Brandon was big and had worked as a bouncer didn't hurt.

And maybe he'd change her luck, because the morning certainly hadn't been going well so far. She hadn't found anything out of order at Marnie's shop, and she hadn't found any footprints in the shrubbery around Marnie's house. Maybe Bolt would shed some light on the mystery at hand — if they could get him to talk.

The truth was Bolt didn't have to talk to

her. It wasn't as if she had a badge. He could throw her out of his house, and if she didn't leave he could have her arrested. And she didn't have any cards to play this time, because something told her that cute and funny wasn't going to do it. Neither was her advanced fashion sense. Although her dad had told her different.

Well, at least she had Brandon along for moral support. Bernie closed her eyes again and sat back in the seat and reviewed what she knew about Bolt. He worked for Marnie, he'd worked construction in the past, and he was a player.

Maybe he had a reason for spooking Marnie, but she sure didn't know what it was. That's what she was going to find out. It would have to be a serious reason, because he was going to an awful lot of trouble to accomplish it.

She spun her onyx ring around her finger while she thought about what her dad would say about getting Bolt talking.

"Give him enough rope and let him hang himself," her dad would advise. "Be an observant listener. Listen to what he's not saying, notice what topics he's avoiding. Start the conversation by asking him to help you with something. Men like that."

As if she didn't know.

Her father would go on. "Then maybe, if you're lucky," he would say, "you can slide into the topic you're interested in. Like maybe you're going to a rave and you'd like some E. Does he know where to get any?"

Bernie sighed.

"Anything the matter?" Brandon asked.

"No. I just wish my dad was doing this."

"What? A failure of nerve?"

"Maybe a little twinge," Bernie said.

"You'll do fine," Brandon continued. "With those boots how could Bolt resist you?"

Bernie grinned. Never underestimate the power of pink lizard cowboy boots. "You know how to pump up a girl's ego."

Now it was Brandon's turn to smile. "That's why I make the big tips."

Fifteen minutes later Brandon pulled up to the apartment development where Bolt lived. Located in the middle of nowhere as the apartments were, the management kept them filled by promising free cable and low rents. Built fifteen years ago, the place was already falling apart.

"You want me to stay in the car?" Brandon asked her when they'd parked in front of apartment 2A.

Bernie nodded. "If you don't mind." She'd probably have a better chance on her own. She'd noticed that men tended to talk to women more when they were by themselves.

Brandon fished the paper out from underneath the front seat. "I'd probably overwhelm him with my presence, anyway."

"Yeah. That's it."

"You mean it's not?"

Bernie laughed as she got out of the Nissan. Then she walked toward Bolt's apartment and rang the bell. No one answered. She tried a second time. No luck. Okay, time to try the apartment next door. Maybe they knew something. She rang the bell. A moment later a girl wearing jeans and a hoodie answered the door.

"I'm looking for Bolt," Bernie told her.

The girl fingered the dragon tattoo on her neck. "Try the health club down the road," she said. "He's usually there."

"Thanks," Bernie said.

"Don't thank me," the girl said. "I wouldn't waste my time on him if I were you."

"Why not?" Bernie asked. This girl wanted to talk. If she was willing to give a little, she might be willing to give a lot.

The girl snorted. "Because he can't keep his dick in his pants. Dr. Phil had a program on it. I should have taped it and given it to him."

"There seems to be a lot of that going around," Bernie said, thinking of Rob.

"Yeah. He thinks just because he hands out stuff he's a big deal."

"He's a dealer?" Bernie asked.

"Are you a cop?" the girl asked.

"Do I look like one?"

"No," the girl replied. "But that doesn't mean anything."

As she watched her stroke her neck, Bernie reflected that the girl sounded as if she had plenty of experience. "Well, I'm not."

"Then why are you asking so many questions?"

"Because he might be causing some problems for someone I know."

"Could he get in trouble?"

"Absolutely."

The girl grinned.

"You don't like him very much, do you?" Bernie asked.

"You got that, huh?"

"Yeah. It was a stretch but I did. How come?"

"He knocked one of my friends up, told her he'd take care of her and the baby, and walked away. No child support. No nothing."

"What happened to your friend?"

"She went back to Ohio."

Bernie asked another question. "Have you ever see him with an older lady? Pretty. Blond hair. Fine features."

The girl twirled a lock of her hair around one of her fingers. "Yeah. I've seen lots of those coming in and out of his place. And now if you don't mind I gotta go." She started to close the door.

"By the way, that's a nice tattoo," Bernie said.

"And those are nice boots," the girl replied as she closed the door.

# CHAPTER 31

"Any luck?" Brandon asked when Bernie got back in the car.

"His neighbor said he might be working out at the gym down the road."

"Let's go get him," Brandon said as he put the Nissan in gear.

Two minutes later they arrived at the gym. As the girl next door had promised it was just down the road.

"So how are you going to do this?" Brandon asked as he pulled into the parking lot in front of the Fitness Center.

"I'm going to blind him with my beauty," Bernie told him.

"I guess that's better than dazzling him with your brains," Brandon said.

Bernie punched him. He gave her the thumbs-up sign as she got out of the car. She walked toward the Fitness Center. Bernie decided the place looked as if it had been a store in its previous incarnation. A smallish store. Not a big box. No one had changed the big plate-glass windows in the front, so Bernie peeked in.

She could see a handful of people working out. The equipment looked old and the machines were right on top of one another. When she opened the door the smell of rancid sweat and rubber wafted out. Bleach would help, Bernie concluded.

People looked at her and then went back to what they were doing. There was no one at the front desk. In fact, there was no front desk and no locker space either from what she could see. Bernie looked around. It took a few seconds, but she spotted Bolt doing bicep curls over in the free weight section. Bernie threaded her way toward him. He didn't see her because he was flexing while studying his reflection in the mirror.

"Looking good," Bernie said when she reached him.

Bolt's jaw dropped when he saw her.

"So how much weight are you using?"

"What the hell are you doing here?" he demanded.

"That's not a polite thing to say to a lady," Bernie replied.

"I repeat. What are you doing here?"

"Would you believe, I was driving by and saw you through the window so I decided to stop and say hello?"

"No. I wouldn't believe that at all."

"Okay, how about, Marnie told me you were sick and I got concerned and drove out here to see how you were? Does that work better for you?"

"I was sick. I had a headache."

"I'm sure," Bernie said.

"I can't believe you came all the way out here for that."

"Someone put some water in one of the vats of chocolate."

Bolt pointed at himself with one of the weights. "And you think I did it?"

Bernie shrugged. "Did you?"

Bolt gave a merciless laugh. "It figures."

"What figures?"

"That Marnie would blame this on me."

Bernie waited. Sometimes silence worked best. But evidently not in this case. Instead of talking Bolt resumed doing his curls.

"Why would she do that?"

"Ask her."

"I'm asking you."

Bolt put his weights down, picked up the white terry cloth towel that was hanging over the weight rack, and said, "A gentleman never tells."

"Does that mean that you and Marnie had something going on?"

Bolt dabbed at his face with the towel.

"I don't believe you," Bernie said, hoping to get a reaction.

Bolt shrugged and tossed the towel back on the rack. He picked up his weights again.

"What could she possibly see in you?"

Bolt smirked. Bernie felt an overwhelming desire to wipe the smirk off his face.

"She sees in me what every other woman does."

Bernie snorted. "What could that possibly be?"

"Ask her."

Bernie moved a step closer to Bolt. "Does she also know that you were supplying her husband with Percosets and E?"

"I never did that," Bolt said.

"That's not what I heard," Bernie said.

"You're nuts," Bolt told her.

He tried to sound confident, but Bernie noticed there was a quaver in his voice that hadn't been there before.

"Yup," she continued. "In fact my informant tells me that you gave some E to Ted the night he died."

"You have no informant."

"Why don't we go to the police and let them decide?"

"Okay, okay," Bolt said. "I sold him a few Percosets when I went to work for him.

So what?"

"And the E?"

"He tried it a few times and gave it up. I think it weirded him out."

"So what were you selling him?"

"Viagra. Really," Bolt said when Bernie didn't say anything. "I figured that's why she came on to me after Ted died."

"I'm not following," Bernie told him.

"It's simple," Bolt said.

"Not to me."

"She wanted to find out what a real man was like."

"I see."

Bolt looked at himself in the mirror and flexed. "It's true. Ask her if you don't believe me."

"I'm going to."

"Good." Bolt turned toward her. "And remember, if you're interested I always have room in my schedule."

"I don't think so."

"You'd be surprised."

"You're right. Maybe I will have to try a real man someday. Too bad that won't be you."

She turned and walked away. "By the way," she told Bolt over her shoulder. "I heard you two started getting together before Ted died."

Bolt picked up his weights again. "Believe what you want."

# CHAPTER 32

"I told you he was a moron," Brandon said when Bernie related her conversation with Bolt.

"Yes, you did," Bernie agreed. "I just didn't believe how big a moron he was. Do you think he was telling me the truth?"

"About him and Marnie?"

Bernie thought back to her conversation with Marnie about the ruined vat of chocolate. She'd kept on saying, "No. He'd never do that to me." Or words to that effect.

"No. That I believe. I was thinking about the Viagra."

Brandon shrugged. "Sure. Why not? It's a party drug now."

Bernie buckled her safety belt. "But why buy it from someone like him?"

"Because it's less embarrassing."

"I suppose."

"I know."

"Do you think that was all Bolt sold him?"

"No. I think Bolt is a full-service pharmacy."

Bernie nodded. "He's probably getting them from someone at the gym."

"Probably," Brandon agreed. "Where to now?"

"You can drop me off at my car."

"Today's my day off. I'm kind of enjoying the chauffeuring business. I'm thinking I may have found myself a new career."

"Are you sure?" Bernie asked.

"I'm sure," Brandon told her. "And anyway, it's my job to keep you from grieving about your recent loss."

Bernie realized she hadn't thought about Rob once since she'd gotten into Brandon's car.

"Well, you're doing a good job," she told him.

"I always do a good job. What is Madam's pleasure?"

"I think I need to go back to Just Chocolate again and talk to Marnie."

Brandon gave a quick bob of his head. "Your wish is my command."

Bernie leaned back in the seat. "I think I could get used to this."

"That's what you used to say back in high school."

"I never said that back in high school."

"Oh yes, you did."

"No, I didn't. How could I? You didn't have a car."

Brandon snapped his fingers. "How could I have forgotten?"

"Amazing, isn't it?"

Brandon put the Nissan in gear and roared out of the parking lot. As they left, Bernie could have sworn she saw Bolt staring out the window at them. The expression on his face was anything but pretty.

It took Brandon about twenty minutes to get back to Marnie's shop. During that time Bernie called Libby and checked in on how things were going at the shop.

"How well are they going?" Brandon asked her when Bernie clicked off.

"About as well as can be expected given the circumstances. Tim discovered a squirrel's nest in the ceiling next to the venting system."

"Do you want to stop by there first?"

Bernie shook her head. She knew that if she did, she'd never get out of there.

"Okeydokey," Brandon said and stepped on the gas.

They headed down Ashcroft. Bernie spent the next ten minutes listening to Dolly Parton and looking at the rich people's houses on Ashcroft and Elm. They were all immaculate with their sloping lawns and winding, carefully shoveled driveways. Even the dusting of snow on their lawns seemed artful.

Fortunately, the mania for McMansionization hadn't hit Longely yet. Bernie hoped it never would. She'd hate to see these houses torn down to make room for bigger ones.

She was just thinking about what a waste it would be when they pulled into Just Chocolate's parking lot. Bernie noticed that it wasn't as crowded as usual. Brandon brought the Nissan to a halt, put it in park, and turned towards Bernie.

"So," he asked, "what's the plan?"

Bernie twisted her ring around her finger. The truth was she didn't really have a plan. "I'm just going to go in and ask Marnie about Bolt."

"Just like that?"

"Just like that. Why?"

"I was thinking you'd try something more subtle. You know, like talking about *Lady Chatterly's Lover* and going from there."

Bernie raised an eyebrow. "I'm impressed you know the book."

"What? You think I'm an illiterate bartender? I took English lit in college."

"I've just never seen you reading anything

but the newspaper." Bernie eyed him specu-
latively. "You just read the dirty parts, didn't
you?"

"Actually we called them the good parts."

"I bet you did."

"I still do."

Bernie laughed. "I think I'm sticking with
my original plan."

"Such as it is."

"Such as it is," Bernie agreed.

"Just remember — any trouble and I'm
your man. I wasn't a member of the junior
varsity wrestling team for nothing."

"That's good to know."

Bernie got out of the car and started
toward the chocolate shop. The closer she
got, the less sure she became of how to
proceed. What was she trying to do here
anyway? She thought about what her father
would say.

She was here to gather information. So the
question was how best to get it: She could
either do a full frontal assault or lurk around
the edge picking up crumbs of information.
In a metaphorical sense. She was still debat-
ing strategy as she walked through the door.

As the parking lot had indicated, the shop
still wasn't busy. The two counter girls were
standing around looking bored, while a

third one was sweeping the floor.

"Is Marnie here?" Bernie asked.

The girl sweeping pointed to the office. Bernie thanked her and went into the back. Three of the candy-making stations were in operation. Cyna was seated at the nearest one, and looked away when she saw Bernie.

"Hi," Bernie said. "I'm looking for your boss."

"In the office," Cyna said without looking up from the potato chip she was dipping in milk chocolate.

"You sell a lot of those?" Bernie asked, regarding the tray that was already three-quarters filled.

"Tons," Cyna mumbled.

They were, Bernie decided, one of those things that sounded weird, but were actually very good. When one combined sweet and salty in one dish the results were usually impressive.

Bernie thanked Cyna and walked toward the office. The door was open and Marnie was working at her computer. Bernie was relieved to see that her office desk looked like the one at A Little Taste of Heaven. When she got close enough she knocked on the door frame. Marnie jumped.

"I didn't mean to startle you," Bernie told her.

Marnie hit a button and the screen on the computer went dark. Then she got up and came outside. "You didn't. What can I do for you?"

"I have a question," Bernie said.

"About the benefit?"

"No. About Bolt."

Marnie crossed her arms over her chest. Bernie noticed that she was wearing a very good, light blue cashmere sweater.

"So you found him?"

Bernie nodded.

"Is he okay?"

"Why shouldn't he be?"

"Because he's sick."

"Not really. He's working out at the gym."

"How do you know?"

"I checked."

"Oh," Marnie said. She seemed nonplussed.

"He says he doesn't have anything to do with the vat of chocolate."

Marnie absentmindedly twirled one of the diamond studs in her earlobe. "I told you he didn't. He would never do something like that."

"That's what you said. He seems to like the ladies."

Marnie shrugged, but Bernie noticed there was a slight tremor under her eye.

"What he does out of work is no concern of mine."

*Right,* Bernie thought. *Of course it isn't.*

"He came on to me," she informed Marnie.

She watched as two bright spots of color appeared on Marnie's cheeks.

"Surprised?" Bernie asked.

"I'm not . . . I mean why should I . . . care?" Marnie stammered.

"I'd care," Bernie told her. "I just found out my boyfriend has been cheating on me, and that doesn't make me very happy at all."

"He's not my boyfriend," Marnie protested, but Bernie thought her protest sounded weak.

Bernie shook her head. "That's not what he said."

"He's lying."

"Somehow I don't think so. Did you take up with Bolt before your husband died or after?"

Marnie still didn't say anything, but Bernie could see her jaw muscles tightening. She clenched her fists, realized what she was doing, and unclenched them.

"Maybe that's why you keep saying that Ted is mad at you. You have a guilty conscience."

Marnie bit her lip. The two spots of color

on her cheeks grew.

"I'm right, aren't I?" Bernie asked.

"No. You're dead wrong," Marnie hissed.

"Really?" Bernie said.

"Yes. Really. I was faithful to that son of a bitch all my life. I never so much as looked at another man and then I find out he's been sleeping around on me. He's been doing it for years. Years." Marnie's face was now completely red. She pointed to the back door. "Now get out of here. Get out of here now."

"Does this mean you don't want my services anymore?"

"Out," Marnie yelled.

"I'm just asking."

As she was leaving Bernie went by the cartons of supplies stacked up on the shelves. There were even more boxes of chocolate than there had been the last time she came. As her eyes passed over the boxes, one of the SKU numbers caught her attention. She closed her eyes while she thought. Yes. She was almost positive. She hurried out to the Nissan.

"We have to go back to A Little Taste of Heaven," she told Brandon. "We have to go back there right away."

# CHAPTER 33

Bernie raced up the stairs to the flat. Brandon was right behind her. She went straight into her bedroom and started looking through her jeans. God, she hoped she hadn't washed the ones she needed. That would be terrible. What pair had she been wearing that night?

Her Lucky jeans? The ones from Seven or the ones from Paper or Diesel? Arrgh. She couldn't remember. Why was she so disorganized? Why didn't she have a folder or a notebook or something? Why was she always doing this? It was crazy making. How many pairs of jeans did she have anyway? Nine? Or was it ten? She went to her closet to check. Her Union Pacific jeans were on the floor.

She was picking them up when she heard, "I thought that was you I saw through the window."

Bernie spun around. Libby was standing

inside her bedroom. Bernie had been so engrossed in her search she hadn't even heard her coming up the stairs.

"You didn't wash any of my jeans, did you?" she demanded of her sister.

Libby gave her an incredulous look. "Why would I do that?"

"I don't know. They could have gotten into your laundry bag by accident."

Libby snorted. "You're a size six, I'm a size twelve. I think when I put them in the wash I'd know they weren't mine."

"Maybe you decided to do me a favor and do them anyway."

"You don't look like a size twelve," Brandon interjected.

"That's sweet," Libby told him.

"I'm a sweet guy," Brandon responded.

"No, you're not," Bernie replied.

"Can I get you some coffee?" Libby asked him. "We're featuring Sumatra and I've got some lemon squares and pumpkin bread from yesterday that's still good."

*Heaven spare me,* Bernie thought as she tapped Libby on the shoulder. Libby turned around.

"We're not playing Martha now."

Libby's face puckered. "I don't understand what you mean."

"I mean we have to stay on task."

"What task? I keep asking, but you're not telling me."

"I'm looking for the piece of paper I took from Ms. McDougal's cabin. I'm positive I stuffed it in one of my jeans' pocket, but I can't remember which pair, not that it matters because it doesn't seem to be there." And to prove her point Bernie gestured to the pile of jeans lying on the floor with their pockets turned inside out.

"Maybe you only thought you put it in your pocket," Brandon suggested. "Maybe you put it in your jacket pocket or maybe it dropped on the floor. That's happened to me a couple of times."

"I was so sure."

"So was I."

Bernie bit her lip, went over to her bed, got down on her hands and knees, and looked under it. Nothing. She got up and dusted off her hands.

"We should go back and look," she said to Brandon. "Just to make sure."

"Excuse me," Libby said. "You still haven't told me what this is about."

Bernie reached for the pair of gloves lying on the bed. It was going to be cold up on the hill. "It's about a SKU number."

"Meaning?"

"I'll tell you when we get back."

Libby put her hands on her hips. Bernie noticed her sister was tapping her foot.

"Tell me you're not going up to Ms. McDougal's cabin now?"

"Okay, I won't tell you."

"Seriously."

"I am serious. I'll be right back."

"Bernie, I still have Tim here."

"You'll be fine."

"That's not the point. The point is that I can't leave if I need something."

"Do you need anything?"

"No. But . . ."

"Well, then there you go."

"Bernie —"

"I'll be back before you know it," Bernie promised as she headed out the door.

"You'd better be," Libby called after her. "And get some butter. We're going to be all out soon. And some parsley flakes."

There might have been more, but Bernie didn't hear it because by that time she was out the downstairs door.

"Are you sure you want to go?" Brandon asked her when they were in the car.

"I'm positive," she answered.

She was thinking about what she'd seen when her cell phone rang. She looked at the screen. It was her dad.

"What's up, Buttercup?" she asked him.

"Whatever's not down, Crocodile."

Bernie listened as he described his meeting with Ted's mom. "She sounds like a nutcase," she said when he was through. There was a word for people who collected animals. Unfortunately, she couldn't think of what it was. She was about to ask her dad when her cell phone started beeping. It was going to die. And then it did.

Brandon turned toward her. "What's up?" he asked.

Bernie explained. Then she fell silent. Things were beginning to fall into place and she wanted a chance to think them through.

They arrived at Ms. McDougal's cabin twenty-five minutes later. Brandon did the same thing he had the first time they arrived and parked the Nissan behind the cords of wood stacked below the house.

"Do you think this is necessary?" Bernie asked.

"You can never be too careful," Brandon told her.

"Of course you can be."

Brandon just shook his head. "I'm not getting into this discussion with you."

Brandon got out of the car and Bernie followed. The wind whipped around her like it had the last time they were up here. She was glad she'd brought her gloves. As they approached the house she wondered if she'd find the paper on the floor. Then she wondered if maybe she was wrong. Maybe she was making things up.

"I wonder if the guy who was living here is still around," Brandon mused.

"How do you know it's a guy?"

"I don't. I'm just making an assumption. Most women wouldn't be living like that."

"This is true. They have more sense."

Bernie looked at the McDougal place. By now they were halfway up the path. At least the climb was easier in the daylight when she could see where she was going.

Brandon turned and looked at her. "You doing okay?"

"Last time I did this you told me I always did okay."

"Last time you did this your heels were lower."

Bernie started to cough and stifled it. "So do you think whoever was here before is still here?"

"I'm thinking that he probably moved on."

Bernie pulled her jacket collar up as far as it would go and snuggled into it.

"He probably swept up the place," she groused.

"Probably," Brandon agreed. "I always clean up after myself when I squat."

"Then why are we here?"

"Because you wanted to come."

"You were the one that suggested it."

"But you didn't have to listen."

"God, you're impossible."

"Always have been, always will be."

"You sound proud of it."

"I am," Brandon replied as he reached in his pocket for his credit card. "I wonder if it makes a difference if I use Mastercard, American Express, or Discover."

"Don't use Discover. No one takes Discover."

By now Brandon and Bernie were at the front door.

Brandon's wallet was out. He paused for a moment to consider the cards in it. "Let's see. I don't want to put any more on my Mastercard. I guess I'll have to use AmEx."

Bernie laughed.

"See what I do for you?" Brandon said as he removed his American Express card from his wallet. He went over to the door, inserted it in the space between the lock and frame, and popped the lock.

Bernie clapped.

Brandon bowed and stepped inside. Bernie followed. She reflected that the place looked the same as it had when they were there before. She pointed at the empty can of tuna sitting on the coffee table.

"I guess that guy is still around," she said.

"Maybe he's planning on wintering over up here."

"Maybe," Bernie said absentmindedly. She was more interested in her immediate problem. "I was standing in the bedroom when I found the paper, wasn't I?" she asked.

"To the best of my recollection you were. You go in and I'll watch."

Bernie nodded and headed toward the bedroom. She didn't know what Brandon had to watch for and she wasn't in the mood to ask. That dratted paper had to be somewhere. She'd been standing, where? By the foot of the bed? She'd read recently that stress affected a person's memory. Rob must have affected her more than she thought, Bernie decided, because she always remembered everything and now she couldn't seem to recall even the simplest thing.

She twisted her onyx and silver ring around her finger while she did what she always did in this kind of situation: She pictured what her father would do. He'd divide the room into a grid pattern, start from one end, and methodically work his way up and down the area until he had covered everything.

"Do it right the first time, then recheck it. That way you don't make any mistakes," he always said.

Bernie had just decided to start at the far left corner when she heard the door slam and Brandon yell, "Wait."

Wait? Wait for what? Bernie dashed out of the bedroom. Through the living room window she could see Brandon tackling someone, and then they were both thrashing around on the ground. By the time Bernie got outside, Brandon had whoever it was pinned to the ground.

"Let me go," the man yelled.

"How can I let you go when you don't exist?" Brandon asked him.

"Jeez," Bernie said when she got close enough to see who Brandon was holding down. "I don't believe this."

"Neither did I," Brandon said. "But here he is . . ."

Bernie finished the sentence for him. ". . . Alive and well."

She squatted down beside him. "So, Ted," she asked, "how's life treating you?"

# CHAPTER 34

Bernie turned to regard Ted Gorman in the back of the Nissan. He looked pretty good for a dead guy. He'd gained some weight since his memorial service, gotten a tan and a better haircut. But, Bernie decided, when you're dead you probably have more time to take care of yourself.

"I thought you were dead. Everyone thought you were dead."

"Obviously I'm not."

"Obviously. But I saw you. You were lying in Ms. McDougal's grave."

"You saw my twin brother."

"What twin brother?"

"The one I was born with."

"How come I've never seen him?"

"Because I just found out I had him a little while ago."

Bernie remembered the advertisement they'd found in the cigar box.

"So how did he get in Ms. McDougal's

grave?"

Ted brushed a piece of dirt off his shoulder. "You should ask my charming wife."

"That will come, but right now I'm asking you."

"Ask her. In fact, I insist on it."

"Okay, then maybe you can tell me what happened to Ms. McDougal."

"You should ask my wife about that too."

"Were you standing in front of her bed the other night?"

Ted shrugged. "I have a right to do what I want. It's my house."

"Not if you're dead you don't," Bernie informed him. "If you're dead you lose all your rights."

"It's the American way," Brandon chimed in.

"The French too," Bernie added.

"But probably not the ancient Egyptians'," Brandon said.

"What do you think?" Bernie asked Ted Gorman.

Instead of answering he looked out the window.

"Fine," Bernie said to him. "Be that way."

"I think I should take you to the police station and let them sort this mess out," Brandon suggested. "This is just too weird."

Ted rubbed his shoulder. "You didn't have

to tackle me. I think you dislocated my shoulder."

Brandon snorted. "Number one: If I dislocated your shoulder you'd be screaming in agony. And number two: What did you expect me to do when I saw you peeking through the window? Say hello?" Before Ted could answer, Brandon turned to Bernie and asked, "So what do you want to do?"

She thought for a moment. "Let's take him to Just Chocolate."

If they took Gorman to the police station she'd never get to hear the story, or at least the unexpurgated version. If they took Gorman to Just Chocolate and put him in with Marnie, she might. After all, what was the worst that could happen? She could always call the cops if things got totally out of control. It might also be interesting to call Clayton and invite him over to Just Chocolate as well. It would save her having to explain things to him later.

"Just Chocolate it is," Brandon said. He put his foot down on the gas and they were off.

They arrived at Marnie's shop half an hour later. During that time Ted Gorman looked out the window and hummed "Onward Christian Soldiers" under his breath.

By the time they reached Just Chocolate, Bernie was ready to make his death a reality.

"Okay," Brandon said as he pulled into a spot in front of the store. "We're here."

He got out of the car first. By the time Bernie got out, Brandon was over by her side waiting for Ted Gorman to emerge.

"Don't worry," Gorman told him. "I'm not going anywhere. This is going to be fun."

"You have a strange idea of fun," Bernie observed.

"Maybe I do," he allowed. He rubbed his hands together. "Let's get this show on the road."

When they walked into the shop one of the counter girls turned white. Ted Gorman smiled and kept walking toward the back room. Then he opened the door and went through. Bernie and Brandon followed.

"Here we are," Gorman announced in a loud voice.

Cyna looked up, lost her color, and collapsed onto the floor. Everyone else was too stunned to do anything. They just stood there gaping. Except for Marnie. She took one look at her husband and flew across the floor.

"You son of a bitch," she hissed.

"That's funny, given what you did to me."

"I did to you? I didn't do anything to you. I wasn't the one that cheated. I didn't make a fool out of you. I didn't lose our money."

"I didn't lose it."

"The hell you didn't."

"It was temporary. You panicked."

Marnie pointed to Cyna, who was lying on the floor. "Don't you want to go over there and see how your sweetheart is doing?"

Ted glanced at her briefly and turned back to Marnie. "She'll be fine."

"She was hysterical when you died."

"That's flattering. I didn't realize she cared that much."

"She shouldn't have. You're not worth it."

"You used to think I was."

"That's before I found out you couldn't keep your pants zipped up."

"So you decided to kill me?"

"I didn't kill you. You're standing right here."

"No. You killed my twin brother."

"If you ask me, one of you is one too many to have in this world."

"Let me tell you, the police will not be amused by your little stunt."

"Oh. And they're going to like yours?"

"What I did wasn't as bad as murdering someone."

"Excuse me!" Marnie put her hands on her hips. "Have you forgotten about the old lady?"

"You mean Ms. McDougal?" Bernie said.

Ted Gorman looked at Bernie and Brandon. "She's lying."

"What is she lying about?" Bernie asked.

"I didn't have anything to do with her death."

"You most certainly did. You caused it. Test the chocolate in the box." Marnie jabbed her finger into his chest.

"What box?" Bernie asked.

"The box of chocolate in her house. But it's probably gone by now. She probably ate it."

Had it been there? Bernie wondered. She'd seen it the first time she'd been in the house, but she couldn't remember if she'd seen it the second time. She was going to ask Gorman when Marnie poked her ex-husband in the chest again.

"Don't poke me," he told her.

"I can do whatever I want." And Marnie poked him for the third time.

Ted pushed her. Marnie was reaching for the frying pan lying on the prep table when Brandon stepped between them.

"Enough," he said.

"Hey," Marnie said while she was trying

380

to get around Brandon. "If I'm going down, so is he." She waved her hand in her husband's direction. "You think you're going to just walk away from this, you have another thing coming. As far as I'm concerned, you've been declared dead, you can stay dead!"

"Get the frying pan away from her," Brandon said to Bernie.

Bernie stepped around and grabbed Marnie's arm. Marnie turned toward her, swinging the pan in her direction. Bernie stepped back just in time to avoid getting hit in the jaw.

"Grab her wrist and squeeze," Brandon yelled as Ted Gorman started running for the back entrance. Brandon tackled him and they both went down in a heap.

"Why don't you put that pan down?" Bernie told Marnie.

"No," Marnie said. "I'm going to kill Ted with it, and if you get in my way I'm going to bash your head in too."

"Lovely," Bernie said. Perhaps they should have taken them to the police station after all.

"You have caused me no end of trouble," a new voice said.

Clayton was standing there. Bernie realized she'd been so focused on what was happening she hadn't heard him come in. She loosened her grip slightly and Marnie slipped out of her grasp, pushed Clayton out of the way, ran toward her late husband, and brought the pan down on his head.

"Get her out of here," Brandon screamed.

"I'm trying," Bernie cried as she came up behind her.

*Bam.* A blow to the head.

"Put her in a full nelson," Brandon yelled.

"I would if I knew what it was," Bernie said.

"Well, think of something," Brandon cried.

Bernie reached over, grabbed hold of the waistband of Marnie's yoga pants, and pulled. *Thank heavens for elastic,* she thought as Marnie's pants came down around her ankles. She took a step forward, tripped, and hit the floor with a thud. The pan went sailing out of her hand and hit Clayton in the stomach. He doubled over.

Meanwhile, Marnie started to crawl toward her husband. Bernie yanked her back. She turned and hit Bernie. Bernie managed to hold on. Marnie turned and did it again. Bernie could feel her grip loosening when she realized that the police were in the room.

*Thank God,* she thought. She wouldn't have been able to hold on any longer.

# CHAPTER 35

"Great brownie," Clyde said as he ate one of the girls' test recipes for the upcoming Valentine's Day benefit.

"You don't think it's too moist?" Libby asked. She worried that people would think the brownie was raw instead of merely underbaked.

"It's perfect," Marvin agreed.

"Can't be improved upon," Brandon added.

"I third that," Sean said.

" 'Third that' is not proper English," Bernie said.

"It's close enough," her dad told her.

Everyone was crowded into the Simmonses' living room. It was tight but it felt right, everyone being together, Libby decided. She passed around a plate of the mint brownies. Everyone groaned but took one anyway.

"Keep 'em coming," Brandon said.

Sean chuckled.

"What's so funny?" Bernie asked.

"Nothing," her dad replied. "I was just remembering how Brandon used to say that when he came over after school and your mom gave him milk and cookies."

Bernie laughed too as she remembered Brandon's milk mustache.

"So where's the benefit going to be now?" Clyde asked Libby.

"At the Longely Community Center," Libby replied.

"I didn't know we had a community center," Marvin said.

"It's five blocks from the new hardware store that opened up," Bernie said.

Libby glared at her. "And now we have to do the whole thing."

"Why?" Marvin asked.

"Because it's hard to cater a benefit from jail," Libby told him.

Bernie looked at her. "Are you saying I should have let this whole thing go until after the benefit?"

"No. I'm not saying that."

"Then what are you saying?"

"I'm just observing that now we have even more work to do than we had before. That's all."

Clyde reached for another of the mint

brownies. "I'll certainly miss the Gormans. Their morals are horrible, but their chocolate is great."

Sean took a sip of his tea. "What do you think will happen to them?" he asked Clyde.

Clyde swallowed. "I guess that depends on how good their lawyers are. Right now the two lovebirds are blaming each other for everything. And of course since we managed to recover the box of chocolates from the McDougal trash pile, that includes two murders: Ms. McDougal's and Ted's twin brother, Eric LeClare. The problem of course is who killed whom."

Marvin shook his head. "What a mess."

"At least your father is happy," Libby said.

"Not really. His stomach still hurts from getting hit by Marnie."

Bernie rolled her eyes.

"I bet he blames me," she observed.

"How did you know?" Marvin asked.

"Because he always does," Bernie said. She sighed. "What was it they said about no good deed goes unpunished? At least someone out front had the good sense to call the police."

Brandon ran his hand through his hair. "We should have taken Gorman to the police station in the first place. Then none of this would have happened."

"No," Sean reassured him. "You did the right thing."

"How do you figure?"

"Well, if you hadn't gotten Ted and Marnie together, it would have taken us a lot longer to figure out what was going on."

"I guess," Brandon said.

Bernie bit off a piece of the double chocolate brownie and conveyed it to her mouth. Maybe there was such a thing as too much chocolate after all, she decided as she swallowed. The middle needed a spoonful or so of something like rum or coffee to cut the chocolate a tad.

"It's true," she said after she'd swallowed.

"I still don't get it," Brandon said.

"Get what?" Sean asked.

"Get what happened."

"It's really pretty simple," Clyde answered.

"Not to me," Brandon said. "To me it's really confusing."

Sean smiled. "You want to fill him in, Clyde?"

Clyde took a sip of his coffee. "Let Bernie start and I'll jump in. After all, she's partially responsible for solving this case."

Bernie got up and took a little bow. Everyone clapped. Bernie sat back down and began.

"This whole thing really began sometime

ago with Ted losing some money, lots of money from what I can gather, on commodities, and pretty soon he was deep in the hole."

"And it doesn't take that long for that to happen," Sean said, ruefully thinking of his brief foray into penny gold stocks.

"No, it doesn't," Bernie agreed. "Anyway, whether he told Marnie or she found out on her own I don't know, but the both of them hatched a plan."

Clyde nodded and took up the narrative. "The plan involved Ted disappearing. After all, if he was gone his debts would go with him — which is not true — but that's what they thought. So they decided to stage a car wreck. All they needed was a body to take the place of Ted's."

"And that's where Ms. McDougal came in," Marvin observed.

"Exactly," Sean said. "Now, they knew that Ms. McDougal had no family, so no one would notice if the grave was tampered with or not. Unfortunately, she was in excellent health, so they decided to help things along —"

"By doctoring the boxes of chocolate that Ms. McDougal received each month," Clyde said. "They sent her the candy and waited."

"Do we know what they used?" Libby asked.

Clyde took a nibble of the double chocolate brownie. "According to Ted it was a combination of Viagra and digitalis — which would make someone stroke out — but we won't be sure until we do some tests. Anyway, after she died and was buried Ted and Marnie dug her up."

"That's probably who the groundskeeper saw sitting in their car," Libby said.

"Probably," Clyde agreed. "Anyway, they staged the accident and everything went great.

"The car went up in flames and burned down to the frame. Marnie played the grieving widow to perfection and Ted hid out in Ms. McDougal's cabin while he made plans to go to Brazil and have his face redone. Then he'd come back, reunite with Marnie, and everything would be like it was before. It was like having the best of both worlds. Unfortunately there was a small problem."

"Cyna," Libby said.

Sean nodded his approval. "Marnie overheard her telling one of the girls at work that she'd been sleeping with Ted."

"I wonder if Marnie knew that Ted was sleeping around," Bernie mused.

"She probably did on some level," Clyde

said. "Most women do. But it's one thing to know and another thing to have it thrown in your face. So Marnie decided to console herself with Bolt. Given the circumstance, it seemed only fair. And then, from what I can surmise, she got to thinking. As long as Ted was legally dead, why not make it permanent? That way she could have a debt-free business and Bolt."

"Makes sense to me," Bernie said. "So Marnie mixed up another batch of Viagra-and-digitalis-laced chocolate — after all, if something works why change it? Now she'd set the candy to harden and went home. She'd invited Ted over to the shop later that evening on the pretext of discussing some things, figuring that she'd try the candy out on him then. However, a curious thing happened."

"Ted's twin brother came by the shop," Libby said.

Clyde nodded. "Ted had just met him and wanted to introduce him to Marnie. But Ted was going to be a little late, so he gave his twin the key to the back entrance so he could let himself in. Which he did. And while he was waiting around he ate some of the chocolate.

"By the time Marnie came in he was lying on the floor convulsing. Marnie assumed it was Ted. She said some not very nice things to him, which unfortunately Ted heard because by this time he'd come in the back entrance. Given the circumstances, Ted did the only possible thing. He slipped out as quietly as he had come in. This left Marnie with a big problem. What should she do with the body? After some thought she decided that the easiest thing would be to bury the person she thought was Ted in Ms. McDougal's grave. That way there was no risk of Ted being found."

"So she called Bolt," Bernie continued, "who pointed out that the ground was frozen and that it would be hard to dig."

Clyde ate the rest of the brownie and wiped his fingers on a napkin. "I have to say he's being extremely cooperative. It's amazing what the threat of jail will do to a person. Anyway, he borrowed Tim Conner's backhoe to dig up the grave, hence the tracks that you all saw. He and Marnie put Ted's twin in the grave and covered him back up, but they didn't do that great a job, which is why the groundskeeper noticed."

"And he called my dad, and my dad called you," Marvin said.

"And we've been running around in circles ever since," Bernie said.

"But I still don't understand why Ted

didn't leave," Brandon said.

"The oldest reason in the book," Sean said. "Revenge. He wanted to make Marnie crazy. And he did for a while. Guilty conscience and all."

Clyde stretched. "And then Marnie cottoned on to what was going on and upped the ante by steering you in his direction. She wanted him caught —"

"And she figured that we'd pin his twin's death on him," Brandon finished.

"Plus several other crimes," Clyde said. He reached over and snagged a rocky road brownie.

Brandon shook his head. "A guy does a crime, you can always trace it back to a woman."

"How do you get that?" Bernie asked him.

Brandon laughed. "Because it's true. You know what they say — *cherchez la femme.*" And he winked at Bernie. Bernie smiled back at Brandon. She'd forgotten what a good time she always had with him.

Sean cleared his throat and took a sip of his coffee. "Absolutely," he said.

"And while we're talking about women," Bernie said to her dad, "I forgot to tell you that Inez is coming by around two."

"Whatever for?" Sean asked.

Bernie grinned. "I believe it has something

to do with the lovely Valentine's Day card you sent her. And I should also tell you that I've taken the liberty of inviting her to the benefit."

"That's wasn't necessary," Sean groused.

"I thought it was," Bernie told him.

"I'm not even sure I'm going," Sean said.

"Yes, you are," Bernie and Libby said together.

Sean looked at his daughters. "You two think you know it all, don't you?"

"Pretty much," Bernie said.

Brandon grinned at her. Maybe, Bernie thought, this Valentine's Day was going to be a good one after all.

# RECIPES

You know the saying less is more? That's not true, especially when it comes to chocolate. Here are some recipes from my friends and neighbors. Bake and enjoy.

### CARM'S CHOCOLATE RICE TORTE

**Piecrust**
   1 1/4 c flour
   1/4 c sugar
   1 egg
   1/4 stick butter
   1 tsp baking powder
   1/4 c milk
   1 tsp lemon rind
   pinch of salt

Mix flour, sugar, baking powder, and salt. Add softened butter, egg, milk, and lemon rind. Mix with hands until it reaches dough consistency. Add a little flour as needed if dough sticks to hands. Refrigerate dough until slightly cooled. With rolling pin, roll out dough and place into 9″ pie plate. Refrigerate extra dough for lattice top.

## Filling

1/4 c white rice
1 c milk
1 egg
1/2 c raisins
1/4 c sugar
1/4 c pine nuts (chopped)
1 tsp lemon rind
6 oz. melted semisweet chocolate
1/4 c dried mixed fruit

Boil rice in water until half done, add milk, and cook until done. Add butter, raisins, pine nuts, egg, sugar, lemon rind, and melted chocolate. Cool and add to crust.

## Lattice Topping

Cut remaining dough in strips. Space them an inch apart and interlap strips first horizontally and then vertically.

Bake at 375 degrees for 40 minutes or until brown.

### SARAH'S CHOCOLATE ORANGE POPPYSEED CAKE

2 1/4 c unbleached flour

1 1/2 c sugar
1/2 c baking cocoa
3/4 tsp salt
1 1/2 tsp baking soda
3 tbsp poppy seeds
rind of 1 orange, grated
1 1/2 c orange juice
1/2 tsp vanilla extract
1 tbsp orange extract
1 1/2 tsp apple cider vinegar

## Glaze

1 c confectioner's sugar
1 1/2 tbsp orange juice
1/2 tsp orange extract

## Filling

Orange Marmalade

Preheat oven to 350 degrees. Butter and flour 2 round layer pans. Combine dry ingredients. Add wet ingredients and mix until well combined. Divide between prepared pans and bake 20 minutes, or until an inserted toothpick comes out clean. Cool and remove from pans. Spread orange marmalade on top of one layer. Combine glaze ingredients. Put other layer on top and spread glaze over top and sides.

# Margaret's Chocolate Mocha Sour Cream Cake

Cream together:

2 c sugar
1/2 c oil (vegetable)
1 tsp vanilla
2 eggs

Measure and sift together:

2 c flour
1/2 c cocoa
1 tsp baking powder
1 tsp baking soda
1 tsp salt

Add 1 c sour cream and 1 c hot coffee to above in large mixing bowl.

Beat all ingredients about 5 minutes on high speed with a hand mixer. The batter will not get very thick. Bake at 350 degrees and test cake after 30 minutes. The cake should be done. If not give it another five minutes. Frost with a buttercream frosting or for a lighter touch, dust with powdered sugar. The cake is very moist.

## MARY'S FUDGE BROWNIES
## WITH SYMPHONY BARS

4 1-oz squares unsweetened chocolate
2 sticks unsalted butter
2 c granulated sugar
1 c all-purpose flour
4 eggs
2 tsps vanilla extract
3 Symphony bars

Melt chocolate over hot water with butter. Cool, then add to remaining ingredients.

Meanwhile, preheat oven to 350 degrees. Add sugar to butter mixture and mix until creamed. Add flour and mix until well incorporated. Add 1 egg at a time. Then add vanilla and mix until all incorporated.

Turn half mixture into a well-buttered 8-inch-by-8-inch pan, then lay bars on batter and finish by pouring other half over bars.

Bake for 25 minutes, cool to room temperature for about one hour, cut into squares.

# ABOUT THE AUTHOR

**Isis Crawford** was born in Egypt to parents who were in the diplomatic corps. When she was five, her family returned to the States, where her mother opened a restaurant in upper Westchester County and her father became a university professor. Since then Isis has combined her parents' love of food and travel by running a catering service as well as penning numerous travel-related articles about places ranging from Omsk to Paraguay. Married, with twin boys, she presently resides in Hastings-on-Hudson, New York, where she is working on the next Bernie and Libby culinary mystery.